MICE

Gordon Reece

MANTLE

First published in Australia 2010 by Allen & Unwin

This edition first published 2011 by Mantle
an imprint of Pan Macmillan, a division of Macmillan Publishers Limited
Pan Macmillan, 20 New Wharf Road, London N1 9RR
Basingstoke and Oxford
Associated companies throughout the world
www.panmacmillan.com

ISBN 978-0-230-75188-0

1 3 5 7 9 8 6 4 2

A CIP catalogue record for this book is available from
the British Library.

Typeset by CPI Typesetting
Printed in the UK by CPI Mackays, Chatham ME5 8TD

Visit **www.panmacmillan.com** to read more about all our books
and to buy them. You will also find features, author interviews and
news of any author events, and you can sign up for e-newsletters
so that you're always first to hear about our new releases.

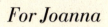

For Joanna

1

My mum and I lived in a cottage about half an hour outside town.

It hadn't been easy finding a home that met all our requirements: in the country, no neighbours, three bedrooms, front and back gardens; a property that was old (it had to have character) but at the same time had all the mod cons – a modern central heating system was essential, as we both hated to be cold. It had to be quiet. It had to be private. We were mice, after all. We weren't looking for a home. We were looking for a place to hide.

We viewed scores of properties with the agent, but if we could make out a neighbour's roof through the trees or hear the drone of traffic in the distance, we'd exchange a subtle glance that struck it off our list. We'd still go through with the visit, of course, patiently listening as the obvious was explained: *This is the main bedroom – this is another bedroom – this is the bathroom.* We would have felt it was somehow rude not to after the agent had driven us so far out into the country, and Mum could as soon have asserted herself over the cocky young man with his gelled hair and constantly trilling mobile phone (*We've seen enough, thank you, Darren, we're not interested*), as fly to the moon. Mice are never rude. Mice are never assertive. And so we spent many Saturdays being shown around properties in which we had no interest whatsoever.

Eventually, however, we'd been taken to see Honeysuckle Cottage.

It wasn't the prettiest cottage we'd viewed – with its brown brick facade, small windows, grey slate roof and smoke-stained chimneys, it looked more town than country. But it *was* wonderfully remote. Surrounded on all sides by acres of farmland, the nearest neighbour was more than half a mile away. The cottage could only be reached by following a tortuous single-track road that meandered its way around the large garden in a wide, serpentine loop. With tight hairpin bends, and hedge-topped banks obscuring the view, it felt more like a maze than a public road. For once we had little trouble believing Darren when he told us that few cars ever ventured down that way, wary of being caught behind slow-moving farm machinery. The long tree-lined driveway we had to negotiate up to the house, with its potholes and sharp dog-leg to the left, only added to the impression that Honeysuckle Cottage was too far off the beaten track for the harsh realities of the world ever to find us there.

It was blissfully quiet, too. When we climbed out of Darren's four-wheel drive on a gusty day in early January, the silence was the first thing I noticed. It was there when the birds in the trees high above us stopped chirruping and Darren paused momentarily in his relentless sales pitch (*I love this house – and I'm not just saying that – I'd live here tomorrow if I could*); it was there, the most wonderful sound in the world – the complete absence of sound.

The owners, Mr and Mrs Jenkins, were an elderly couple. They met us at the door, all stringy grey hair and ruddy cheeks, nursing mugs of tea against their chunky cardigans, bursting into hearty laughter when no one had said anything particularly funny. Mr Jenkins explained that they were having to move back into town because of Mrs Jenkins's health – a 'dicky ticker' as he put it – and they didn't want to be out here 'in the sticks' if anything went wrong. They were heartbroken to be leaving, he said, and assured us that they'd had thirty-five wonderful years in the cottage. *Yes, thirty-five wonderful years*, Mrs Jenkins repeated after him, like a woman used to being little more than her husband's obedient echo.

They took us on the usual awkward tour of the house: too many people trying to squeeze into the narrow hall and landing, the bumbling confusion (*After you – no, after you*) at every doorway. As we went from room to room, I could feel Mr Jenkins's stare return to me again and again, trying to work out how a shy, middle-class girl had come to get those nasty scars on her face. I was relieved when they took us out through the kitchen and into the back garden so that I could drop back and avoid his prying blue eyes.

Mr Jenkins was an expert gardener and he was determined we should know it. We trudged behind him
around the back garden while he showed off his fruit
trees, his vegetable patch, and his two sheds. They were
the cleanest, most organized sheds I'd ever seen: every
tool hung from its own hook; even their gardening
gloves had their own pegs, labelled *Jerry* and *Sue*. He
showed us his fetid compost heap, exclaiming proudly,
'Here she is – my pride and joy!', and took us down to
the row of cypresses he'd planted when they first moved
there. The trees now towered more than ten metres
high, and as he expounded on the health of their bark,
I peered cautiously through the thick foliage. Beyond
them was nothing but the dun-coloured furrows of the
farmers' fields, stretching away into the distance.

Mr Jenkins was especially proud of his front garden.
The wide lawn, shaved as close as a bowling green,
was bordered by innumerable plants and shrubs, which
still showed patches of bright colour here and there
in spite of it being the dead of winter. 'It's important
to have some winter bloomers,' he told Mum, 'and
plenty of perennials, or else you lose all your colour
during winter.' Mum, trying to change the subject, said
she didn't know very much about gardening, but Mr
Jenkins took this as an invitation to repair the gap in
her education there and then. He began a long lecture
on the different types of soil. 'Now this soil,' he said, 'is
a chalky soil. It's a little dry, a little *hungry*. It needs a
lot of farmyard manure, garden compost, turf . . .' I
wandered away, unable to listen to him as he churned

on and on – 'leaf mould . . . artificial fertilizer . . . lime-
stone strata . . .' I thought I heard him say 'dried blood'
at one point, but decided I must have misheard.

I kept walking, the irritating voice fading to a dull
murmur behind me, until I found my path blocked
by a large oval rose bed cut in the centre of the lawn.
The roses had been pruned back ruthlessly and seemed
to raise their amputated stumps to heaven in protest.
The whole bed had a forlorn look. With its great mound
of turned-over soil, it reminded me of a freshly dug
grave.

Looking around at the other plants and shrubs in the
garden, I realized I knew the names of hardly any of
them. If I was going to be a writer, surely that was something I should put right. Writers always seemed to know
the names of flowers and trees; it helped to make them
sound more authoritative, more Godlike. I made up
my mind that the first thing I'd do when we moved in
(because I already knew from the dreamy look on Mum's
face that this was going to be our new home) would
be to learn the names of every flower and tree in the
garden – their common names *and* their Latin names.

When I came back to Mum's side, Mr Jenkins was
unable to keep his curiosity at bay any longer.

'And what happened to you, my dear?' he asked,
indicating with a vague wave of his hand that he was
referring to my scarred face.

Mum instinctively pulled me close to her and answered for me.

'Shelley had an accident. An accident at school.'

2

Mum bought Honeysuckle Cottage with her share of the money from the divorce. Her *mouse's* share. My dad – a family lawyer, believe it or not – had left us eighteen months earlier for his secretary, a girl an incredible thirty years younger than him, with a lewd baby-doll face and a cleavage always on display (she was only ten years older than me! And I was meant to see her as my *new mother?*). The financial and child-care aspects of the divorce had dragged on for the best part of a year. Dad fought my mum as if she'd been his bitterest enemy, rather than his wife of eighteen years, and he tried to take everything away from her – even me.

Mum gave in on issue after issue – she gave up her right to a share of his pension, she gave up her right to alimony, she even gave back some of the gifts he'd bought her during the marriage, as he'd petulantly demanded – but she refused to give me up. The court took the view that being an exceptionally bright fourteen-year-old, I was able to make up my own mind about who I wanted to live with. Since I desperately wanted to stay with Mum, my dad's custody application was eventually thrown out of court. When he realized that he couldn't punish Mum for her years of devotion by taking me away from her, he promptly emigrated to Spain with Zoe. Having apparently loved me so much that he wanted me to live with him, he left without even saying goodbye and I hadn't heard from him since.

The conveyancing went through with unusual speed, and we moved into Honeysuckle Cottage at the end of that January. It was one of those psychotic winter days when the sky is full of louring black clouds one moment, and the next the sun is shining brightly as if spring has come early – only to be snuffed out once again by gruesome clouds bringing a bitter wind and spots of cold rain.

The removal men, chewing gum and reeking of body odour, traipsed back and forth through the cottage in their muddy boots, dropping loud hints about how thirsty the work made them and how they could 'kill for a cuppa'. Mum obediently brought them out mugs of milky tea on a tray and added three or four sugars as they directed, and they sat around on the gravel drive drinking and smoking, perched on the tea chests they should have been moving. One of them saw her looking at the nasty gouge they'd made in the side of her piano and called out blithely, 'We didn't do that, luv. It was already like that.' She scurried back into the house (*mice are terrified of confrontation*) and they all had a good laugh.

They bullied her into paying them in cash – including for the half hour they'd sat drinking her tea and imitating her 'posh' accent – and then finally drove away, leaving their discarded cigarette butts suspended in the axils of the flowers.

I had no regrets about swapping the luxurious house in town, where I'd lived nearly all my life, for the modest comforts of Honeysuckle Cottage. The house had stopped being my home when the divorce proceedings began; after that it became the *matrimonial home* – a valuable piece that the lawyers on both sides manoeuvred to take, like two crafty chess players. A *matrimonial home* can never be a happy home.

There were too many memories there for me – both good and bad. I wasn't sure which were the more painful: my dad dressed up as Santa Claus when I was seven, passing me a little golden hamster that sat trembling in his gently cupped hands; my dad, dangerously drunk, literally kicking down the front door seven years later when it was his turn to have me for the weekend and I was refusing to go with him; my parents' fifteenth wedding anniversary when they danced cheek to cheek in the lounge in front of all their friends to Eric Clapton's 'Wonderful Tonight'; three years later, my dad pushing Mum away from him with such venom that she'd fallen over backwards onto the floor and broken one of her fingers. *In that very same lounge . . .*

There was another reason I was relieved to be leaving the *matrimonial home*, a reason I was loath to admit even to myself. It was the temptation to keep loving my dad. In spite of the disgusting way he'd treated Mum and me, in spite of my best efforts to paint him as blacker than black in my mind, the blood bond was still hard to break. Everywhere there were reminders of his other side, of how kind he could be and how much fun we used to have together. There was the tree house in the copper beech that he'd made for me when I was six or seven; the beautiful bookshelves he'd put up in my bedroom before I started secondary school, and the leather-bound collection of children's classics he'd brought me back from London (it was Dad who'd encouraged me to be a writer, *he'd* planted that seed). In the garage, where he used to work out and which still smelled faintly of his sweat, there was the old dartboard on which we used to play hysterical games of Round the Clock.

But perhaps the most poignant reminder of my dad came every time I looked in the mirror – and saw his hazel eyes staring back at me. I'd never been as close to Dad as I was to Mum, but when we had tender moments, when I was a little girl and he held me high in the air above him as if trying to see right through me in the bright sunlight, somehow it was even better.

I kept this secret from Mum, of course, as it would have hurt her deeply. But as long as we stayed in the *matrimonial home* that treacherous temptation persisted, and if Mum and I argued for any reason it would suddenly grow stronger. With the move, I was hoping this Trojan horse emotion would weaken and eventually disappear altogether.

*

Honeysuckle Cottage was a refreshing new start. I loved the kitchen with its old-fashioned pantry, terracotta-tiled floor and scrubbed pine table – it was always warm and cosy no matter how bleak the weather outside, so that we ended up eating all our meals there. I loved the way the lounge ran into the dining room without a dividing wall, so even when we were doing different things I always felt Mum was close. I loved the open fireplace with its chimney breast of craggy grey stone, the varnished oak mantelpiece, the neat little lozenge shapes of the mock-Tudor windows. I loved the worn wooden staircase, with the fourth stair from the bottom that squealed loudly no matter where you placed your foot on it. I loved my bedroom with its exposed beams and the built-in window seat, where I could sit and read for hours in the purest, clearest light I'd ever known. I loved opening the curtains in the morning and seeing a patchwork of ploughed fields, instead of the identical red-brick 'executive homes' of suburbia, each with its BMW or Mercedes parked on the drive outside. Most of all, I enjoyed being able to drag a chair into the back garden, where I'd sit and watch the clouds slowly forming and re-forming in the sky above me like melting wax in a lava lamp.

Staring up at the sky, I liked to imagine that I lived in a simpler, more innocent time – ideally a time before there were any human beings at all, when the earth was one vast green paradise and cruelty, hurting for the pleasure of hurting, was completely unknown.

3

Mum had been a brilliant young lawyer, headhunted by a top London law firm while she was still at university. She'd taken the job on graduating, but it hadn't worked out for her. She'd hated living in London, with the aggressive crowds, the packed rush-hour tubes, the drunken winos with their bloodied faces (*London is no place for a mouse to live*), and after four years she'd decided to move to the country. She took a job at Everson's, the largest law firm in town and that was where she'd met my dad, eight years her senior and already a partner. After dating for little more than six months, he'd asked her to marry him.

I've often wondered, given how different they were and how the marriage was to end, why Dad chose her and why she let herself be chosen by him. I've no doubt he was attracted to Mum – her wedding photographs show how pretty she was, with her dark features and bashful smile. But I'm sure he also saw a challenge in conquering the heart of this awkward, stand-offish girl with her first-class degree and imposing reputation for procedural brilliance. Maybe after Mum's experiences in

London (her flat was burgled, her handbag snatched in broad daylight) she wanted someone strong like Dad to protect her. Perhaps she thought that his strength would magically rub off on her. It might just have been his good looks and smooth charm that won her over; Dad was always suave – even as a little girl I was jealously aware of the effect his easy smile had on other women.

When I was born four years later, my dad insisted Mum give up work in order to stay at home and look after me full-time. He didn't want his daughter being passed around from nanny to nanny like some parcel, he said; he didn't want his daughter coming home from school to an empty house because both parents were out working, he said; his salary was more than enough for us to live on and there wasn't any need for them both to work, he said. His insistence had nothing to do (of course) with the fact that Mum was on the verge of being made a partner herself. It had nothing to do (of course) with the fact that she was generally held to be the best lawyer in the firm and that her quicksilver mind often left him feeling inadequate and stupid.

Mum dutifully did what he wanted. He knew best, after all; he was older, he was a partner, he was a *man*. How could she have resisted him, even if she'd wanted to? How can a mouse resist the cat? So she gave up the job she loved, and for the next fourteen years dedicated herself to looking after me and the house – cooking, shopping, washing, ironing – while my dad gradually worked his way up to become senior partner at Everson's.

When he walked out on her, she was forty-six years of age. Her legal knowledge was hopelessly out of date – withered away like fruit left to moulder on the tree. Her solicitor's practising certificate hadn't been renewed for fourteen years.

The only job she'd been able to find was as a legal assistant at Davis, Goodridge & Blakely, a law firm in one of the seedy back streets in town behind the railway station. The partners used her long absence from the law as an excuse to offer her a laughable salary – 'Take it or leave it', they said – and, of course, she took it. She was given a desk in a small office that she shared with two of the secretaries, to make clear that she was seen as little more than another secretary rather than as a qualified lawyer in her own right.

But the partners quickly realized how competent she was, and were astonished at the speed with which she caught up on what she'd missed. Blakely, the sleazy crime partner, unloaded a shameful number of his clients onto her and used her as a personal assistant and general dogsbody; Davis, the head of the personal injury department, began to pass her more and more of his problem files, the ones he'd got into such a mess he had no idea what to do with them next. By the end of her first year Mum was carrying some of the firm's most difficult cases and being paid less than the secretaries.

Brenda and Sally, the secretaries who shared Mum's cramped office, thought her move out of town into

Honeysuckle Cottage was a mistake and didn't hesitate to tell her so. 'Shelley's nearly sixteen now, Elizabeth,' Brenda said. 'She's going to want to meet up with friends in town in the evening—'

'That's right,' said Sally. 'She'll be going out clubbing every weekend if she's anything like my one. You're going to spend your whole life going backwards and forwards to town dropping her off and picking her up.'

Mum tried to keep her private life *private* – or as private as it was possible to keep it without offending Brenda and Sally, who were happy to offer up the most intimate secrets of their marriages without the slightest embarrassment.

Mum just blushed and mumbled something about not minding it really and that she was sure Shelley wouldn't take advantage. This had met with great cries of protest and derision: *Elizabeth, you're such a soft touch!*

Brenda and Sally were always saying this sort of thing to her – Elizabeth, you're too nice! *Elizabeth, why do you put up with it? Elizabeth, why don't you stand up for yourself?* They'd watched her meekly accept a pay rise that was downright insulting, they'd seen Davis and other lawyers in the firm dump their problems on her desk and barely thank her when she solved them, they'd seen Blakely regularly sidle up to her at five minutes to five and ask her to work late or to 'look at this file over the weekend' because he knew she was too weak to say no. A day rarely went by when either Brenda or Sally didn't have cause to cry out, *Elizabeth, you're such a soft touch!*

She didn't tell them the truth about me, of course. She didn't say that I wouldn't need lifts into town to meet my friends from school because I didn't have any friends from school. Not a single one. She didn't tell them that I'd been the victim of a bullying campaign so vicious I'd had to be withdrawn from school altogether and was now receiving tuition at home. She didn't tell them that on the advice of the police, my new address had been withheld from my school in case the girls concerned discovered it.

4

The girls concerned. The three girls concerned: Teresa Watson, Emma Townley and Jane Ireson.

They'd been my best friends ever since we were put in the same class at the age of nine. We played together every breaktime (skipping, hula hoop, hopscotch, granny's footsteps), we sat together every lunchtime in the school canteen to eat our packed lunches. We regularly met up at each other's houses over the weekends and during the long school holidays. We were an inseparable little clique, a club. We even gave ourselves a name, the JETS – an acronym made from the first letters of our first names.

Looking back now, I can see that things had started to go wrong between me and the other three long before the bullying started.

When we were eleven, twelve, thirteen, we would have been seen as good girls. We took our schoolwork seriously – comparing our answers after the weekly spelling test, colouring in every map as if it were the ceiling of the Sistine Chapel, ringing each other up after school to discuss difficult homework. I always came top of the class in English and art; Emma (nicknamed 'Pippi Potter' for her bright ginger hair and round glasses respectively) seemed to have a gift for maths; Jane, the most serious of the four of us, played the cello and was in the school orchestra and a Saturday music-school orchestra as well; Teresa, with her pretty eyes and strawberry blonde hair, wanted to be an actress and was mad about drama. We talked in class, I'm sure, like all children, but we were terrified of the teachers; we would never have dreamt of answering back and I can't remember any of us getting into serious trouble.

At around fourteen, however, the others started to change. And I didn't.

Emma exchanged her glasses for contact lenses and had her beautiful hair cut into a punk style – shaved close above her ears, a crest of flaming red spikes on top. Jane gave up music and just seemed to stop caring about her schoolwork altogether. She started dyeing her hair black and painting her nails to match. She filled out and grew big-breasted, and when she was made up she could easily have passed for eighteen. Jane was constantly getting into trouble with the teachers, but nothing they did – not detentions, not suspensions – seemed to bother her in the slightest. It was as if she'd rejected everything to do with school and was like a convict in prison, just bitterly counting the days until her release.

But it was Teresa Watson who changed the most. She

shot up to five foot nine seemingly overnight. She went from being pudgy and cute to thin and sullen-faced. Her body became lean and bony and hard-looking, her face gaunt, her angular cheekbones jutting out like ledges of rock. She started to wear clothes that brazenly challenged the school's dress code – green ten-up Doc Martens, low-cut hipsters, skimpy crop tops that left her long, pale midriff bare. She wore a silver stud through her left eyebrow even though the head teacher told her again and again she wasn't to come to school like that. She grew her hair long and wore it parted in the centre and pressed flat to her scalp. As her body took on this spare hardness, so something hard appeared in her green eyes, something hard and unforgiving. Something vaguely threatening.

In light of what happened next, I've often thought about the way their looks changed around the same time that their behaviour towards me started to change. And I've wondered if there was any connection. Does the way we look affect our personality? Or does our personality affect the way we look? Does the warpaint turn the tribesman into a fierce warrior? Or does the fierce warrior put on the warpaint to advertise his cruelty? Does a cat always look like a cat? Does a mouse always look like a mouse?

Whatever the truth might be, the fact was that I didn't change. I still worked hard in class and crammed for my tests and coloured my maps. I still came top in English and art, but now I often finished top in history,

French and geography as well. I still jumped out of my skin if a teacher shouted in class. I kept my hair in the same style I'd worn it in since I was nine – straight, shoulder-length, with a fringe. I grew a little taller but didn't lose my puppy fat – I still had rolls on my belly, and my thighs rubbed together when I walked. I didn't start wearing make-up to school like they did, as Mum was always telling me it wasn't good for my skin. When I did get spots I left them (Mum said squeezing them left scars), while the other girls dug theirs out with their sharp varnished nails and smeared over the tiny wounds with foundation. I didn't wear earrings, neck-laces, bracelets and rings as they'd started to, as I was allergic to anything that wasn't pure gold, and I didn't really like jewellery – it just seemed to get in the way, and I was scared of losing it. I wore the same plain blouses, jumpers and skirts to school that I always had, with the same clumpy shoes with side buckles (Teresa called them my 'orthopaedic shoes'), while the others grew increasingly obsessed with the clothes they wore and the way they looked.

I noticed that they never seemed pleased to see me any more when I sought them out in the schoolyard or in the canteen. When we were together now the atmos-phere was different, as if they were enjoying a joke I was excluded from. They seemed to look me up and down with vague disgust, and for the first time in my life I began to feel self-conscious about how I looked, embarrassed by the doughy fat bulging over the waistband of my skirt, my little-girl fringe, the crop of whiteheads on my chin.

It was seeing the way they looked at me, the withering expressions on their faces, that gave me the first inkling – an inkling I still wasn't ready to believe – that my best friends had started to find me repulsive.

We didn't play games together any more at break, even though I would have liked to, as they considered it babyish. Instead, they wanted to slump apathetically behind one of the classrooms, where the teachers couldn't see them, and play on their mobile phones, increasingly contemptuous of me for not having one (Mum couldn't afford one for herself – I was hardly going to ask her for one of my own). When they weren't playing on their mobiles, they seemed to talk almost exclusively about subjects I had no interest in – pop music, clothes, jewellery, make-up. And more and more they talked about boys.

I was the only one who didn't have a boyfriend. I was fourteen, about to turn fifteen, but I still didn't really understand the attraction. Most of the boys at my school were rough and uncouth. They played football as if it was a mania and fought vicious brawls in the corridors; they swore all the time in a desperate effort to sound tough, and tried to embarrass the girls with their gross sexual suggestions. For years we'd disliked boys and kept away from them. Now Teresa, Emma and Jane all had boyfriends and talked about them endlessly. They talked about their tattoos, the apprenticeships they were doing, the cars they were customizing, the injuries they'd picked up from fights or from sport. But what they liked discussing most was what they were planning to do with their boyfriends on the weekend – what films they were going to see, what club they were going to try to get into, how they'd wear their hair, the bag they were going to buy to match the jeans they were going to buy. At the end of some lunchtimes I'd realize I hadn't spoken a single word during the whole hour that we'd been together.

I know now with hindsight that I should have stopped hanging around the three of them much sooner than I did and tried to make new friends. I should have just accepted that we'd grown apart. But it wasn't so straightforward at the time; although I knew things were changing between us and I could sense their growing hostility towards me, I didn't grasp just how serious it was – after all, we'd had plenty of little spats over the years that had quickly blown over. And besides, it was impossible to imagine school life without them. I had no other friends at school – I'd had no *need* to make other friends. I'd always had Teresa, Emma and Jane. We'd been best friends since we were nine. We'd loved each other like sisters. *We were the JETS.*

I had no idea how toxic their feelings towards me had actually become. And I had no idea how much danger I was in.

5

The bullying began around March of my fourth year in secondary school. We were still living in the *matrimonial home* at the time – Dad had left us more than six months before – and our move to Honeysuckle Cottage was still some ten months away.

I've never really understood precisely what triggered it. I know I won the school short-story competition around that time, and was presented with a small silver cup at morning assembly. I know we were weighed and measured in physical education then, too, and I'd been the heaviest girl in the class. I know I was very teary that March as my dad's custody application was on the twenty-fourth, and even though Mum's lawyer assured me it wasn't going to happen, I was still terrified that the judge would order me to go and live with him and Zoe. Our form teacher, Miss Briggs, who knew all about the divorce, was very attentive to me over that period – if she saw I was upset she didn't hesitate to put her arm around me and take me off to her office to talk my spirits back up over a cup of peppermint tea. Perhaps they were jealous of this attention, perhaps they were jealous because I'd won an important school prize, perhaps being officially the fattest girl in the class I suddenly lost all right to be treated like a human being . . . I don't know. I have no idea. Perhaps cruelty just has a logic all of its own.

It began slowly with wisecracks and put-downs which could have been seen as leg-pulling at first, but pretty soon lost any trace of good humour and were revealed for what they were: hostile, mean, designed to hurt. I was shell-shocked. After so many years of friendship, the fact that my best friends didn't like me any more left me reeling, bewildered. I tried to keep my distance from them, but I was their entertainment now, a new diversion they'd discovered to help get them through the tedium of school. They came looking for me at break and lunchtime, and although I tried desperately to hide they would invariably find me. In a grotesque mockery of the games we used to play together, they'd dance around me, their arms linked so I couldn't escape, shouting the worst insults they could think of until they'd succeeded in making me cry: *Your dad left 'cause you embarrassed him, you fat retard! Shelley's mum puts her tampons in for her!*

But this name calling quickly bored them. They needed to raise the level of spite a few notches for the game to keep their interest.

They started to vandalize my personal property. Every day I came back after break to find some new intrusion, some new violation: all my coloured pencils snapped in two; a piece of history homework I'd spent hours on scissored into ribbons; Tippex poured onto the neat brown-bread triangles of my sandwiches; the contents of the wastepaper bin emptied into my school-bag; a worm as long as a shoelace squashed inside my English exercise book; 'pizza face' and 'fat pig' scrawled in black marker on the back of my wooden ruler; all my lucky troll's mauve hair pulled out and his face scribbled over with biro; two hard pieces of dog turd stuffed inside my Hello Kitty pencil case.

I couldn't tell the teachers because I was sure it would only make things worse for me in the long run. I didn't want to give my persecutors an excuse for even more horrible outrages – I didn't understand then that the cruel don't need an excuse for their actions. I also had a queasy lack of faith in the school's ability to protect me. I'd noticed how the teachers – even Miss Briggs – would turn a blind eye to Teresa, Emma and Jane's behaviour, pretending not to have heard the swear word, not to have seen the flicked finger – anything for a quiet life.

I should have told Mum, I realize that now, but I was ashamed to. I was ashamed to tell her that I'd been singled out for this treatment, as if I carried some stigma that marked me as different from everyone else. What made it worse was that Mum knew these girls – she'd made them tea, she'd driven them home, she thought they were my best friends. I couldn't bear the thought of her knowing how much they hated me. And I dreaded the questions she'd inevitably ask –

What did you do? Did you do something to upset them? – because, deep down, I couldn't shake the feeling that somehow what was happening was my fault, that somehow I was to blame.

Besides, telling Mum or the school would have meant confronting my tormentors, and I was incapable of that. I just didn't have it in me. I just didn't have that sort of character. I was a mouse, don't forget. It seemed more natural to me to say nothing, to suffer in silence, to stay very still and hope not to be seen, to scurry along the skirting board searching for a safe place to hide.

The only person I seriously thought of telling was my dad. Until Zoe came on the scene he'd always been protective of me. He'd even tried to 'toughen me up', as he put it, so that I'd be able to defend myself, nagging me to go running with him, even trying to persuade me to take up judo – compensating or *over*-compensating for what he saw as Mum's 'bad influence'. I indulged in fantasies of Dad springing into action to protect me now, coming to my rescue like a comic-book superhero.

But I knew full well that Dad was no superhero. I remembered how boorish and arrogant he was towards the end, how secretly vulgar (I'd once found a *Hot Sluts* magazine hidden in his briefcase). I was sure Zoe would have been poisoning his mind against me (*Shelley's a whingy little namby-pamby mummy's girl*). And why wouldn't she? She didn't want to share any of his money with me. I doubted Dad would do anything to upset Zoe. I doubted he'd do anything to risk losing that provocative mouth, those porn-star breasts.

I had a contact number for him in Spain and very nearly called him – but the thought of Zoe picking up the phone made my stomach turn over.

Dad wasn't in my life any more.

6

My silent submission didn't save me. In time, my 'best friends' turned their aggression from my belongings onto me directly.

The first time it happened was just after lunch one day. Jane held me by my hair while Teresa and Emma stuffed a bread roll down the front of my blouse. Then they wrestled with me, trying to squash the roll and make it as messy and uncomfortable for me as they could. When I tried to pull it out, Teresa slapped me hard in the face. The blow, the loud smack, took everyone by surprise – even Teresa – and I could have sworn she was about to apologize when her features suddenly hardened again. She greedily seized my hand and bent my fingers back. The searing pain choked my screams to silence.

After that, it was easy for them. After that, physical violence became the norm.

I wrote down everything they did to me in my diary, sitting in my room after school, a chair against the door in case Mum should try to come in. These entries make strange reading today, and not just because what happened on my sixteenth birthday – my very own 9/11 – makes them look trivial in comparison. I'm struck by how devoid of emotion the entries are, almost as if I'd been describing something that was happening to somebody else. In the same diary there are pages and pages full of emotional outpourings about Mum and Dad's divorce, but as soon as the bullying starts the entries become shorter and more reticent, and as the intensity of the violence increases they grow even more clipped, almost matter-of-fact – a world of suffering reduced to the briefest of sound bites, the story of the crucifixion written on the back of a matchbox.

> May: *Jane pushed me over the low wall on the way to art and into one of the prickly hedges . . . Emma called me a lesbian and pulled the hair clips out of my hair – with a lot of my hair too . . . Emma clicked her lighter in my face and threatened to set me on fire . . .*

> June: *Teresa tried to give me a 'dead leg'. She kept missing the spot and made me keep still until she got it right. Have a massive bruise now. Mustn't let Mum see it . . . Jane and Teresa threw one of my shoes behind the IT building. Teresa kicked me hard on the shin when she saw I'd got it back. Nearly passed out . . . Teresa jabbed me with a compass in the backside during geography. Went to the bathroom and there was blood in the back of my knickers . . .*

I recognize this somnambulant, hollowed-out tone now when I see the survivor of the landslide, the victim of the bomb blast on TV. *There was a loud bang. There was a lot of smoke.* I understand that the greater the trauma the less adequate words become until, I imagine, when we face the greatest test of all, only silence seems appropriate.

But that June I almost found my voice. That June I almost threw off my paralysis and spoke out . . .

School had finished for the day. I had to go to my flute lesson, but Teresa, Emma and Jane wouldn't let me out of the classroom. They corralled me behind the desks, and when I made a dash for the door they caught me and pulled me to the back of the room.

Jane got me in a headlock and, egged on by the others, tried to push my head into the sharp metal edge of the windowsill. I remember unexpectedly breaking free and running for the door again when something heavy – one of the huge physics textbooks – thumped into my back with such force that I bit my tongue.

Just then, Miss Briggs came into the classroom and the girls quickly turned away from me and pretended to be busying themselves at the bookshelf. Miss Briggs picked up the papers she'd come back for and was turning to go when she noticed me – frozen to the spot, struggling to fight back the tears.

'Is everything all right, Shelley?' she asked.

And that's when I nearly told her. That's when the confession nearly burst out of me on a flood of choking

sobs. But then I caught Teresa's eye – as cold and piti-
less as a shark's – and lost my nerve.

'Yes, Miss,' I said. 'Everything's fine, Miss.'

I had to work hard to keep Mum from finding out what
was going on. I wore long sleeves all the time to hide
the bruises on my arms, and scarves to cover up the
scratches on my neck. I had to wear pyjamas instead
of my usual nightie, or she'd have seen the yellow and
black bruises that peppered my shins and thighs like
the symptoms of some horrible new disease.

I also became adept at cleaning myself up before Mum
got home from work. Locking myself in the upstairs
bathroom, I washed the stains out of my jumpers and
skirts where I'd been pushed over or held against a filthy
wall – I even sewed back buttons that had been torn off
when they were dragging me around by my shirt front.
Time and again I methodically cleaned out my school-
bag with soapy water to remove whatever filth they'd
smeared inside it. Luckily I'd always been rather scatty
and forgetful, so Mum readily believed me when I told
her I'd lost my lunch box or hair clips or coloured pencils.

My greatest fear was that they'd start sending me
abusive emails and Mum would find out what was going
on that way. Although we'd rarely emailed each other,
I knew they had my email address and I was terrified
that one day Mum would open a message full of sick,
foul-mouthed abuse. So every morning I'd get up early
and slip downstairs to check the emails before Mum

came down. But the girls concerned were too smart to get into cyber bullying. They knew an email could be seen by Mum and traced back to them, and they were having way too much fun to risk that.

They only broke their Internet silence once. One Saturday morning I opened a message from a sender I didn't recognize, already fearing the worst. It was a pornographic photo – a man doing something disgusting to a woman – an image so vile that even today I don't want to think about it. It was still on the screen when Mum came up behind me, asking if there were any messages. I only just managed to press Delete in time (*No, Mum. No new messages*).

I put it down to a Saturday-night Bacardi Breezer binge when they'd been too blasted to think straight, and it never happened again.

But in spite of my best efforts, I knew Mum sensed something was wrong. I could feel her antennae probing, trying to get inside my head and find out what it was about me that had subtly changed. If she hadn't been so busy that summer with the Jackson file – a personal injury case Davis had shamefully neglected and then given to Mum to prepare for trial – I'm sure she would have worked it out.

I counted down the days for the school year to end and at last – *at last!* – the summer holidays arrived to save me.

At the end of July Mum and I left the claustrophobic greyness of the *matrimonial home* and went on holiday

– two weeks in a self-catering cottage in the Lake District. We were blessed with glorious weather. We walked in the mountains, we hired bikes and followed the trails marked by splodges of red paint on tree trunks and boulders, we swam in the lakes. We wandered around the pretty villages looking at antiques and gorging ourselves on cream scones with jam in the library-quiet tea shops.

In the evenings we cooked extravagant meals together and read for hours. Mum worked her way through the cottage's collection of dog-eared romances, stopping to read the funniest passages out loud to me. I read *Macbeth*, which was one of my set texts for my exams the following year, methodically noting down all the words I didn't know in an exercise book I'd bought specially. I couldn't help imagining the three witches with the faces of Teresa, Emma and Jane – those three unnatural hags had intervened in my life just as the three witches had in Macbeth's. But what fate, I wondered, did my three witches have in store for me? As I read on, I was surprised to see that it was *Lady Macbeth* who had engineered King Duncan's murder and not Macbeth as I'd thought, and I found myself wondering, in the light of what my 'best friends' had done to me, whether women were the gentler sex after all. Was it possible that women were actually crueller than men?

There were times on that holiday when I completely forgot about Teresa, Emma and Jane and their punches and insults and the sting of their kicks, when I completely forgot about the dad who'd walked out of my life when I'd still needed him so much. When Mum and I were swimming in one of the freezing lakes, giggling and screaming and whooping with the cold, or when I was following closely behind her as we climbed a winding mountain path, the nervous cows getting slowly to their feet at our approach, I actually forgot the painful details of my life and was happy.

But September soon came round again. As the time to go back to school came closer, I grew listless, headachy and feverish. Every time I thought about school my stomach burned acidly. I had no appetite, and at mealtimes I had to fight back the nausea and force myself to finish everything on my plate so that Mum wouldn't get suspicious. I couldn't concentrate on anything. I couldn't read two lines.

The night before school started I lay in bed unable to sleep, trying to steel myself for what lay ahead. Next year was exam year. If I did well enough, I'd be able to stay on at school and start working towards university in earnest. I was sure the girls concerned had no intention of staying on and would leave after the exams. That meant I just had to make it through one school year (*keeping very still, hoping not to be seen, scurrying along the skirting board searching for a safe place to hide*), and then it would be over. I was confident that I could survive one year.

I thought it was even possible that the bullying might have stopped when I went back, that the long six-week summer holiday might have broken up its momentum, like a firebreak can stop the fiercest forest fire in its tracks. After all, they had exams like I did and, even though they had no interest in going on to university, they still needed good grades if they wanted to get good jobs. Perhaps they'd be too worried about their results to concern themselves very much with me. Perhaps the bullying would lessen. Perhaps it would stop altogether. Perhaps . . .

I was wrong, of course. From the first day back at school the bullying started again. If anything, it seemed that they'd missed their regular fix and were trying to make up for lost time.

The bullying ratcheted up yet another notch.

Dutifully, I recorded my shell-shocked telegrams from the front line of my secret war in my diary – my diary which had remained gloriously blank over the summer.

> September: *Teresa punched me in the face in the girls' toilets. Had a really bad nosebleed that wouldn't stop. Told Mum I fell over in the corridor . . . they held me down and Teresa pulled my blouse and bra right up and took a video with her mobile. She said, 'Your ugly tits are going to be all over YouTube' . . . they pushed me up against the toilet block wall and took turns to spit in my face . . .*
>
> October: *Teresa hit me on the head with her bag when I was drinking from the water fountain.*

*Deep cut in the roof of my mouth . . . they waited
for me after school and beat me up. Teresa sat
on top of me and farted right in my face. When
I got back home I was sick twice. Managed to
clean everything up just before Mum got back . . .*

What made me realize that I was never going to make it through a whole year – that I wasn't going to make it through the *first term* – was an incident that happened later that October.

I began to notice a strange smell around my desk one morning after break – a faint sour smell that seemed to grow worse as the day went on. I could still smell it around me as I walked home and I started to suspect it was coming from my sports bag. As soon as I got home I sat on the lounge floor and emptied everything out – maybe my towel was fusty or I'd overlooked a dirty sock or something. But my gym stuff all smelled fine. I searched inside the bag, feeling around in all the pockets with my hand but I couldn't find anything. I couldn't work it out. I could still smell that sickly sour smell.

I'd picked up one of my gym shoes to see if the sole was soiled when something inside it became dislodged and dropped onto my bare leg. When I saw the blind black eyes, the gaping mouth, the rigid claws, I screamed and screamed and kicked my legs frantically until it slid off me onto the floor. I backed away into a corner and sat there hugging my knees tightly, sobbing uncontrollably, rocking back and forth on my haunches like a lunatic. It was a long time before I was calm enough to pick up the dead sparrow and carry it outside to the bin.

After that I knew they'd won; that's when I knew I couldn't endure the fear and the pain and the humiliation any longer.

One Thursday night I sat in my bedroom and thought it all through quite matter of factly. Even if, by some miracle, I did summon up the courage to tell on them, I was still convinced it would only make my situation worse; the head would summon them to his study and they'd deny everything. There was no direct evidence against them (no one in my class would dob on them) so it was my word against theirs. Without proof, the head, who was weak and ineffectual, and paranoid about any kind of bad publicity for the school, wouldn't take any action. If I told on them, they'd be free to persecute me with even greater determination, greater viciousness. It was too late to transfer to a new school with only two terms left before my exams. And besides, even if I did transfer, they knew where I lived.

They could easily wait to ambush me or, even worse, they might decide to bring their campaign of hatred into my home – *my home!* – the only place where I still felt safe from them. I couldn't bear the thought of Mum finding some obscenity stuffed through our letterbox. Anything, anything, other than that.

There didn't seem to be any way out of the miserable existence I found myself living. Or rather, there seemed to be only one.

I planned it all out sitting at my desk, as if it was just another homework assignment. I decided to do it two days later, on the Saturday, when Mum went to do the big weekly shop at the supermarket just outside town. I usually went with her, but this time I would plead a headache. After a great deal of thought, I settled on the best way to do it (the beam in the garage where Dad used to hang his punchbag; the thick belt from my towelling dressing gown) and tore a sheet of paper from an exercise book to write a final message to Mum.

But even though I sat there for more than half an hour, the words just wouldn't come. I still couldn't bring myself to tell her about the bullying, not even in a note, a note she wouldn't read until after I was dead. I didn't really understand why I couldn't confide in her. All I could think was that no matter how close we are to someone else, there are limits, frontiers between us that we just can't cross, things that touch us so deeply they can't be shared with anyone else. *Maybe*, I thought, *it's what we can't share with others that really defines who we are.*

I'd been doodling unconsciously while turning the still-born phrases over in my mind, and when I looked down at the piece of paper I couldn't help smiling bitterly when I saw what I'd drawn. It was a mouse. And around its neck was tied a thick hangman's noose.

I knew I was timid; I knew I had a tendency to cry easily – to tremble and lose my voice at the smallest reprimand or sign of aggression. But it had taken the months of bullying for me to understand finally that this was what I was: *a mouse, a human mouse*. And at the same time, I realized that this drawing was the most eloquent statement I could leave behind me. I folded the sheet over, wrote *Mum* on it and left it in my top drawer, where it would be easily found.

And that's how my life would have ended, like the lives of so many other weak little mice before me – hanging from a home-made noose, my feet turning in smaller and smaller circles, my hands twitching spasmodically – if my tormentors hadn't sprung their cruellest trap the very next day.

That vicious attack, ironically, saved my life.

7

I remember the attack that could have killed me far less clearly than most of the others.

I'd gone to the girls' toilets at break as I'd been having really bad period cramps all morning. I thought I heard Teresa and Emma talking, but when I came out of the cubicle there were just some younger girls mucking around by the paper-towel dispenser. I went to wash my hands. The water was cold and I let it run to warm up. I'd just squeezed some turquoise liquid soap into the palm of my hand when I was suddenly grabbed around the neck and jerked violently backwards.

I caught a brief glimpse of Jane's flushed face and the terrified juniors running away as I was swung round hard into the cubicle door. My forehead cracked against the doorframe and, completely stunned, my head ringing, stars exploding in front of my eyes, I slid on some soggy tissue paper and ended up in a sitting position on the wet floor.

I was aware of Emma and Teresa kneeling close beside me, holding me still, almost as if they were trying to help me. I heard a click-clicking sound close to my face and Emma's voice say: *This is how you cook a pig.* Teresa and Jane burst into throaty laughter – and then they were gone.

I sat dazed on the floor for what seemed like a very long time. I dabbed at my nose, which had started to bleed, and felt a strange prickling sensation creeping over my scalp. I was getting unsteadily to my feet when one of the juniors came in and saw me. She let out a piercing horror-movie scream, then turned and ran out again.

Managing to stand upright, I walked slowly, shakily, towards the mirror to clean myself up before the next class. But when I looked for my reflection, *I wasn't there*. There was a girl my shape and size wearing the blouse and skirt I'd put on that morning – but she had no face. Instead of a face there was a swirling ball of orange flame.

I still hadn't recognized the horror in the mirror when Mr Morrison burst in. He came running towards me (*I saw it all in slow motion*), roaring like a soldier charging into battle (*but I couldn't hear anything*), and tearing off his jacket (*that's when I knew the girl in the mirror was me*), he held it up like a blanket (*I called out for Mum*) and threw it over my burning head (*but no sound came*).

And then everything went black.

While I was in hospital, Mum found my diary. She was looking for my favourite baby-blue pyjamas when she stumbled on it. She broke the lock open and read everything. Appalled and horrified, she took it straight to my school and showed it to the head teacher.

Mum told me later that the head had ordered the three girls to his office, insisting that Mum stay while he conducted the interview (I could just imagine how she must have squirmed, as reluctant to confront them as I had been). Apparently Teresa, Emma and Jane weren't the slightest bit intimidated by his summons; to them the head was little more than a joke, an obese, bumbling clown straight out of a third-rate sitcom. Nor were they fazed when they saw Mum. She said they slouched, sniggering and grinning, in their chairs, eyeing her with contempt, all memories of her past hospitality and kindness to them forgotten.

The head read out some of the most damning extracts from my diary and then demanded, 'Well? What do you have to say about this?'

And they had a lot to say, according to Mum. All shouting out at the same time, they angrily denied bullying me and protested that they'd been nowhere near the girls' toilets when I was attacked. I could hear their three voices entwining like a cat's cradle into one: *She's just trying to get us into trouble! She's a freaking weirdo! It's all a pack of lies!*

This was the only time Mum said she spoke. It pained me to imagine how much it would have cost her. How with red face and trembling lips she'd managed to say: *Shelley doesn't lie.*

Emma immediately snapped back at her, 'If it's all true, then how come she never told *you*?' And Mum had fallen silent again.

Leaning forward in her chair towards Mum, Teresa said with a barely concealed smirk, 'Maybe Shelley went into the girls' loos to have a smoke and had some sort of accident with her lighter. Maybe she'd gone into the toilet to *light up*, Mrs Rivers.' Emma and Jane had to cross their legs and bite their cheeks so as not to burst out laughing at her wicked joke.

Later the same day, they were interviewed by the police. They took these interviews much more seriously. Each girl was led separately into one of the sound-proofed rooms at the local station, where a detective questioned them about the attack.

I could see it all: the three of them denying everything in teary, frightened voices while their parents held their hands and comforted them, convinced that their precious daughters were incapable of doing anything as barbaric as setting another girl's hair on fire. The three of them telling lie after lie, carefully repeating the alibi they'd worked out together beforehand, while their solicitors sat tensed like jack-in-the-boxes, ready to jump up and object to any question they deemed inappropriate for their vulnerable young clients; demanding absolute fairness for girls who didn't even know the meaning of the word.

Meanwhile, I lay in Lavender Ward, a twelve-bed women's ward in the local general hospital. According to the consultant, I'd been very lucky. He tried to explain what had happened, but I hadn't followed him very well. I'd been saved by the fact that the flames had shot upwards, pulling all my hair up with them. This had been helped somehow by a draught coming in through one of the toilet windows. It meant that the fiercest heat of the fire was above my head rather than on my face. It also seemed that my hair had only been on fire for a short time: it had felt so much longer, he told me, because I'd been in shock and shock slows time down to a snail's pace.

Miraculously, I'd only sustained second-degree burns to my neck, forehead, right ear and left hand – which I must have put into the flames without realizing what I was doing or feeling any pain. My eyes and hearing were completely unaffected. Not even all of my hair had been burned. One visit to a good hairdresser to trim it into a new short style and, apart from a raw red patch at the back, it would be as if the attack had never happened. There were scars, of course – an ugly red-and-white marbling across my forehead and neck – but he assured me that these would fade in a relatively short period of time.

I was given painkillers and several injections; the burns were smeared in a cold, sweet-smelling cream and lightly dressed. I could have gone home that afternoon, but the consultant said that since I'd gone into shock and passed out, he wanted to keep me in for a few days just to be on the safe side.

It took a long time to get off to sleep that first night with all the unfamiliar noises and activity going on around me. The truth is that a hospital doesn't really sleep at night; it just rests a little, that's all. The night nurses passed up and down the ward attending to the patients who'd buzzed them or called out for them in hoarse whispers; patients slopped back and forth to the bathroom in their slippers; a new patient was brought in on a gurney at three o'clock in the morning; screens were wheeled into position around the bed of an elderly woman at the far end of the ward and my consultant briefly appeared, red-eyed and unshaven, to tend to her. Even if the ward had been completely silent, the light from the main corridor that blazed away all night would have made falling asleep difficult.

Yet strangely – in spite of the trauma I'd been through and the uncomfortable freezing sensation on my face, neck and hand – I felt happier lying under those tightly tucked-in sheets than I had for months. Everything was out in the open now. Mum knew. The school knew. The police knew. The hospital knew. It was as if the enormous burden I'd been struggling to carry all on my own had suddenly been lifted by a sea of helping hands. It was other people's concern now – adults, professionals, experts in this type of thing. I was free from it at last.

I felt wonderfully at peace in the special atmosphere of the hospital. I loved the regularity of the routine (*a cup of tea at three, visiting time at five, dinner at seven*); I loved the nurses in their neat white uniforms who always stopped to have a little chat with me, knowing I was the youngest patient on the ward. I even loved the sharp pine scent of the disinfectant that pervaded everything, and the muzak they played for the elderly ladies in the afternoons – bland, woozy tunes from another time that were somehow strangely comforting. I enjoyed the company of the other women, who fussed over me and made me laugh with their outrageous jokes and bad language. They spoiled me terribly, insisting that I have the sweets and chocolates their relatives had brought in for them and refusing to take no for an answer.

There were plenty of other mice in the ward – maybe that's why I felt so at home. There was Laura in the bed next to me, a fifty-one-year-old mouse, whose husband had beaten her with a baseball bat because she'd burned his dinner. There was eighteen-year-old Beatrice in the bed opposite, whose joky banter was darkly contradicted by the heavy bandages on her wrists. We all shared the same secret bond, what I called with bitter irony *the fellowship of the mouse*. I liked to amuse myself by imagining the fellowship's badge that we'd wear on our breasts: a mouse in a trap with a broken neck, and our motto 'Nati ad aram' in a curling scroll – *born with the victim gene*. Was that Mum's real legacy to me?

Sitting in my bed flicking through a magazine or idly doodling in my sketchbook, I felt relaxed and optimistic about the future. In their sadistic desire to hurt me, Teresa, Emma and Jane had ended up hurting themselves more. They were likely to be prosecuted for what they'd done to me – they could even end up being sent to prison. At the very least, they'd be expelled from school. Either way, they'd disappear from my life forever. I'd return to school and everything would go back to normal.

Normality! Glorious, dull, mundane normality! I couldn't think of anything more wonderful!

8

My optimism began to fade soon after I was discharged and found myself back in the *matrimonial home*, surrounded by gloomy memories of my parents' failed marriage and my failed friendships.

Mum and I had a visit from a police inspector who dryly informed us that they weren't going to press charges against the three girls I'd accused (the word *accused* made it sound as though they thought I was *lying*!). There simply wasn't enough evidence, he explained. No other students had actually witnessed them setting fire to my hair. The parents of the younger girls – who had at least seen them throw me into the door – had made it clear they weren't going to let their daughters become involved in a criminal trial. Unless one of them confessed to the crime and gave evidence against the other two, there was just no way a successful prosecution could be brought – and I knew hell would freeze over before that ever happened.

A week or so later a letter came from the school's head teacher. Mum and I read it together at breakfast. He began by wishing me a speedy recovery on behalf of all the staff and students (all the students?) and then he broke more bad news. Following 'a thorough investigation', he wrote, he'd found no independent evidence to back up the 'allegations' I'd made in my diary. All three girls 'strenuously denied' waging a bullying 'campain' (*misspelt!*) against me and 'disclaimed all knowledge' of the 'unfortunate incident' on the twenty-third of October. He said he'd received 'strong representations' from the parents of the three girls, 'forcefully protesting their innocence' and pointing to the police's decision not to prosecute as proof that they had no case to answer. In light of this, 'the school board has decided that no disciplinary action will be taken against Teresa Watson, Emma Townley and Jane Ireson'.

The letter went on to say that the school had in place some of the toughest anti-bullying policies in the country, and took great pride in its exemplary anti-bullying record. He hoped Mum was not considering bringing any legal action against the school – but if she was, he 'advised' her that it would be 'robustly defended'. The final paragraph read:

> We look forward to welcoming Shelley back
> into our community at the earliest opportunity.
> We don't need to remind you, of course, that
> this is a vitally important year for Shelley, with
> her GCSEs due to take place next June, and
> therefore every effort should be made to ensure
> that her absence from the classroom is kept as
> brief as possible.

So not only was there to be no criminal prosecution, but they weren't even going to be expelled for what they'd done to me – they weren't going to be disciplined in any way at all!

There are people who would have roared up to the school and torn that letter to pieces in the head's face; there are people who would have got on the phone to the national press and denounced the school and its lily-livered head in banner headlines; there are people who would have got the local TV station down to their house to film the scars on their face and neck. There are people who would have done anything to ensure that those girls were punished for what they'd done and that their viciousness was publicized the length and breadth of the country . . .

But we weren't that sort of people. We were mice. Meekly, we thanked the police inspector for his time and accepted that there could be no prosecution. Meekly, we accepted the head's decision not to discipline the three girls. Meekly, we accepted, we submitted, we said nothing, we did nothing, because weak submission is all that mice know.

By the second week of November I was no longer in any pain or discomfort. There was really nothing to stop me from returning to school. Except that I knew Teresa, Emma and Jane were waiting for me. And when the three of them got me alone next time . . . what then?

While Mum was at work, I moped about the *matrimonial home*. I sat in front of my dressing-table mirror futilely trying to do something with my cropped hair. It didn't suit me at all – it made my face look mannish, my head too big for my shoulders, and showed my ears, which I'd always hated. With squeamish disgust, I examined my forehead and neck, the burns stretching their cobwebby brown fingers over my pale skin like some foul alien membrane. (*Why weren't they fading? He said that they'd fade!*)

And my thoughts began to return to the beam in the garage, the towelling belt of my dressing gown . . .

Then I received the best news imaginable. The head, mistaking our pathetic silence for defiance and terrified of bad publicity, wrote us another letter. This time it contained a proposal: if Mum would agree not to bring any court action against the school and not to discuss 'the incident of the twenty-third' with any 'news media (including newspapers, television, radio and Internet)', I wouldn't have to return to school. Instead the school would arrange for the local authority to provide tutors to teach me at home right up to my exams in the summer – which I would also be allowed to sit at home. In addition, they'd strongly recommend to the exam board that the coursework I'd already submitted should receive a ten per cent 'uplift' in light of 'the difficult circumstances under which it was prepared (but for which the school makes no admission of liability) . . .'

Mum signed the agreement there and then, while I whooped and danced for joy around her, and sent it back to the school by return post. I was delirious with happiness. *I didn't have to go back to school! I didn't have to face my tormentors!* With tutors coming to the house five hours a day five days a week, I was sure I'd do really well in my exams. I'd go back to school liberated from the girls concerned and begin studying for university. I'd make a whole new set of friends. My life would start all over again . . .

To celebrate, Mum made my favourite dinner that night: duck in orange sauce with roast potatoes, peas and broccoli, followed by apple pie and ice-cream. To my surprise, she placed a bottle of red wine on the kitchen table along with two large glasses.

'You know you're breaking the law, Mum?' I teased as she poured the wine into my glass and it glugged and splashed deliciously. 'I'm not legally allowed to drink for another two years. *And* you're a lawyer!'

'I think you deserve it.' She smiled.

I noticed how tired she looked – the lines under her eyes etched a little deeper, more strands of grey in her dark frizzy hair – and I realized how hard all this had been for her, too. *That's the curse of mothers*, I thought, *doomed to feel their children's pain as sharply as if it were their own.*

'You do too, Mum.' I smiled, and we clinked glasses.

'Anyway,' she added, 'you're sixteen in – what is it – four months? If sixteen's old enough to get married, it's old enough to have a glass of wine.'

Halfway through the meal the phone on the breakfast bench rang, and Mum hurried to swallow the food in her mouth before answering. She made pained, comical faces as she stood chewing by the phone, moving her head from side to side, rolling her eyes, chewing and chewing and chewing but still unable to swallow. I giggled uncontrollably at her antics, no doubt helped by the wine, which had gone straight to my head. At last she was able to pick up the receiver. It was Henry Lovell, her lawyer. He told her that the couple who'd expressed an interest in buying the *matrimonial home* had now made a formal offer, which 'the other side' (meaning her husband, my dad) had accepted.

'So . . . how's the house-hunting going?' he asked.

'It's not,' Mum said. 'We've not even started!'

'Well, you'd better get your skates on,' he warned her. 'I understand these people are desperate to move in as soon as possible.'

We drank the whole bottle of red wine as befitted a double celebration, and the next morning I woke up with my very first hangover. But even the gimlet pain in my temples couldn't dampen my spirits. No more school. No more Teresa, Emma and Jane. No more humiliation. No more suffering in silence. No more pain. And, to top it all, the *matrimonial home* had been sold. We were getting out of that house of horrors, that museum dedicated to a failed marriage, at last!

Six weeks later I was standing in the front garden of Honeysuckle Cottage contemplating the funereal mound of the oval rose bed.

9

Our life in Honeysuckle Cottage quickly settled down into a pleasant routine.

We had breakfast together every morning at the pine table in the kitchen. I'd prepare everything (taking no little pride in getting it all *just so*) while Mum flew around in her usual morning panic, speed-ironing a clean blouse, sending last-minute emails or searching high and low for something she'd lost. We had a rota – toast one morning, cereal the next – which we kept to religiously even at weekends.

Mum would leave at around a quarter past eight, as she had a much longer commute to work now. We'd say goodbye exactly the same way every day like an old married couple – I'd give her two glancing kisses in the hallway, remind her to drive carefully, and then stand at the door to wave her goodbye as the ancient Ford Escort crunched its way slowly down the gravel drive. She'd always glance back and give me a final little wave, her fingers pressed together like a glove puppet taking a bow. When she'd gone, I'd do the washing-up from breakfast and the night before, listening to the news on the radio, and then I'd go up to my room and get dressed.

At ten o'clock on the dot, my main tutor, Roger Clarke, would arrive. Roger taught me English language and literature, history, French and geography, the five subjects I was most confident of getting A grades in. Roger and I would work at the large table in the dining room, sustained by endless cups of tea, which Roger said I made so strong 'you could stand the spoon up in it'.

Mum hadn't been keen at first on the idea of a man coming to the house to teach me, but after she was assured he'd been thoroughly vetted, and after meeting him for herself, she relented. She must have seen that Roger didn't pose any threat to me because Roger was a mouse too. He wore the badge of the mouse fellow-ship on his chest just like I did, just like Mum did, and I instantly felt a kinship with him.

He was only twenty-seven, but he'd already lost most of his hair due to a condition brought on by stress. All that remained were two hardy patches just above his ears. Perhaps to compensate, he'd grown a thick blond moustache. He was anorexically thin and wore round tortoiseshell glasses that hugely magnified his green eyes. When he spoke, his Adam's apple bobbed up and down in his throat like a hardboiled egg. In spite of his slightly odd appearance, I felt comfortable with Roger right away, and quickly realized what a gifted teacher he was; with his softly spoken explanations, things I'd found difficult to follow at school suddenly seemed quite straightforward.

Roger and I got on really well. He was much more like a friend than a teacher. During our regular 'concentration breaks', he gradually told me more and more about himself. He'd got a first-class degree at university in history and then trained to become a classroom teacher. It had always been his ambition to teach – both his parents had been teachers, and he'd seen how much satisfaction and pleasure their work had given them.

For Roger, however, the reality had been very different to the fantasy. He'd found himself in a school where few of the children had any interest in learning. Because of the way he looked he was detested by the pupils, who nicknamed him the foetus. He'd had terrible discipline problems with his classes. In the five years he'd stuck it out, he'd been assaulted by pupils *eleven times*. His car had been keyed and the tyres punctured so often that he'd eventually sold it and walked to and from school instead – a round distance of more than four miles. He couldn't take the bus because he was too frightened that pupils from his school might get on.

Eventually, after a pupil had headbutted him in the mouth and knocked out one of his front teeth, Roger had a nervous breakdown and was forced to resign on health grounds. When he was better he'd returned to university to write a research paper on the origins of the First World War (*one of the greatest mice massacres in history*). He'd been struggling financially, as his grant was very small, and a friend had suggested he put himself forward to the local authority as a personal tutor for those children too sick or too terrified to attend school. I was only his second pupil.

With Roger, my former reticence disappeared and I readily told him my own story: about my dad, whose sex life was more important to him than his own daughter; about the JETS and how they'd knocked me almost unconscious and then set my hair on fire.

'It's amazing,' I said to him one day, 'that I was a pupil and you were a teacher and we were both victims of school bullies.'

His brow furrowed as if he wanted to draw some distinction because of our ages, but then he smiled as if to say: *What's the use denying it when it's true?*

'We've got a lot in common,' I said.

His distorted green eyes lingered on my face. 'Yes, Shelley, we've got a lot in common.'

At one o'clock we'd stop work and Roger would leave to drive back to his flat in town, never tiring of his parting quip – 'Glad I brought a ball of wool with me or I'd never find my way back to civilization again!'

I'd prepare myself something light for lunch – a salad, usually – and sit and watch the news on TV. Mum's caseload was so heavy that she had to work through her lunchtimes, making do with a hurriedly nibbled sandwich at her desk. While Blakely, Davis and the other partners gorged themselves at the local bistro, bragging and bellowing like the fat cats they liked to think they were, Mum sat in the empty office quietly and efficiently correcting their mistakes.

After lunch I'd burrow into whatever novel I was reading at the time, sitting upstairs on the window seat in my
bedroom in that glorious lucent light. If it was warm –
and there were some beautiful days that February – I'd
sit outside and read, always careful to keep the scars on
my forehead and neck well covered from the sun.

At two-thirty Mrs Harris, a short combative woman
in her fifties with dyed orange hair, would arrive. I
didn't get on with her anywhere near as well as I got
on with Roger, and this wasn't only because she taught
me maths and science, my least favourite subjects.

Mrs Harris had been teaching mice like me for years
and over that time her sympathy had been completely
eroded away. She'd come to the conclusion that we were
nothing more than shirkers – spoilt and over-indulged
children who couldn't face up to the realities of life.
I once made a remark about my scars to her, and she
turned on me with derision.

'Scars? Scars? You call those *scars*? You should go
down to the hospital and see what *real* burns look like.
A bit of make-up and no one would notice your scars.
That's the problem with young people today – too vain,
only think about themselves.'

I bitterly resented her attitude, but was too weak to
speak up in my own defence. I felt I'd seen plenty of
life's realities – *too many*, in fact. I doubted Mrs Harris
had, or she'd have been more understanding.

Mrs Harris would leave at four-thirty and I'd work
on whatever homework I had until Mum got back at

around six-thirty. If I'd finished my homework I'd practise my flute, my music stand set up beside the piano so I had a view out onto the front garden while the light lasted. If I didn't feel like playing my flute, I'd read more, or get out my watercolours and paint. As I wasn't very good at just making pictures up, I'd get one of the big art books down from the lounge bookshelves and copy a particularly beautiful horse or an interesting landscape. Sometimes I'd have a go at painting one of the objects on the sideboard in the dining room – the wooden bowl of potpourri, or the vase of dried flowers, or one of the many china and glass knick-knacks Mum had collected over the years. Most of these ornaments were presents to Mum from her mum (Mum had never had the heart to tell her they weren't really her thing). They were hideously kitsch – a Beatrix Potter hedgehog, a Victorian flower girl with rosy red cheeks, a little boy fishing with a string tied to his big toe, a glass dolphin breaking the water, a miniature thatched cottage – yet, strangely, the more kitsch they looked, the more they amused us and the more attached to them we became.

It was the evenings at home with Mum in Honeysuckle Cottage that I enjoyed the most. When she got in from work, I'd make her a cup of tea and we'd sit at the kitchen table and chat. We adopted a custom we'd seen in a Michelle Pfeiffer film, *The Story of Us*, where a family take it in turns to describe the highs and lows of their day during the evening meal.

My highs were usually things like getting a good mark from Roger, or reading a particularly exciting chapter in my novel, or doing a painting that turned out really well. Lows were feeling depressed about the scars that still clung to my neck and forehead, or thinking about my dad and feeling angry with him for walking out on us the way he did. Mum's highs were settling cases successfully and being praised by grateful clients; her lows usually involved the odious Mr Blakely speaking rudely to her – sometimes he even swore at her – or trying to rub up against her in the photocopying room.

Mum would always try to be encouraging, insisting that my scars were healing, and I'd try to be the same about Blakely, although there wasn't much I could offer beyond platitudes. She couldn't risk losing her job. She needed it. *We* needed it. But on the subject of Dad it was much more complicated. Not far beneath the surface of my anger towards him there was a guilty pining. Those Greek soldiers were perilously close to pouring out of the Trojan horse's belly and hacking into the bonds that tied me and Mum together, and I could see her stiffen when I mentioned him. I was terrified of hurting her, alienating her, acutely aware that I was friendless, that I'd be lost without her.

After we'd had our tea, Mum would change out of her work suit and then we'd prepare dinner together. We both loved food and cooking, and we liked to try complex recipes from our countless cookery books. Sometimes we spent a good two hours in the kitchen chopping up vegetables on the heavy marble chopping board Mum had brought back from Italy one year, while the saucepans hissed and bubbled on the stove.

After dinner we'd sit in the lounge with the central heating turned up high, and a fire blazing in the grate if it had turned really chilly outside. Usually we read our novels (although Mum often had reading to do for work) and listened to classical music. I'd grown up listening to classical music, as it was one of Mum's great passions – she was a competent amateur pianist – and although I'd tried to like pop music, somehow it had never really taken root. We loved Mozart and Chopin, Tchaikovsky and Brahms, but our absolute favourites were the operas of Puccini. With no neighbours for miles around, we could turn the stereo up full blast and revel in the tragic beauty of *La Bohème* or *Madam Butterfly*.

Apart from the news, we didn't watch much TV. It seemed to consist of nothing but depressing documentaries on crack addicts in New York or Aids in Africa, cheap and badly acted soap operas, or reality TV shows that were facile beyond belief. But we did like movies, especially romantic comedies, and we always looked in the paper to see if any good ones were scheduled. Our favourites were oldies such as *You've Got Mail* and *Sleepless in Seattle* with Tom Hanks and Meg Ryan, and Hugh Grant classics like *Notting Hill* and *Four Weddings and a Funeral*, that sort of thing. We didn't like the modern ones – they just seemed vulgar and crudely sexual, and I felt embarrassed watching them with Mum. We both had a soft spot for George Clooney and would happily put up with all the macho posing and incomprehensible plots of the *Ocean's Eleven* series just to watch him. Every now and again he'd look a certain way or say something, and remind me a little – just a little – of my dad. I never mentioned this to Mum, of course, but I often wondered if she had the same thought.

We got into the habit of having a mug of hot choc-olate at around ten o'clock, and by eleven we were usually both falling asleep curled up together on the sofa.

Lying dozing there with my head resting on Mum's shoulder, a chocolate moustache drying on my upper lip, my novel slipping to the floor from my sleepy fingers, Brahms's violin concerto or Tchaikovsky's sixth sym-phony unfolding exquisitely in the air around me, I'd luxuriate in the safe, warm atmosphere of Honeysuckle Cottage. And sometimes, as I watched the orange flames of the fire licking and crackling in the grate, I'd think about Teresa Watson and what she might be doing just then – dancing at a club, drinking lager in some crowded smoky pub, snogging her boyfriend on the back seat of his car, and I'd think: *I wouldn't change places with you, Teresa Watson, not for all the world.* I know I'm a mouse and I know I'm hiding from the world here in my snug little nest behind the wainscoting, but my mouse's life is full of all the good things there are in the world – art, music, literature . . . love.

It might only be a mouse's life but it's a good life, it's a rich life, it's a *wonderful* life.

10

Spring came early that year. A mild February made way
for a warm March. The cherry trees burst into frothy
pink blossom, and a few days later we awoke to find
the apple trees dressed in white. We made plans to
bake pies when they bore fruit later in the summer,
to eat with great dollops of vanilla ice-cream. As I'd
promised myself, I learned the names of all the flowers
in the garden, and one Sunday morning took Mum on a
guided tour, introducing her by name to all its flowering
inhabitants. I finished at the oval rose bed, announcing
with a courtly flourish of my hand, 'And last but not
least, the hybrid perpetual, Rosa Hybrida Bifera . . .'

As the days grew longer we began to spend more and
more time out of doors. We now took our after-work
cup of tea onto the back patio, sitting on the white plastic garden furniture Mum had picked up in town for
next to nothing. At the weekends we spent hours potter-
ing about in the garden. We mowed the lawn – which
was no small task since the gardens ran to nearly three
acres and we'd allowed the grass to grow longer than it
ever had under the iron reign of Mr Jenkins. I went back

and forth dumping bins filled with cut grass onto the sweating compost heap at the back of the garden, remembering with a smirk how Mr Jenkins had presented the slimy pile to us with all the glowing pride of a proud parent.

Mum got very excited about the vegetable patch and the idea of cooking vegetables that she'd grown in her very own garden. She wanted to grow even more vegetables than Mr Jenkins had planted, and she also wanted to grow herbs like rosemary and thyme to flavour her cooking. Since there wasn't enough room in the existing plot, she decided to extend the vegetable patch back towards the cypress trees. So one Saturday morning, after a trip into town to buy shovels and a pitchfork, we set to work, turning over an area the size of two double beds until it was a rich brown porridge. We threw ourselves into the work with a will, glad to be doing something physical for a change, but we had no idea how exhausting we'd find it. When we woke up the next morning we could hardly move – even picking up the kettle hurt, while walking up or down the stairs was agony.

In our silly moods, we played croquet on the front lawn or stretched a net between the fruit trees and played badminton. Mum, who was tall and rather gawky, was terrible at sports, and when she missed the hoop from just a few inches away, or swiped wildly at the spiralling shuttlecock and hit nothing but air, we would both collapse, helpless with laughter.

MICE

It was so good to live in the country, and not to have any neighbours for miles around. You could talk, laugh, shout – scream even – at the top of your voice, and no one could hear you. It was such a change from the *matrimonial home*, where you always felt self-conscious when you went into the garden because it was over-looked on all sides, and where you had to whisper so that the neighbours – whose shapes you could see moving behind the bushes – wouldn't hear you.

In the evenings we played duets together in the lounge, something we seemed to have got out of the habit of doing since Dad had left. We had lots of music for flute and piano and one day, idly looking through them, I'd found one called *Russian Folk Songs* we'd never even opened. This became our absolute favourite and we worked our way through the entire book that March. The flute parts were catchy and quite easy to play, while the piano parts were tricky and tested even Mum occasionally. They were the sorts of tune that got stuck in your head and we'd both be whistling and humming them the next day. If I made a particularly horrendous mistake, we'd both get the giggles so badly it would take us half an hour just to work our way through a few bars. I really enjoyed these duets, and I was enjoying playing the flute – which I'd given up and started again countless times – more than I ever had.

I would look at Mum sometimes as she stood on tip-toe struggling to free the shuttlecock from the branches of a cherry tree, or pulled a comic face as I sent her

croquet ball bouncing away down the garden, and feel
overcome with love for her. With her tall, awkward
body, her large hands that she never seemed to know
what to do with, her dark, frizzy hair no amount of
combing could tame, she looked so . . . so *vulnerable*
that I'd just have to run over and throw my arms around
her and hug her as hard as I could.

I knew money was tight, so when Mum started trying
to find out what I wanted for my sixteenth birthday
I just gave her a short list of books. When she asked
incredulously if that was really all I wanted, I said, yes,
that I had everything I could possibly want.

This wasn't exactly true, of course. There *was* something I wanted, but it would have been far too selfish to
ask for it at that time. Mum was driving around in a car
only fit for the scrap yard and going to work in suits
more than fifteen years old. I couldn't remember the
last time she'd bought herself anything new. Meanwhile we always ate well, there was always money for
new clothes and shoes for me, for a book or a magazine
I wanted, a DVD or a trip to the cinema. I saw how she
always put my needs before her own, and there was no
way I was going to abuse that.

But there was something I wanted. Something I
wanted very much – as much, if not more, than I'd
wanted a flute when I was a little girl. I wanted a laptop: one of those sleek new laptops I'd seen when I was
out shopping with Mum that were so slim, so light you

could slip one into a shoulder bag and it'd take up no more room and weigh no more than a file of papers.

We already had a desktop computer in the small front room of Honeysuckle Cottage that Mum used as her office. This computer was nearly ten years old (Dad, of course, had taken the newer computer with him when he'd left), which made it prehistoric. It was already displaying the idiosyncrasies of the aged – it regularly froze up for no good reason, it often wouldn't shut down properly, and it was slow, slow, *slow*! I used it when I needed to go on the Internet, but I never felt very comfortable when I was on it; I knew it was really Mum's work computer, and I was terrified of accidentally deleting a client's statement or a complicated schedule of damages that had taken her hours to work out. I preferred to write my essays in longhand rather than struggle with the beast, as we nicknamed it, but I knew how much easier having my own computer would make my homework. I'd be able to move paragraphs around, delete whole sections I didn't like (rather than scribbling them out like a four-year-old), check my spelling and know exactly how many words I'd written at a glance, which would save a huge amount of time when Roger set a strict word limit.

My thoughts were already starting to move beyond A levels to university. A laptop would be a huge advantage with all the essays I'd be expected to write, and I even saw myself taking notes on it during lectures if I could learn to type fast enough.

But what really excited me was the thought of how a laptop could improve my own creative writing. With a laptop, I might be able to embark on something really long – I might even be able to write my very first novel . . .

I said nothing, though. I knew that if Mum had even an inkling that I wanted a laptop, she'd buy it for me – even if it meant she had to go to work with holes in her shoes and ladders in her tights.

11

March ended and April began. Our routine carried on pleasantly – Roger came in the mornings, Mrs Harris in the afternoons. I studied hard and was on course again to do well in the exams that were now only two and a half months away. Mum still did the work of three people and put up with Blakely's rudeness and his wandering hands with meek resignation.

My birthday grew closer, and I felt a little flutter of excitement at the thought of turning sixteen. I received money from my elderly grandmother in Wales, and some far-flung relatives sent birthday cards that Mum displayed on the sideboard. A really sweet card came from the hospital, signed by the nurses who'd looked after me there. I was stunned to get a letter from the police forwarding a cheery 'Birthday Greetings!' from my school, signed with 'heartfelt best wishes' by the head teacher. I tore it into pieces and threw it straight in the bin.

Even though I tried not to, I couldn't help looking out for something from my dad. But nothing came. This splinter of petty cruelty worked its way deep under my skin, and the harder I tried to ignore it the more it irritated me. I still couldn't really believe that our relationship was over, that I was never likely to see him again. I knew he had our Honeysuckle Cottage address and I began to suspect that Mum had intercepted a present from him – I even scrabbled frenziedly through all the bins one day. But when I thought about it rationally I knew Mum couldn't be hiding anything from me – the postman didn't usually come until long after she'd left for work. The truth was that Dad hadn't called me when I came out of hospital, so why should he get in contact just because I was turning sixteen? It was clear that as payback for taking Mum's side and choosing to live with her and not him, he'd consigned me to the rubbish bin, that he'd choked off all the affection he used to lavish on me like turning off a tap.

My birthday, April the eleventh, fell on a Tuesday that year. The night before, Mum rang around six to say she'd be home late – she'd been caught by Blakely, who'd asked her to see a client who could only come in after normal hours (*you're such a soft touch, Elizabeth!*).

I'd finished my homework early and had been drawing at the dining-room table, but instead of going back to it I decided to make myself useful and prepare dinner. I still hated lighting the gas after what had happened to me at school, but if I kept it down low I sometimes managed not to scream when I put the match to the burner. I cooked a spaghetti bolognese, which turned out really well and was just about ready to serve up when Mum put her key in the door.

'What's all this?' She smiled as she came into the

kitchen. 'I thought it was *your* birthday tomorrow, not mine.' She kissed me and her nose was cold on my warm cheek.

'You're freezing,' I said, putting my hand up to the cold spot on my face.

'Yes, it's turning cold out there. It's starting to rain.'

I put on *La Bohème* while Mum got changed, set two places at the kitchen table, and lit some scented candles. I opened a bottle of red wine and poured out two glasses, then recorked the bottle and put it back in the rack in the pantry. I'd learned my lesson after the first time – one glass was quite enough.

Mum came down in her tracksuit bottoms and her comfiest polo neck jumper just as I finished dishing up. We toasted my 'nearly birthday' and tucked in. We played our usual game of highs and lows. Mum had won a case against a local bus company that she'd never expected to win; Blakely had shouted at her in front of Brenda and Sally because she'd brought the wrong file to him at the magistrates' court that morning (Mum said she'd brought the file *he'd asked for*). I'd struggled with the equations Mrs Harris had set me that afternoon, only getting three out of ten right; I'd taken down our book on Goya and copied one of his pictures called *The Sleep of Reason Produces Monsters*, and although I'd made the legs of the man who'd fallen asleep at his desk a little too short, I was really happy with the owls and bats and cats, *the monsters*, that were creeping menacingly up on him.

During the meal, I became aware of Mum's gaze lingering on my face.

'What?' I asked. Since my face had been scarred, I'd become sensitive to being looked at too closely.

'Nothing,' she replied dreamily. 'I just can't believe that my little girl is going to be sixteen tomorrow. Sixteen! It seems like only yesterday that I was breast-feeding you.'

'Please, Mum, I'm *eating*!'

'The time goes by so quickly.' She sighed, slowly shaking her head. 'You always had a good appetite, you never said no to the breast.'

'Mum, you're not going to go off down memory lane again, are you?'

'No, no, not if it embarrasses you – I promise I won't go down *mammary* lane . . .'

I was in the middle of swallowing a mouthful of wine, and nearly choked laughing. When I'd recovered, she still had that dreamy look in her eye.

'We'll have a proper celebration tomorrow, Shelley. We'll go out somewhere really nice.'

'There's no need, Mum.'

'Yes, there is.' She circled her index finger pensively in a little pool of red wine on the table. When she spoke again her eyes were moist.

'I want to say I'm sorry, Shelley.'

'What for?'

'For letting you down. For not protecting you from those awful, *awful* girls.'

My reply was so strangled it barely carried to her. 'You didn't know.'

'But that's just it. You should have been able to come to me.'

I drew patterns in my spaghetti sauce with the tines of my fork.

'Why do you think you couldn't tell me, Shelley?'

'I don't know.' I shrugged. 'I felt – I was sort of – paralysed. And embarrassed.'

'That hurt me more than anything else, you know – that you didn't feel able to confide in me. It was *my* fault. I was still feeling sorry for myself after the divorce and I was preoccupied with work. I closed you out.'

I knew it wasn't Mum's fault – *I* decided to keep the bullying secret from *her* – but at the same time it was deeply comforting to hear her take the blame on herself.

'I wish – sometimes – that you weren't so much like me, Shelley.'

'Don't say that, Mum.'

'I mean, I wish that you'd turned out more – I wish that I could have been more—' She couldn't find the right words. Whatever she wanted to say, it was too complicated, too sensitive. She abandoned the attempt and looked pleadingly into my eyes. 'The world is such a *hard* place, Shelley!'

She wiped away what could have been a tear from her cheek and tried to smile, but then her expression changed as if she'd been struck by a thought so weighty it forced her to collapse slack-shouldered into her chair.

'Maybe I was wrong to move us out here. Maybe I was wrong to take you out of school. It might have been better if we'd tried to face—'

'*No!*' I was seized with panic. 'I don't want to go back to school!'

Mum reached across the table and took my hand in both of hers. 'You don't have to,' she soothed me, 'you don't have to.'

She pressed my hands so tightly that they hurt. 'I won't let you down again, Shelley. I promise you that.'

I found the piercing intensity of her expression disconcerting and I had to look away. When I looked up at her again, I was relieved to see it had given way to a gentle, reflective smile.

'I want you to know how proud I am of you,' she said, 'how proud I am of the way you've dealt with all the terrible things that have happened to you.'

'*Mum.*'

'No, I mean it. You've been amazing. Calm, sensible. No hysterics, no self-pity. We'll go somewhere really nice. A really swanky restaurant. OK?'

No self-pity. I remembered the belt from my towelling dressing gown, the beam in the garage where Dad used to hang his punchbag . . . but decided to let it go.

'OK, Mum.' I smiled. 'OK.'

After dinner we played another duet from our *Russian Folk Songs*, something called 'The Gypsy Wedding' that had a fast stomping beat I just couldn't keep up with.

Every time Mum reached the halfway point, I was woefully behind and in fits of giggles. I was making hundreds of mistakes, and the more mistakes I made the harder we both laughed.

We were both very sleepy that night; Mum was dropping off even before the ten o'clock news came on. It was full of some boring political scandal that I couldn't face sitting through. I gave Mum a hug and a kiss and climbed upstairs to bed.

I lay awake for a long while, listening to the light rain falling against my window, enjoying the dying moments of my life as a fifteen-year-old. In the morning I would be sixteen. *Sweet sixteen and never been kissed*, that's what they always said. And for me, that was true. I never *had* been kissed.

And for the first time in my life I felt that I wanted to be. I wanted to have a boyfriend. I wanted to be kissed. Perhaps when I was sixteen, when my scars had all healed up, I'd meet someone. Someone handsome like George Clooney but with the boyish innocence of a young Tom Hanks; someone loyal and sincere who wouldn't leave you when your looks started to fade and the crow's feet came . . .

Something was stirring inside me, quickening into life in the same way that the garden of Honeysuckle Cottage was quickening into life outside my window in the gentle spring rain, sprouting green shoots, opening sticky buds, unfurling virgin petals. When I woke up I would be sixteen. *Old enough to get married*, Mum had said. I felt as though I stood on the threshold of exciting new experiences, new emotions, new relationships, and I yearned for them as the butterfly in the chrysalis yearns to spread its fragile wings and fly.

Thinking these thoughts, I fell into a sweet, delicious sleep.

12

My eyes snapped open and I was instantly wide awake. Even though I'd been sunk in the depths of a deep, deep sleep, the unmistakable pig squeal of the fourth stair had reached the part of the brain that never sleeps. I had no doubt what I'd heard, and I had no doubt what it meant: *someone was in the house.*

The fluorescent display of the alarm clock on my bedside table said 3:33.

I could feel my heart pounding in my chest like something with a life of its own, like a rabbit writhing and twisting in a snare that grew tighter the more it struggled. I strained to hear above the booming roar in my temples. My ears probed outside my bedroom door – the landing, the staircase – like invisible guard dogs, constantly sending back information: *silence, silence, silence, there's only silence: we can find nothing.* Could I have been mistaken? But I knew I wasn't. I'd heard the fourth stair scream under a person's weight.

Sure enough, after what seemed like an eternity of waiting there came the groan of another stair, a higher stair: *someone was in the house.*

I was paralysed with fear. Since my eyes had opened I hadn't moved a muscle. It was as if a primitive instinct – to keep absolutely still and not make a sound until the danger had passed – had taken control of me. Even my breathing had become so slow, so shallow that it made no sound, and didn't move the quilt the tiniest fraction. I thought about the rounders bat I kept under the bed 'in case of burglars', but I was power-less to reach down to grasp it. Something stronger held me frozen and immobile. *Keep still*, it ordered, *don't make a sound until the danger's passed*.

The footsteps continued up the stairs – louder now, as if the intruder had given up trying to be quiet. I heard a body bump heavily into the cabinet on the landing (*drunk?*) and a voice swearing (*a man*).

I heard him open Mum's bedroom door. I knew that he'd switched her light on, because the thick darkness in my room lightened infinitesimally. I heard Mum's voice. Sleepy. Confused. Frightened. Then the man's voice, a stream of aggressive, guttural grunts that sounded more animal than human. 'Wait,' I clearly heard Mum say. 'My dressing gown.' Then I heard them both walking towards my bedroom.

My door shushed open against the thick nap of the carpet, and my light exploded into white blinding life.

Even though they were both in my bedroom I still didn't move (*keep still, don't make a sound until the danger's passed*). I lay as still and helpless as if my neck had been broken.

Mum said my name to wake me, but I couldn't answer. She said it again louder, closer to my bed. Finally she appeared in my vision. Her pale face was still battered by sleep, her hair wildly disordered in a way that would have been funny in other circumstances, her dressing gown pulled on hastily, its belt hanging loose. She saw that I'd been awake all the time and that I knew exactly what was happening.

'Shelley, darling,' she said, 'don't be frightened. He just wants money. If we do everything he says, he's going to go away and leave us alone.'

I didn't believe her and I could tell from the trembling of her hands and the catch in her voice that she didn't believe it herself. When a cat gets into the mouse hole it doesn't go away leaving the mice unharmed. I knew how this story was going to end. He was going to rape me. He was going to rape Mum. Then he was going to kill us both.

With a tremendous effort, I finally managed to move my left leg to the cold outer edge of the bed. With that, the millennia-old spell was broken and I was able to sit up and reach for my dressing gown.

The burglar was younger than he'd sounded. He was a weedy youth of no more than twenty with a thin weasel face and long black hair that hung in his eyes and coiled around his neck in greasy rats' tails. He wore a scruffy olive-green bomber jacket and filth-encrusted jeans that hung so low on his hips they seemed on the point of falling down.

From five feet away I could smell the stink of alcohol that surrounded him like an invisible mist. He was clearly drunk, but he was *more than drunk*. He was unsteady on his feet and his unhealthy pale face oozed with sweat. He was barely able to stay awake; his eyelids kept drooping, flickering wildly with the effort to remain open. His eyes glazed over and rolled up into his head and he seemed to be on the point of passing out, when he suddenly came to with an ugly jerk of his shoulders, looking all around him as if trying to recollect where he was.

He held a huge knife in his right hand – the type hunters use to gut rabbits.

He stood at the top of the stairs, swaying crazily from side to side like a man on the deck of a storm-tossed ship (*would he fall? Please God, let him fall down the stairs and break his neck!*) but he didn't. He motioned with the knife for Mum and me to go down.

Trembling and terrified, we obeyed him.

I went first, the floorboards ice-cold beneath my bare feet. Below me I could make out the front door at the bottom of the stairs. Outside was the safety of the darkness, a hundred places to hide. If I made a dash for it, could I get out in time? The chain was pulled across. If I fumbled with that . . . and he was right behind Mum with that savage knife.

I stepped off the last stair, and the chance – *our last chance?* – was gone.

He herded us into the lounge and switched on the lights. I was freezing after the warmth of my bed, and began to shiver uncontrollably. Instinctively Mum wrapped her arms around me and started rubbing me vigorously to warm me up, but my shaking didn't stop. I realized I wasn't shaking with cold. I was shaking with fear.

'Stay here,' he grunted. 'Don't do anything or you'll get this!' and he jabbed the knife violently at Mum, the serrated edge passing just a few inches from her left eye.

He negotiated the half-dozen paces into the dining room with difficulty, as if the floor he walked on was banked sharply at forty-five degrees, and he was evidently relieved when he reached the table and could steady himself against it. Mum and I stood hugging each other in the middle of the lounge, Mum whispering to me over and over again, 'It'll be all right, Shelley, it'll be all right.' I buried my face in her neck and squeezed my eyes tight shut. *Please let this all just be a nightmare*, I prayed, *please say this isn't really happening!*

I could hear him talking incoherently to himself as he rifled through the drawers in the sideboard and the antique writing desk. As his searching grew more frantic, I heard the bowl of potpourri get swept to the floor, the birthday cards slapped into the air like a flock of cardboard birds, the vase of dried flowers shatter into pieces on the parquet. All the time, he kept up a nonsensical, babbling commentary punctuated with fits of childish giggles and explosions of vicious swearing.

'What's he looking for, Mum?' I whispered.

'I don't know, darling. I'm not sure he knows. Don't worry. He'll be gone in a minute.'

Listening to that stream of gibberish coming from

the dining room, I had the sickening realization that the burglar wasn't really *there* with us in Honeysuckle Cottage at all, that he was tripping on whatever cocktail of drink and drugs he'd taken. All this – Mum and me standing shivering in our dressing gowns, the drawers he was casually yanking from the writing desk and emptying onto the floor – for him, all of this was merely a dream. It wasn't real at all. He could stab us with his hunting knife and it would mean nothing to him because we didn't exist, we were just phantoms in a dream, his mind, his reason, was elsewhere – drugged, asleep. And I knew very well what the sleep of reason produced.

I looked up from Mum's shoulder to see him walking towards us, dragging two dining-room chairs with him. He put them back to back and told us to sit down.

'We're gonna play musical chairs,' he said, and burst out laughing as if he'd just made the funniest joke.

'Yeah – that's right,' he said, 'we're gonna play musical chairs. Like in school with the teacher. Laa dee laa dee laa dee laa. Stop! Who's got the chair? I've got the chair! Who's got the chair? I've got the chair! Laa dee laa dee laa dee laa!'

With another wild jag of the knife, he gestured for us to sit down. We reluctantly let go of each other and did what he wanted. I instantly regretted it because now I couldn't see Mum at all – only the fireplace and the piano – and I felt my fear intensify and panic rise in my breast. I closed my eyes and took deep breaths, trying to drive the hysteria back down.

The youth stood just a few feet away to my left, silent, like an actor who's unexpectedly forgotten his lines. His eyelids began to flicker wildly again and his eyes slid upwards until all I could see were the discoloured whites. His head slumped forward. It was almost as though he'd fallen asleep standing up. The knife hung limply in his hand just held by the tips of his fingers.

I stared at him, expecting him to suddenly snap out of it, but he didn't. He stayed immobile, like a clockwork toy that has run itself down. *If I throw myself at him now,* I thought, *right now, the knife will drop harmlessly to the floor and Mum will pick it up.* Without the knife he wasn't a cat in the mouse hole at all – he was only a kitten, and a sick, disorientated kitten at that. If I rushed at him now, when he was off in one of his trances, I could knock the knife from his hand. I could do it. I should do it. I had to do it . . .

But slowly his eyelids unglued themselves, his grey irises with their pencil-point pupils dropped back into place, and he stared directly at me. He smiled vacantly and smacked his chops like someone waking from a deep sleep with a foul taste in their mouth. His grip tightened on the knife. He brought it up to his face and used the back of his hand to wipe away some bubbly dribble that was running down his chin.

I was too late. I was too late again.

'Yeah,' he said slowly, beginning to remember where he was. 'Yeah – we're gonna play musical chairs.'

He groped around in his pocket and pulled out a ragged jumble of rope.

13

'You don't have to tie us up,' Mum said, trying to sound as calm and reasonable as she could. But I could hear the fear in her voice. If he tied us up, we'd be completely at his mercy; we couldn't even run away if he started to use his knife. We'd be as helpless as the turkeys I'd seen in the market at Christmas, trussed up in a squalid corner, pathetically awaiting the butcher's hatchet.

'It's really not necessary,' Mum went on. 'We're not going to do anything. Take whatever you want – there's jewellery in the red box in my bedroom, and there's cash under my mattress – take it. We won't call the police. I promise.'

The youth stood stock still, his face strangely distracted. Perhaps he was considering what she'd said; perhaps his trip was taking him through a particularly scary loop the loop at nauseating speed.

Then he laughed, wiped his mouth with the back of his hand again and began to tie Mum's wrists together. 'I gotta tie you up,' he said. 'That's why I brought the rope.'

He knelt on the floor and tied her legs together, and

then crawled over on his hands and knees to me. He tied my legs over and over again, lost in the action of taking the rope round and round my ankles. I watched his greasy head bobbing around me and tried not to breathe in his fetid stink. When he finished my legs he found he'd used up nearly all the rope. He grabbed my wrists and pulled them roughly towards him and bound them tightly in the raggedy end that was all he had left. There was just enough to tie a tiny knot.

'There,' he said, 'that'll stop you going anywhere!'

He got up slowly from his knees, breathing heavily. He held his stomach and grimaced as if he were about to be sick. He cracked a loud sour belch.

'Sorry, ladies,' he said. 'Sorry, madam. Sorry, *madame*. I shouldn't have had them eggs. Them eggs was off.'

There was a long silence. An unbearably long silence. I couldn't see him, but I sensed he was standing in front of Mum. I tried to look over my shoulder, but he was in the blind spot directly behind me and I couldn't catch even a glimpse of him. *He's going to stab her*, I thought. *The killing's going to start right now. He's going to kill her and then he's going to kill me. He's not interested in stealing anything. He's come here to kill us. He's going to slit our throats in our own lounge. This disgusting pig is going to slit our throats.*

I tugged at the rope tying my hands but it was tied too tightly and wouldn't give. There was nothing I could do. I slumped back in my chair and waited for it to begin.

'I need a bag,' he said. 'I didn't bring a bag.'

'There are – there are some bags under the stairs,' Mum suggested tentatively. I was relieved to hear her voice again.

'I brought the rope, but I forgot a bag,' he said, like a little boy apologizing to the teacher for not coming to school properly prepared.

'Under the stairs,' Mum repeated gently. 'There's a sports bag there. You can have the sports bag.'

'I'm going upstairs now. I'm getting the money and all them jewels. And if you try anything while I'm gone, I'm gonna kill you. I'm gonna kill *both* of you. You understand?'

'Yes,' Mum said.

'You understand?' he brayed.

'Yes, we understand completely,' Mum repeated in a voice that was as compliant as she could possibly make it.

There was another long, uneasy silence.

'You want the sports bag under the stairs,' Mum prompted. 'It's red.'

'I know what I want, lady! I know what I want!' he shouted petulantly. 'Don't you tell me what I want! Don't *you* tell *me* what *I* want!'

For a moment he seemed to hesitate, as though he was tempted to work this spark of anger up into a real blaze, but when he spoke again his voice was more subdued than angry. 'I know what I want, lady. I know what I'm doing. Don't you worry about that . . .'

Then he was gone. I heard him rummaging under the stairs and dragging out the sports bag, then his heavy sleepwalker's footsteps clomping up the stairs.

'Mum?' I whispered. 'What are we going to *do*?'

'Just keep calm, Shelley. If we panic, then he'll panic as well. We have to stay calm.'

'But he's going to kill us!'

'No, he's not. He just wants money. When he thinks he's got all there is, he'll go – that's all he's interested in.'

She was wrong. I was sure she was wrong, but there was no point in arguing. We were both tied up. There was nothing we could do now but wait. Something heavy thumped to the floor in the room above us. A little later we heard him flush the toilet in the bathroom.

I stared at the piano, its lid still open, *Russian Folk Songs* still turned to 'The Gypsy Wedding' from the night before. There was my flute, still balanced on the velvet seat of the piano stool where I'd left it. It was impossible to believe that just a few hours earlier Mum and I had been playing a duet in that very room, that we'd been laughing and giggling as I struggled to keep up with the frenetic pace of the music. Now we sat trussed up and terrified, waiting to see if a drug-addled burglar was going to kill us or let us live.

With a sick smile, I remembered that it was officially my birthday. *Happy birthday to me!* How many people, I wondered, had died on their birthday? Now there was irony for you. I was going to say something to Mum, but thought better of it. My morbid observations weren't going to help the situation.

I surveyed the bookshelves on either side of the craggy vertebral column of the chimney breast. There they all were – *The Complete Works of Shakespeare, War and Peace, Madame Bovary, Crime and Punishment, Pride and Prejudice, Don Quixote, Oliver Twist, Les Miserables* – a worthy selection of the classics of Western literature packed tightly onto those walnut shelves. Above them were our books on art and artists – enormous illustrated volumes on the Renaissance, the Impressionists, Modernism, Degas and Vermeer, Michelangelo, Turner and Botticelli. Just below these in our 'music section' was the thirty-volume *Lives of the Great Composers* that we'd ordered from the Music Lover's Book Club, neatly arranged in alphabetical order from Bach to Wagner.

Yes, there they all were, all the gods and goddesses of art, literature and music. All the deities of middle-class culture. But for the first time in my life as I looked up and down their ranks, instead of feeling awe and admiration for them, I only felt loathing. More than loathing, in fact – *disgust*. They made me want to be sick.

It was all lies. It was all one gigantic fraud. They pretended to be about life – *real life* – but they weren't connected with real life at all. Real life had nothing to do with novels or poems, it had nothing to do with landscapes in oils or abstract paintings of red and yellow squares, it had nothing to do with the organization of sounds into the formal harmony of music.

Real life was the complete opposite of order and beauty; it was chaos and suffering, cruelty and horror. It was having your hair set on fire when you'd done no harm to anyone; it was being blown up by a terrorist bomb as you walked your children to school or sat down in your favourite restaurant; it was being kicked to death in a back street for the meagre pension you'd just collected; it was being raped by a gang of drunken strangers; it was having your throat cut by a drug addict who'd broken into your house looking for money. Real life was a massacre of the innocents *every day*. It was an abattoir, a butcher's shop, draped with the bodies of countless mice victims . . .

And all this culture, all this art, was simply a trick. It allowed us to pretend that human beings were noble, intelligent creatures who'd left their animal past behind them long ago and had evolved into something finer, something purer; that because they could paint and write like angels they *were* angels. But this art was just a screen that hid the ugly truth – that we hadn't changed at all, that we were still the same creatures who had cut into the warm bellies of the animals we'd killed with sharpened stones and vented our anger on the weak with frenzied blows of a blunt club. Pretty paintings and clever poems didn't alter our real nature one bit.

No – art, music and poetry didn't reflect real life at all. It was just a refuge for cowards, a delusion for those too weak to face the truth. By trying to absorb this culture, all I'd done was make myself weak, weak and helpless, unable to defend myself against the human beasts that inhabited this twenty-first-century jungle.

'He's going to kill us, Mum. I know it for sure.'

'Shelley, you've got to stay calm. Just do what he says.'

'You don't understand the danger we're in! He's high on drugs! *He's going to kill us!'*

What kind of justice was this? What kind of God would let this happen? Hadn't Mum and I suffered enough? Dad had walked out on us and left us to struggle on by ourselves while he luxuriated in the Spanish sun with his twenty-four-year-old slut. I'd been so badly bullied that I'd had to leave school and be taught at home. My face had been left scarred with the marks of others' spite. And now out of all the houses that this walking time bomb could have broken into, he'd broken into ours, just as we were starting to build a new life together, just as things were beginning to get better again.

What more did we have to suffer now? Rape? Torture? What crime had we ever committed apart from the crime of being weak, the crime of being mice? What harm had we ever done to deserve such relentless punishment? Why wasn't this happening to Teresa Watson and Emma Townley? Why wasn't this happening to the girls who'd bullied me so badly that I'd wanted to take my own life? Why wasn't this happening to my

dad and Zoe? Why was this happening to us? Again?
Hadn't we suffered enough?

'Mum?'
'Yes, darling?'
'Mum, this rope's beginning to give. I think I can get
my hands free.'
And then I smelled the chemical tang of alcohol and
knew that he was back in the room.

14

He walked past us, carrying the red sports bag, its sides straining to contain all the objects he'd stuffed inside. It seemed he'd grabbed anything that had come to hand – I could even see the family-sized bottle of shampoo from the bathroom protruding from one of the zippered side pockets.

He went into the dining room and began sweeping the knick-knacks from the top of the sideboard into what little space was left in the bag. All the while he stared glassily at the wall in front of him like a blind man, almost oblivious to what he was doing. He didn't seem to notice when any of the miniature glass animals or china figurines missed the bag and fell to the floor, but just carried on sweeping, sweeping, like a robot.

But what I couldn't take my eyes off, what I stared at in disbelief, was the knife. He'd left the fanged hunting knife on the dining-room table. *He was unarmed.*

My hands were free now. I left them lying loosely in my lap, the rope still ineffectively coiled around them, and began to work on my legs. The rope must have been years old, and as I forced my ankles apart I could feel the dry prickly strands snapping one by one.

'Mum!' I hissed, turning right around in my chair to bring my lips close to her cheek. 'This rope's so old that—'

'Hey!'

I jumped as if a firecracker had gone off under my chair. He was staring straight at me, an ugly dog snarl curling around his lips and nose.

'No talking!' he screamed, the veins standing out in his forehead and a shower of spittle spraying from his mouth. It was so loud that I still felt the words echoing round and round the room long after he'd said them.

When he couldn't fit anything more into the bag, he walked towards us, the knife still lying forgotten on the table behind him. He stood in front of us, rocking queasily backwards and forwards. Under the bright ceiling light, his skin was greasy with sweat and deathly pale; he wore a pained expression like a child who'd eaten too much at a party and now had raking stomach ache and knew he was going to be sick. I could see the hairs on his top lip and chin – not a man's bristles, but the ugly, sparse whiskers of an adolescent.

'I'm goin' now,' he said.

But he didn't move. He stayed swaying unsteadily in front of us while his eyelids began their now-familiar flickering and his eyes rolled up like those of an epileptic about to fall into a seizure. His head lolled onto his chest and slowly, slowly he began to topple forwards.

The sound of the bag thudding to the floor brought him around too late to stop his forward momentum. He fell heavily against me. His greasy face rubbed against mine and I inhaled the nauseating stench of his foul breath. He kept his face close to mine, laughing quietly to himself, enjoying the fear and disgust he aroused in me. I kept my hands tight together, praying he wouldn't see that I'd managed to untie them.

'Fancy a snog?' he said.

I closed my eyes tightly and clenched my teeth, ready for his disgusting assault. But it didn't come. He pushed himself upright.

'I don't want to snog you,' he said. 'You're an ugly, stuck-up bitch.'

I opened my eyes a fraction and saw his olive-green shape hovering at my side.

'What's all that –' he grimaced – 'what's all that *crap* all over your face?'

I couldn't speak. I'd been so frightened for so long now I felt I couldn't take much more. I felt as though my pounding heart was going to give out at any second and I was going to die of fright, like I'd heard hunted animals did even before the hunters' dogs seized them in their jaws.

'What is it, eh?'

Silence. A long uncomfortable silence.

'What is it?'

'She was in an accident at school,' Mum answered hurriedly.

With a speed I wouldn't have thought him capable of, he wheeled around and punched her hard in the face. I felt her whole body rock violently sideways in the chair behind me.

'I didn't ask *you*!' he shouted.

'I'm sorry,' Mum said, still thinking clearly even in the full shock of the blow, trying to placate him, trying to stop him from losing his temper and spiralling out of control.

'I had an accident at school!' I cried, trying to get his attention back to me and away from Mum as his arm drew back, readying to strike her again. 'I got burned in a fire! They're scars! I'm scarred now!'

He unclenched his fist, and his arm dropped back down to his side.

'Yeah – well, you're a mess.'

'Yes, I know,' I said, trying to keep him talking, trying to keep his attention on me.

'Your old mum's prettier than you are.' He hiccuped, triggering another sour belch.

He picked up the red bag and tottered drunkenly away. He walked right past the hunting knife without so much as a glance in its direction, and disappeared into the kitchen.

We heard nothing for a long time.

'I think he's gone,' Mum whispered.

As if that were his cue, he walked back into the lounge carrying a large gift-wrapped box in his arms. It was decorated with a bright red bow, and balanced on top of it was a pink envelope with my name written on it in Mum's neatest calligraphy.

'What's *this*?' he demanded.

'It's my daughter's birthday present,' Mum answered coldly.

'What is it?'

'It's a computer, a portable computer.'

'Nice one!' he exclaimed delightedly, as though the gift had been bought especially for him. 'I'm goin' now. You'd better not call the police or I'll come back.'

His eyes closed and a vague smile passed over his face as if he were enjoying a private joke. They opened again but only just, struggling to push up lids that had become unbearably heavy. He looked around him as though trying to remember where he was, what he'd been saying. 'Yeah, that's right,' he drawled, 'I'll come back and do you. Understand?'

'Yes, we understand,' Mum said. 'We won't call the police. We promise.'

He stood rooted to the spot for a long time, lost in the convoluted labyrinths of his trip. He mumbled something and tried to belch but nothing came up. His eyes closed and I'd just decided that he'd slipped into another one of his strange trances when they suddenly flicked open again like a doll's. He stared fixedly at me with such cold, piercing, homicidal intensity that I had to look away. *The bloodletting's going to start now, the bloodletting's going to start right now, just when we thought he'd gone away and left us in peace! The frenzy's going to start now . . .*

He teetered forward and the pink envelope slipped off the laptop and clacked onto the floor. At this sound he drew himself up straight again, smacked his chops loudly and licked his lips.

'I'll come back and do you,' he said again, so quietly it was almost inaudible.

He fumblingly reorganized the laptop, turning it onto its side and gripping it under his left arm. As he did so, the beautiful red bow fell off and spiralled to the floor like an autumn leaf. Then he tacked his way slowly back to the dining room. He paused at the table and I was sure he was going to pick up the knife this time. But he just seemed to look right through it, as if it were invisible or some hallucinatory dagger of the mind, before he reeled into the kitchen and disappeared from sight.

I listened to him in the kitchen struggling to let himself out with my computer under one arm and the red sports bag in the other, too far gone to put one down and open the back door with a free hand.

'It's over,' Mum said. 'He's really going now. I told you he wouldn't hurt us.'

Yes, it was true this time. He really was going, taking away with him my sixteenth birthday present clasped tightly against his stinking jacket. The gift Mum had carefully wrapped up and decorated with a pretty red bow and put out on the kitchen table last thing before she went up to bed so that it would be there for me when I came down to breakfast in the morning, a wonderful birthday surprise. The laptop that with her mother's intuition she'd known I wanted, that she couldn't afford but that she'd been determined I should have, no matter what she had to go without herself.

He was going – leaving behind him a jagged gouge on Mum's cheek from his bulky signet ring and a storm-coloured bruise engulfing her right eye. He was going – leaving behind him two defenceless women he'd systematically humiliated, tormented and abused as if it were the natural order of things, as if it was his *right*.

To this day I still don't know exactly what made me do what I did next. Perhaps it was seeing that pallid, vicious thug carrying away my birthday present, the symbol of all my future ambitions; perhaps it was outrage at what he'd done to Mum; perhaps it was because he'd called me ugly; perhaps the truth is that we all have a limit to what we can endure – *even mice* – and that when that limit's passed something just snaps. Perhaps it was merely the way Mum's beautiful red bow had floated so slowly, so pathetically to the ground . . .

I tore away the few remaining strands of rope that tied my legs, grabbed the knife from the dining-room table, and ran out into the garden after him.

15

He'd only gone a short distance to where the patio met the grass of the lawn, still within the yellow patch of light the kitchen threw out into the darkness. He heard me coming, and glanced back over his shoulder before continuing unconcernedly on his way, as if he'd seen no more than a cat going about its catty business – not a screaming girl running at him with a knife.

I thumped the knife into the gap between his shoulder blades with all my might.

I couldn't believe how hard his back was, like stabbing the trunk of a tree – the blade stopped two inches short of the hilt and it took a huge effort to pull it out again. At the blow, he let out a long sigh and dropped the laptop and the red bag. He leaned forward as though he'd been punched in the stomach, and half-turning, glared up at me with a look of outraged innocence on his face.

'What did you do *that* for?' he moaned, as if I'd played some tasteless practical joke on him.

I struck at him again and again, half-closing my eyes, not wanting to see the wounds the knife was making, not wanting to see the blood.

Still bent double like a soldier under sniper fire, he headed back towards the kitchen, his left arm raised to try to ward off the worst of my blows. I thought, *Good! I want you back inside the house! I don't want you to get away from me!*

He got into the kitchen and tried to close the back door against me, but he wasn't fast enough and I shoulder-barged my way inside. He staggered towards the pantry, trying to put the pine table between us, but again he was too slow. I ran alongside him, stabbing him at will, taunting him like a picador taunts the bull as he jabs his spear into the animal's streaming flanks. He went round and round the table and I followed him, stabbing, stabbing, stabbing.

'*We're playing musical chairs now!*' I screamed at him. '*We're playing musical chairs now!*'

I'd struck him so many times by then I'd lost count. He seemed to be growing weaker, and he collapsed against the sink, upsetting the plastic drainer full of plates and dishes from the previous night and sending them crashing to the floor. As he tried to recover his balance, one of my blows nicked the side of his neck and blood suddenly jetted out like water from a burst pipe. He clapped his hand to the wound and hunched in the corner by the bread bin, his back turned to me.

I just wanted him to lie down, to stop moving, to stop being any sort of threat to us. I contemplated the back of his ripped and bloody jacket, trying to judge where his heart would be, and struck as hard as I could. Just at that instant, he twisted away. The knife met the thick bone plate of his shoulder blade with such force that it was jarred out of my hand and went skidding away across the floor.

I saw the expression on his face change from cowering submission to a mocking, murderous triumph as he realized the tables had turned in his favour, and before I could even look round to see where the knife was, he launched himself at me.

My knees buckled, and with all the burglar's weight on top of me, I fell heavily backwards onto the floor. I landed on something sharp and hard that ground against my coccyx, and I screamed out in blinding pain. I knew at once what it was. I was lying on the knife!

He writhed on my chest, dragging himself up my body, trying to push back my chin with his forearm to expose my throat. Blood streamed from his neck wound like wine from an upturned bottle. It poured into my face, a never-ending river, flowing over me, filling my mouth so I had to spit and gasp for air as if I were drowning, stinging my eyes like soap, blinding me completely.

His face was pressed up against mine now, our lips almost touching in a hideous parody of a lovers' kiss. He was trying to get his hands around my neck, but I frenziedly beat them away and clawed wildly at his face. Every time he tried to pin my hands to the floor I twisted out of his grip and dug my nails back into his eyes. I was flailing and screaming, desperately trying to push his suffocating weight off me so that I could get my hand to the knife trapped against the small of my back. If I could just roll him off me for one second and reach the knife then I'd have the advantage again. If I could just get my hand to the knife . . .

But he was too strong. In spite of the wounds he'd suffered, in spite of the blood he was haemorrhaging from his neck, he was still too strong for me, and he finally managed to get both his hands around my throat. I felt a sudden vice-like pressure cut off my air supply. Pinpricks of white light exploded in the darkness behind my eyelids, and I knew with absolute certainty that I was about to die if I didn't breathe in the next few seconds. I managed to squint my burning eyes open and saw his contorted face in repulsive close-up. His pupils were hugely dilated with adrenalized frenzy, his yellow teeth gritted with effort as he choked the life out of me; a thin thread of pink spittle dangled from his lower lip. And I thought, *This is the last thing I'll ever see.*

Something started to give in the middle of my neck; something was on the point of snapping. I'd managed to get my fingertips to the knife, but now all the strength was draining from me. My arms flopped uselessly by my sides. I hadn't drawn a breath for a very long time. The pinpricks of white light became bigger and bigger until there was only white light. *So this is what dying is like,* I thought, *this is dying – this is the white light they talk about* – and I stopped fighting him, even in my mind, and closed my eyes and gave up and waited for death to come, the actual moment of death to come, and then there was an enormous crack and as if by magic all his weight was gone and the terrible pressure on my throat was suddenly taken away.

When I opened my eyes again I saw Mum holding the chopping board in both hands, its white marble surface spattered with dark blood. She'd struck him with such force that he'd been lifted right off me and pivoted sideways so that only his legs still touched me, lying across mine at an oblique angle.

Amazingly, he was still conscious, his two eyes staring wildly out of a mask of bright crimson blood. He was up on his forearms, trying to drag himself under the kitchen table before another blow could fall. But Mum wasn't going to be denied. I watched her lining up the blow, picking her spot carefully, tightening her grip on the board's short handle so there would be no slipping, no mistake. Then she raised it high above her head.

I closed my eyes as it started to descend. I dreaded seeing the obscenity it would make when it struck. But I heard the sickening mushy noise and felt a hard fragment of the burglar's skull ricochet off my cheek.

16

The clock on the kitchen cooker said 4:57.

I sat propped against the washing machine, hungrily sucking air into my burning throat. Mum sat at the table, her head in her hands, sobbing quietly.

The burglar was dead. There was no doubt about that. His body was sprawled on the floor, his head and torso under the kitchen table. His jacket was bunched up around his ears, his right arm stretched out in front of him as if he'd been reaching for something when he died.

I couldn't see his face from where I was sitting – thank God – just the back of his head, grotesquely mis-shapen after Mum's killing blow. A lake of blood was spreading out around him, a veritable *sea* of blood, glistening in the bright electric light. It crept slowly over the tiles in thick oily tongues, and lapped against the bottoms of the cupboards, the cooker, the prickly coir fibre doormat by the back door, the dusty heating pipes beneath the breakfast bench. I thought of that line in *Macbeth* that I'd found so odd, when Lady Macbeth, remembering Duncan's murder, says: 'Who would have thought the old man to have had so much blood in him?' I understood it completely now. I wondered idly if Shakespeare had ever killed anyone – how else could he have known so exactly what the aftermath was like? *Who would have thought the skinny burglar to have had so much blood in him?*

The red tide threatened my feet, stretched out in front of me, and I pulled them back a few inches to avoid contact with the syrupy pool. But I didn't move – I was simply too exhausted. Besides, I was already covered in his blood. My hands were slippery with it, my hair matted, my nightdress spattered and stained, my towelling dressing gown that had soaked it up like a sponge was heavy with it, my mouth was full of its sharp metallic taste.

The next time I looked at the clock it was 5:13.

I tried to speak, but my throat burned and only a hoarse croak emerged. After a while I tried again, and this time it was a little easier.

'Mum?'

She sat at the table, lost in thought, her head still propped up by the columns of her forearms as though it was unspeakably heavy. She looked up when I spoke, but it took a moment for her eyes to return to the present.

'Mum, shouldn't you call the police?'

She smiled sadly and shook her head. 'That's what I've been sitting here trying to work out, darling.'

I didn't understand what she meant and thought she was in some kind of shock. 'We have to call the police,

Mum,' I said gently. 'We've got to tell them what's happened. They'll call an ambulance. I need to go to hospital – my neck – it's killing me.'

But she didn't go to the phone. She remained seated at the kitchen table, her bare feet perched on the struts of the chair to keep them out of the pool of congealing blood. With the right side of her face swollen, her eye puffy and half-closed and ringed by black and purple bruising, she didn't look like herself any more – it was almost like looking at a completely different person.

'Mum?' I prompted her again. 'The police? I need to go to hospital.'

But still she didn't move towards the phone.

'Shelley . . .'

'Hm?'

'What happened when you ran into the garden? I couldn't see – I was still struggling to untie my legs. I saw you take the knife. What happened then?'

'I stabbed him,' I replied.

'Where?'

'In his back.'

'Did he have a weapon?'

'No.'

'How many times did you stab him before I found you in the kitchen?'

'I don't know . . . lots . . . lots. Mum,' I groaned, 'when are you going to call the police?'

Her reply took me completely by surprise.

'I don't want to go to prison, Shelley.'

'What are you talking about?' I croaked. 'What do you mean, *prison*?'

'I don't want to go to prison,' she repeated coldly, flatly. 'And I don't want you to go to prison either.'

'What are you talking about, Mum? You're not going to go to prison. He broke into our house. He had a knife. We were defending ourselves, for God's sake. He was strangling me – if you hadn't come along when you did, he would have *killed* me!'

I thought she was being completely pathetic. I wanted help to come. I wanted to go to hospital and have the pain in my throat taken away. I wanted to have all the sticky sour blood washed off me and to be clean again, to smell of soap and talcum powder and to lie in a crisp cool hospital bed and be fussed over by nurses. Above all, I wanted to sleep, to sleep for hours and hours, and to forget the horror I'd just lived through . . .

To my amazement, when I looked at Mum again she was laughing – not a happy laugh, but a morbid, bitter laugh.

'If only it were that simple, Shelley . . . but it isn't.' She patiently collected her thoughts before she spoke again. 'He was leaving the house when you chased after him. He was unarmed—'

'*Unarmed!*' I exclaimed in disbelief. 'He's a man. I'm just a girl.'

'It makes no difference! He was *leaving* the house. *You* had the knife and *he* didn't.'

'Mum, you're being ridiculous. It was self-defence.

He tied us up. He hit you in the face. I didn't know whether he'd really gone, or if he was about to come back and kill us both. He'd already come back once – I couldn't take any chances. The police would never take his side against us . . .'

'Shelley, I'm a lawyer. I know what I'm talking about. If we call the police, their forensic people will search every inch of this house. They'll quickly work out that he was *outside* the house when you attacked him. We'll have to admit that you had the knife then and he was unarmed. They'll have no choice but to prosecute us—'

'Prosecute us? Prosecute us for what?'

'For murder.'

'For *murder*?' I couldn't believe what I was hearing. Surely she was in shock, surely she was just talking nonsense . . .

'There'll be a trial. Three or four court appearances beforehand, perhaps as long as a year to wait before the trial itself. There'll be publicity, lots of publicity, the press will have a field day – this is just the kind of thing they love. I'll lose my job. Blakely won't want the firm to be connected with anything as messy as this. If we're lucky, we'll have a sympathetic jury who'll take our side – they'll understand that we were in fear of our lives, that it's impossible to think rationally when you're so terrified.'

'And what if we're unlucky?'

'If we're unlucky and we get a bad jury or a particularly good prosecutor—'

'Then what?'

'We could be convicted of murder.'

'But how? This is insane!'

'The law says you can use force to defend yourself against an attacker but only *reasonable* force. The jury only has to decide that one of those wounds – *just one* – that you gave him with the knife wasn't reasonable and if it was potentially fatal—'

'What does that mean?'

'If he'd have died from it later, whether I'd hit him or not. If that's what the medical evidence concludes, you could be found guilty of murder.'

I sat in stunned silence. Put like that, everything suddenly seemed very different.

I *had* been defending myself. I *had* been defending Mum. I *did* think he might come back . . . but it was also true that I hadn't wanted him to escape, that I'd been pleased when he'd run back into the kitchen. I remembered how I'd taunted him and struck at him as we ran round and round the table, how I'd aimed the blow at his back where I thought his heart would be as he'd huddled in the corner by the bread bin, so that he'd stop moving *for good*. If I was really honest, hadn't I meant to kill him? And if I'd meant to kill him, wasn't that murder?

I shouldn't have gone after him. It was a stupid, stupid mistake. And if I had to be punished for it, so be it, but I didn't understand why Mum should suffer for what I'd done.

'What about you though, Mum? You hit him when

he was strangling me. You saved my life. How could that be murder?'

'That's true, Shelley, that's true, he was strangling you. But I hit him *twice*. That second blow . . . I knew you were out of danger. I knew he was no longer a threat. I could have called the police then and who knows, he might be in the hospital now, he might even have gone on to recover from his injuries. But I didn't. I hit him again. Deliberately. I – I don't know what came over me. But the truth is, *I wanted to kill him*. I know it was done in the heat of the moment, but if the jury decides that second blow wasn't reasonable – then I'm guilty of murder.'

'I don't believe this,' I whimpered. We'd beaten off the weasel-faced burglar's murderous assault, but he still remained a threat to us. Even though we'd killed him, he could still destroy our lives. 'What are we going to do, Mum?'

'I don't think I could survive it,' she said. 'The trial, the reporters, the publicity. And prison – prison would kill me.'

'What are we going to do, Mum?' I moaned. *'What are we going to do?'*

The clock said 5:56 when Mum spoke again. A watery grey light was beginning to seep in through the kitchen window, the birds in the trees outside were chirruping joyously, welcoming in the morning as if this were a new day just like any other.

'I think we should bury him in the garden,' she said.

17

And that's what we did. We buried him in the garden.

'Surreal' is the only word to describe the hour that followed. It was as though Mum and I had stepped into a bizarre hall-of-mirrors world where familiar reality was warped into absurd and grotesque shapes. I *knew* that it was all really happening, but at the same time I couldn't *believe* that it was all really happening.

Mum and I pulling on our wellington boots so that we wouldn't have to wade into that sticky pool in our bare feet when we seized the burglar's legs and pulled him out from under the table.

The two of us debating whether to bury him in the vegetable patch or the oval rose bed as rationally, as calmly, as if we'd been discussing which wallpaper to pick for my bedroom (we finally chose the oval rose bed, as the veggie patch was too far to drag him and too close to the road).

The way the burglar's body resisted our first tug, as though he'd become stuck in that congealing gravy.

Mum and I dragging a corpse (*a corpse! A dead human being!*) through the dew-wet grass while the birds twittered hysterically in the trees around us, and the day, a beautiful warm spring day, dawned.

The burglar's head bumping down the concrete steps that led to the front garden and the oval rose bed (I winced at each bump and then told myself: he can't feel anything – he's *dead* – and I realized that death was still too enormous for me to grasp, that I still couldn't rid myself of the idea that he must feel something).

Mum lurching backwards when his trainer came off in her hand and taking a pratfall straight out of a home-video bloopers show.

The two of us, staggering around the garden, help-less with laughter, while the corpse lay face-down on the grass, its right arm outstretched before it like a resolute swimmer.

Mum and I walking to the shed to get the shovels – not to plant vegetables this time, but to plant a corpse, to plant a skinny, pallid twenty-year-old man in the chalky soil of our front garden.

Returning with our tools to find a large ginger cat we'd never seen before and have never seen since, licking the blood from the tips of the corpse's fingers (it slunk away reluctantly at our approach and disap-peared through an impossibly small hole in the hedge).

Looking up from our digging to see a farmer, perched high atop a ludicrous Heath Robinson piece of farm machinery, come roaring down the narrow lane and right past the house not more than a hundred and fifty metres from where we stood; watching him glance quickly in our direction and salute us with a stiff straight arm which he kept aloft until he'd passed out of sight.

We waved dazedly back at him, two women in blood-stained nightclothes burying a body in our front garden at half-past six in the morning.

There was just enough room to fit the corpse in the rose bed without having to uproot any of the rose bushes. The top layer of soil was wet after the night's rain and our sharp spades cut through it easily. It was sticky and clung to the blades and we had to use our boots time and again to scrape them clean. The deeper we dug, however, the more difficult it became. Two feet down, the soil seemed unaffected by the rain and as hard as rock.

I started to sweat profusely. I felt dizzy and light-headed and had to take off my heavy dressing gown before I could carry on. We were both too weak, too exhausted from lack of sleep, to make much of an impression against this stubborn stratum, and as we hacked away fruitlessly at the soil, the day was growing lighter every second. I began to feel horribly exposed and visible, even though there was no one around to see us – the farmer had long gone, the lane was deserted, and the surrounding fields were as still and silent as a photograph. I found myself remembering one of my religious education teacher's favourite sayings: *The eye of God sees all.*

At three feet deep, Mum stopped, red-faced and breathing heavily from the exertion.

'It's not deep enough, Mum,' I said. 'Animals might be able to dig him up.'

'It'll have to do, Shelley. We've just got to *hide* him. We've got the house to clean up yet.'

We dragged the body to the very lip of the narrow trench, and then pushed him in using our feet and our spades, not wanting to touch something so disgusting with our hands. To my horror, he came to rest on his back, and I found myself staring at that weaselly face yet again. The same face, yet different, subtly changed by death.

The eyes were half-open, but they were glassy, un-focused. His eyebrows, completely relaxed now, had dropped low on his forehead, forming a dark Neanderthal ridge. His jaw must have been dislocated by Mum's blow, because the bottom half of his face was twisted sharply away from the rest. The fracture had forced his mouth open and his lower teeth now protruded slightly above his top lip, giving him a fierce, animal look like a boxer dog. His left arm lay straight by his side, the hand on his thigh as if strumming a guitar, while his right arm, stiffened into the position in which he'd died, was extended high above his head like a keen student who knows the answer to a difficult question.

And maybe he does know the answer to a difficult question, I thought, *the most difficult question of all – what happens to us when we die?*

The shallow pit we'd dug wasn't long enough to fit the burglar's straightened right arm. The forearm and hand remained protruding out of the mud, a grotesque new five-petalled flower in the garden. Rather than dig any more, Mum stepped gingerly down into the hole and seized the corpse's arm and tried to bend it down towards the top of his head. Rigor mortis had already started to set in, and the arm kept slipping from her grip and straightening itself as though the burglar was deliberately resisting her – even in death.

Mum was horribly pale when she stepped up out of the hole.

We shovelled the soil back on top of him. I buried his feet (one foot in its trainer, the other in a ragged green sock), his legs, his left hand, his waist, but I couldn't bring myself to throw any dirt over his head. When I saw Mum dump a shovelful of soil onto his face, I winced (*mud was going in his eyes – mud was going in his mouth!*) and then kicked myself for being such a baby.

He can't feel anything – he's dead!

When we'd finished, the youth had completely disappeared from the face of the earth. There was Honeysuckle Cottage, there was the neat front garden, there was the oval rose bed, there were the rose bushes already showing here and there a precocious pink bud. But the corpse had vanished without trace.

We leaned on our spades, drunk with fatigue, taking a moment before we started on the next horrendous task – cleaning up the blood in the kitchen.

It was then that I heard the noise. Soft, muffled, a

series of musical notes like a bird or maybe even an insect. It stopped and then a few seconds later it started again, the same set of musical notes. Mum and I looked at each other, confused. The noise stopped. It started again. I looked around at the bushes and flowerbeds to see what it could be, and then it dawned on me. I knew that tune. I'd heard it many times before, in the street, in cafes, in restaurants, on trains . . .

It was the ringing of a mobile phone. And it was coming from the oval rose bed.

18

The burglar's mobile must have rung more than twenty times before it finally rang off. I realized I'd been clenching my fists and gritting my teeth the whole time, as though enduring an agonizing physical pain.

Mum rarely swore but she swore now. A staccato outburst of ugly expletives.

'Oh my God!' I whined. '*Omigod!*'

We both stared in horror at the rose bed as if we'd seen the soil form itself into a mouth and start to speak.

'What are we going to do, Mum? What are we going to *do*?'

Mum was silent for a long time before she answered. 'We've got to dig him up. We've got to get that phone. We can't risk it ringing again and someone hearing it . . . and the police will be able to trace it, they'll be able to pinpoint its exact location. We've got to get it out of there.'

She raked her hand through her hair, her brow knotted with anxiety. '*Dammit!* I should have gone through his pockets! Whatever was I thinking?'

The thought of digging up the corpse and searching

through its pockets was simply too much for me. I slumped down on the grass.

Mum glanced at me over her shoulder. I was struggling to bite back the tears. I felt unnaturally hot, feverish. I was short of breath, but even taking great lungfuls of air didn't seem to help. I didn't want to see that face again. I didn't want to see that face with mud in its eyes and mud in its mouth. I didn't think I could bear that . . .

'I'll do it, Shelley,' she said as if reading my mind. 'But we haven't got a lot of time. Go back inside, get the mop from the kitchen cupboard and start cleaning up the floor. Don't walk anywhere else – *stay in the kitchen* – we mustn't tread blood all over the house.'

'OK, Mum,' I said in little more than a whisper. But I didn't move. I felt weighed down by the futility, the stupidity, the wrong-headedness of what we were doing.

'Someone's looking for him already, Mum. Someone's already trying to find him. We're never going to get away with this. We're bound to get caught!'

She turned towards me a face made strange and sinister by the livid purple bruising.

'It's too late to worry about that now,' she said, her voice oddly hollow, as if her mind was elsewhere, perhaps already steeling herself to the grisly task she was about to perform.

Just then the burglar's phone rang again, and I jumped as if I'd had an electric shock. I got quickly to my feet and hurried across the lawn back to the house.

I couldn't bear that sound! *I had to get away from that sound!*

That cheery eight-note sequence repeating itself over and over again sounded to my ears like the burglar's laughter – taunting us, mocking us from the darkness of his shallow grave.

When Mum came into the kitchen thirty-five minutes later, her face was more drawn, more haggard than I'd ever seen it before.

She emptied one of her dressing-gown pockets onto the breakfast bench. There was a flattened packet of cigarettes, a Zippo lighter, a worn leather wallet, sweet wrappers, a bunch of car keys with a football keyring and the mobile phone.

'I've turned it off,' she said.

She delved into the other pocket and waved a wad of crumpled notes at me. 'And look at this! He had all the money from under my mattress in his back pocket – nearly two hundred pounds! I can't believe I didn't look in his pockets before we . . .' Her voice trailed off.

'We've had hardly any sleep, Mum. We're not thinking clearly.'

'Well, we've got to start thinking clearly from now on – or we *will* get caught.' She put her hands on her hips and chewed her bottom lip as she always did when she was agitated. 'We've got to think. We've got to *think.*'

She was trying to suppress her panic, her horror and

revulsion; she was trying to deal with this bloodbath as she would a problem tossed onto her desk at work – as a mental puzzle, an intellectual challenge. All she had to do was bring the full force of her brilliant mind to bear on it, her common sense, her methodical attention to detail, and she would solve it like she solved all the other problems.

It was only then that Mum looked around the kitchen and noticed the work I'd done. I'd picked up all the pieces of broken crockery and put them in a cardboard box by the back door. I'd set about cleaning up the worst of the blood with the mop, filling and emptying bucket after bucket of water at the sink, watching the water I poured away gradually change from dark crimson to the faintest of pinks. I'd dried the floor off as best I could with the tea towels that were to hand and was just about to start on the bloodstains on the walls and benchtops when Mum had come back.

'Well done, Shelley,' she smiled. 'You've got rid of the worst of it.' She glanced at the clock on the cooker. 'Seven twenty-three. That's good. We're doing well for time.'

Then her face became concentrated again. *The problem. She had to address the problem.*

She took a thick roll of black bin bags out of the drawer under the sink and snapped one off.

'Listen to me carefully, Shelley,' she said. 'We've got to get rid of everything that's bloodstained and everything that can prove the burglar was ever in this house.

We'll put it all in bin bags and we'll hide them upstairs in the spare room until we can get rid of them safely.'

She swept the burglar's little pile of personal possessions into the bin bag, then picked up the box of bloodstained crockery and tried to fit that in. I held the neck of the bag open for her to make it easier, then brought over the tea towels I'd used to dry the floor and dropped them into the bin bag too.

'Where's the knife?' she asked.

I took it from the draining board where I'd left it and gave it to her, trying not to look at the gore dried thick and dark like treacle on the blade. She wedged it deep inside the cardboard box.

She looked around her for other bloodstained objects, and noticed the doormat. She knelt down and folded this too into the bin bag. I mopped up the pink rectangular stain it had left behind.

Mum tore off another bin bag. She took off her blood-flecked dressing gown and stuffed it inside.

'Where's your dressing gown, Shelley?'

I had to think for a minute and then I remembered. I'd left it by the rose bed.

'Can you run and get it, please, darling, and it can go in here with mine. It'll have to be destroyed, I'm afraid – we can't risk washing it.'

I didn't want to go anywhere near the burglar's grave, but I couldn't say no – not after what Mum had just forced herself to do. I raced across the lawn, trying not to look at the oval rose bed, trying not to think about a voice coming from under the soil (*Fancy a snog?*) or a cold hand seizing my ankle. I grabbed the towelling bundle and sprinted back to the house as fast as I could.

Mum put my dressing gown in the bin bag with hers.

'Now give me your wellies,' she said, and that word, with its aura of childhood innocence, sounded weirdly out of place in that kitchen, at that moment.

I sat on a chair and tugged them off. Mum took hers off too, and flung both pairs into yet another bin bag.

'OK,' she said wiping her forehead with the back of her hand. 'I'm going to really scrub everything in here – cupboards, walls, *everything*.'

She disappeared into the louvred kitchen cupboard where we kept all the household cleaning stuff, and emerged a few moments later with a plastic bowl, scrubbing brushes, a pile of clean tea towels and an enormous bottle of disinfectant. I looked at her in her nightie and bright yellow rubber gloves, her hair a ragged bird's nest, and felt the urge to burst out laughing again as I had when the burglar's trainer had come off in her hand and she'd been catapulted backwards.

'*People in the audience sometimes laugh out loud during the grisliest scenes in* Macbeth,' *Roger had said to me once.*

'*Why?' I'd asked.*

'*Because horrible things are funny.*'

I managed to beat down the urge to laugh – which was probably a good thing in light of the desperate resolve on Mum's face.

MICE

'What do you want me to do, Mum?'

She didn't answer me. She was filling the bowl with hot water, absorbed in the details of the problem – how to rewind time, how to make the house look just as it had before the burglar broke in, how to clean the kitchen so that the police wouldn't find a single spot of blood. I had to ask again.

'I think you'd best go upstairs and shower and get all that blood off you,' she said, as she yanked off another bin bag. 'Put your nightie in here when you take it off and any towels that you use. Even if they don't *look* bloodstained, they will be . . . and we can't afford to take any chances.'

19

For the second time in my life I looked at my reflection and was unable to recognize myself. The face of a savage stared out at me from the bathroom mirror – not a sixteen-year-old middle-class English girl, but a primitive savage with a face daubed in the blood of the kill, eyes wide with the excitement of battle, hair stiff with dried blood and sticking up in jagged stipples. It was a shocking sight and it took several seconds before I could accept that the savage in the mirror *was me*.

I rubbed my cheek with my index finger and the dried blood flaked off like rust, leaving a trail of russet powder on the white ceramic of the sink. I examined the grey smudges on my throat, two dark half-moons on either side of my windpipe, where the burglar had tried to strangle me. My throat still stung and I could feel something odd, something lumpy, every time I swallowed. My eyes were completely bloodshot save for a few microscopic blobs of white floating here and there. I remembered reading that the police could tell if a person had been strangled by the burst blood vessels in their eyes. Something to do with lack of oxygen in the blood. *How close had I come to death?* My head throbbed, and I felt so tired I could have curled up on the bathroom floor and gone to sleep right then and there.

A huge wave of depression crashed over me and swept me away. What a mess! What a disaster! *And it was all my fault.* I'd turned an unpleasant but commonplace domestic burglary into a disaster of monumental proportions, a calamity so shocking, so sensational it would be blazoned across the front pages in banner headlines.

In all likelihood I'd ruined my life and Mum's life for good. We were never going to get away with what we'd done. No one gets away with murder, there's always some clue, some loose end that they miss. The police always catch them sooner or later. We'd end up in prison, we'd both end up in prison. And all because I'd lost control. All because I'd refused to listen to Mum. She'd *told* me to stay calm, she'd *told* me not to panic. She'd *told* me that he wasn't going to hurt us. What had come over me? Why hadn't I listened? I'd ruined everything. I wanted to disappear, I wanted the ground to swallow me up.

Yet beneath all the guilt and self-recrimination there was something else, another emotion, stubborn and rebellious, refusing to bend to the dominant mood. It was as if in a piece of classical music, beneath the slow, sad weeping of violins and cellos, a tinny trumpet could just be made out, playing a different tune altogether –

something defiant and brash, like a military march. What was it? What was this emotion – unfamiliar, rude, independent, causing trouble like a drunk at a wedding?

I looked at my bloodshot eyes, the bruises on my neck. He'd really tried to kill me – he'd really tried to choke the life out of me while I'd lain helpless on the kitchen floor. I remembered the determination and hatred on his face, how my air supply had ceased suddenly, absolutely, as if a valve had been shut off. And he would have done it, he would have wrung the life out of me and then gone into the lounge and done the same to Mum . . . but we'd turned the tables on him. The cat had got into the mouse hole, but this time the mice had killed the cat.

When I looked at myself in the mirror again, I was surprised to see my white teeth flashing. I was smiling broadly. And then I knew what that discordant emotion was: *it was exhilaration*.

My nightie was stuck to me where the blood had dried and I had to peel it off like a plaster. It felt so good to stand under the hot rain of the shower and let the hard drops hammer soothingly on my scalp. I watched the blood disappearing down the plughole in a slurping pink whirlpool with an odd satisfaction.

Was there some mysterious connection, I wondered, between women and blood? Hadn't I been washing away blood since the age of twelve, washing it off my

hands, washing it out of my clothes? That was something boys knew nothing about. Was blood somehow
the special domain of women? Was this why so many
women became nurses? I remembered the nurses at
the hospital: those women who never fainted at the
sight of blood, who never looked away, never winced,
because blood held no fears for them, blood was an
old friend.

I worked the soap up into a thick lather and plas-
tered myself with it, enjoying the noisy smacking and
squelching. I wanted to scrub every inch of my body
clean, to make it immaculate, to step from the shower
with a completely *new skin*. As I rinsed off the soap, I
glimpsed in the mirror behind me the nasty welt where
I'd fallen on the knife. Just above my buttocks, a raised
black lump the size of a fist surrounded by an angry red
inflammation.

I reached for the shampoo to wash my hair, but
it wasn't in its usual place and I remembered with a
shudder that the burglar had taken it. I washed my
hair with soap instead, softening it with some condi-
tioner from a little green bottle that had stood on the
bathroom shelf for so long its lid was covered in dust.
When I'd rinsed out all the suds, I set about washing it
all over again.

I dried myself thoroughly and put the towel in the
bin bag where I'd already put my nightie, then wrapped
myself in another towel and secured it under my arm.
I put my favourite moisturizer on my face, working in

the cold milk with circular movements of my fingertips, and I anointed my hands in Mum's hand cream with the strong vanilla scent. I cleaned my teeth to get rid of the disgusting taste of blood that still lingered in my mouth, brushing and brushing until the minty toothpaste was burning so much I couldn't keep it in my mouth a second longer.

When I'd finished, I rubbed away the steam and looked in the bathroom mirror again. The savage had disappeared, washed away in a torrent of cleansing hot water, and I was myself once more, my hair soft and limp, my face scrubbed so vigorously my cheeks glowed. Lady Macbeth's words after Duncan's murder drifted into my mind.

A little water clears us of this deed.

But she'd been proved hopelessly wrong; water had cleaned away the blood from her body, but it couldn't remove the memory of what she'd done from her mind. Guilt over Duncan's murder had eventually driven her insane . . .

What would it be like for Mum and me? Would we be able to wash away what we'd done with a little water? Or would our minds be affected too? Would we be able to return to a normal life with the burglar rotting away under a mere three feet of soil in our front garden? Would we be able to lie to the police when they came knocking at our front door? Can mice lie like that? Can mice gag their consciences and sleep peacefully when they're surrounded by so many dark secrets?

And then a thought occurred to me. After what we'd done – killing the burglar, burying his body in the garden – maybe we weren't mice any more.

But in that case – *what were we?*

20

When I came out of the bathroom I saw Mum disappearing into the spare room, carrying two of the black bin bags. When she came out, I held up the one I'd put my nightie and towel in. 'Do you want this one?'

'Yes,' she said, in barely more than a whisper. 'I'll put mine in there too.' Her face was drained of colour, blanched, and she winced suddenly with pain, but before I could ask her if she was OK she'd slipped past me into the bathroom and locked the door.

While I was in my bedroom drying my hair I thought I heard her retching, but the noise had stopped when I clicked off the hair dryer to listen.

I got dressed in a pair of faded blue jeans and a white blouse, and tied a red scarf around my neck to hide the bruises. Even though it was going to be a warm day, I put on a thick pair of socks and my chunky-soled walking boots. When I stepped into the kitchen again, I wanted to have a good half-inch of vulcanized rubber between me and those tainted tiles.

Mum was still in the bathroom when I walked past, although I couldn't hear the shower running. I was turning at the top of the stairs to go down when I caught sight of the black bin bags in the far corner of the spare room. Mum had piled them up around the mop and bucket like sandbags protecting an anti-aircraft gun.

I stopped. The sight of them excited me strangely. I didn't have to reflect for long before I realized why. *In one of those bin bags was the burglar's wallet.* And inside the wallet, I was sure, there'd be something which would have all his personal details on it. His name. His address. His date of birth . . .

I was seized by the sudden, overpowering urge to know what the burglar's name had been. To know the name of the man I'd killed.

I listened at the bathroom door trying to hear what Mum was doing. I knew she'd go mad if she discovered me trawling through those blood-soaked objects just after I'd showered and put on clean clothes. I heard her tugging up the zip of her skirt. She was still getting dressed. She'd be some time yet, I thought, and I slipped silently into the spare room.

I was looking for the bag with the doormat and the broken crockery in it, the one she'd swept his mobile phone and wallet into. I knelt on the floor and started to run my hands over the bin bags one by one. It felt like a macabre parody of childhood Christmases, when I'd sit beneath the Christmas tree, squeezing and shaking my presents, trying to guess what they were. The bag stuffed with our dressing gowns was easy enough to identify, as was the bag with only our wellington boots inside. I thought I'd found the right one, but when I untied the neck it only contained the red sports bag (now emptied of its contraband), the marble chopping board, the wrapping paper from my laptop and the forlorn red bow.

Just then I heard Mum cough and fumble with the bathroom doorhandle and I jumped up and darted out of the spare room. On the landing, I called to her just in case she'd heard me.

'Mum? Do you want anything to eat before you go?'

Even the thought of food made me feel nauseous. I felt as if my appetite had been destroyed for all time; it seemed impossible to imagine wanting to eat food ever again. I was sure Mum would be feeling exactly the same.

'No, sweetheart,' she answered weakly. 'Just coffee, please – very strong coffee.'

Mum had worked hard while I'd been in the shower. All the smears and smudges of blood – on the cupboards, the pine table, the bread bin, the washing machine, the tiles around the sink – had disappeared. She'd taken down the blood-spattered kitchen curtains (no doubt upstairs in one of the black bin bags) and the kitchen was flooded with golden spring sunshine. The bench-tops, the sink, the draining board gleamed in the bright light, and the kitchen floor – which she'd scrubbed and dried again – positively sparkled.

Mum had left the back door open to help the floor

dry. Outside, I could see that she'd hosed down the patio – washing away our bloody boot prints and the glistening red slug trail the body had left as we'd dragged it over the paving stones. The open back door made me feel suddenly uncomfortable. *What if we hadn't actually killed the burglar but only wounded him? What if he was dragging himself across the lawn towards the house right at that very moment?* I ran to the back door, and slammed it shut and pulled the bolt across, ashamed at myself for being at the mercy of such childish imaginings, but at the same time power-less to resist them.

Mum had worked a similar miracle in the dining room and lounge. The ragged pieces of rope had gone from the floor. The two chairs were back in their proper places. My flute was returned to its case, *Russian Folk Songs* slipped inside the stool and the piano lid closed. The contents of the sideboard and the antique writing desk had been carefully picked up and put tidily away in their drawers. The potpourri had been swept up and was back in its wooden bowl on the sideboard. Every fragment of the broken vase had disappeared and its identical twin – which had stood on the cabinet on the landing – now held the violet spray of dried flowers instead. All the ornaments had been put back in the exact spot they'd occupied when I'd gone up to bed at ten o'clock the night before. Miraculously, they'd sur-vived their mistreatment at the hands of the intruder unscathed – save for the miniature thatched cottage, whose chimney, I saw on closer inspection, had been snapped off.

Mum had put all my birthday cards back on the sideboard and I noticed she'd added her card to them. It read, 'On This Special Day' and showed a close-up of a pink rose, its petals sprinkled with dewdrops. I looked inside and read the inscription: *To my beautiful, darling daughter Shelley. Sweet sixteen! May this year be one that you'll remember for the rest of your life.*

I smiled crookedly at the irony. My birthday wasn't more than a few hours old, and I already knew that I would never (*What did you do* that *for?*) ever forget it.

I made a large pot of coffee, adding six spoonfuls instead of the usual four, thinking that we'd need all the help we could get if we were going to stay awake all day. I took the coffee and cups through into the dining room. I didn't want to be in the kitchen. It wasn't only that without the curtains the light was too bright for my sore eyes. It was as if in some strange way last night's struggle was still going on in there, the stabbing, the struggling, the screaming, like a movie playing non-stop in an empty cinema . . .

It was just after eight when Mum came down, dressed in her navy blue suit and carrying her briefcase ready for work. I was amazed at how expertly she'd managed to disguise the injury to her face. She'd bathed her eye and radically reduced the swelling around it, then put on grey and purple eye shadow, cleverly camouflaging the real greys and purples of the bruising. She'd covered up the gouge on her cheek with heavy foundation, and brought her hair forward (she usually hooked it back behind her ears) to further disguise the swelling. Someone would have had to look at her pretty closely to guess that she'd been punched hard in the face.

'Your eye looks amazing, Mum – how did you do that?'

'I didn't always hate make-up, Shelley. I was sixteen myself once, you know.' She tried to wink at me, but her eyes watered with pain.

She sat down and took several noisy gulps of her coffee.

'How's your neck feeling now, sweetheart?' she asked.

'It's still sore. It hurts when I swallow. I think something's damaged – pushed out of place.'

Mum looked at me anxiously. 'I'll get you something in town today.'

'I don't think cough sweets will help,' I said, trying to control the sudden irritation I felt. 'I need to see a doctor.'

'If it doesn't get any better we'll go the doctor's, but it's a risk, Shelley.'

'I don't know how I'm going to get through today, Mum,' I whined. 'I'm so tired! Can't I just call Roger and Mrs Harris and tell them I'm ill?'

'Absolutely not!' she snapped with a fierceness that brought the heat to my cheeks. 'We mustn't change our routine in any way today – we've got to act *normally*. If the police come asking questions, the fact that you cancelled your classes or that I didn't go in to work today is just the sort of thing that will arouse their suspicions.'

Then she smiled warmly at me and squeezed my hand, and I knew she was saying sorry for snapping. 'I know it's not going to be easy, Shelley, but you'll do it, I know you will.'

I sat glumly in resigned silence. I didn't want her to go to work. I didn't want to be left on my own in the house. Not with that *thing* lying buried out there in the front garden.

'Mum?' I said, broaching something that had been worrying me all morning. 'Do you think that farmer saw us?'

'He saw us – he definitely saw us,' she replied, 'but I don't think he *saw us*, if you know what I mean. He was too far away and he was going too fast. He just saw two women tending their garden in their dressing gowns, that's all – nothing too out of the ordinary in that. Not in the country, anyway.'

I smiled, relieved that she was so unconcerned. My smile morphed of its own accord into an enormous yawn. 'God, I can hardly keep my eyes open!'

Mum held my chin between her thumb and fore-finger and looked at me closely. 'Your eyes are very bloodshot. If Roger or Mrs Harris say anything, just tell them we drank too much wine last night celebrating your birthday and that you're suffering from a bad hangover this morning.'

'That's a good idea,' I said. 'That's just what it feels like.'

Mum drained the dregs of her coffee, all the time glancing anxiously at her watch, then collected herself in that peculiar mother-hennish way she had that always warned me she was about to say something important (*Shelley, darling, your daddy wants a divorce . . .*). She squeezed my hand and looked deep into my eyes. 'Look, Shelley, I've no idea what's going to happen today. The cottage is as clean as I can get it in the time I've had, it should be OK, but keep people out of the kitchen whatever you do, and don't let anyone go upstairs under any circumstances. If –', and she squeezed my hand more tightly before continuing – 'if the police do come, call me straight away. Tell them your mum's on her way and she'll be here within an hour. *Don't let them into the house* – even if they have a warrant. They'll wait, I'm sure they'll wait. But should the worst happen and you are arrested, don't say *anything* to *anyone* – do you hear me? Refuse to answer any of their questions. You can tell them you're following my strict instructions if you like.'

With that she stood up. 'I've got to go. I mustn't be late.'

I stayed where I was, still shocked by her words: *should the worst happen and you are arrested . . . you are arrested . . . you are arrested . . .*

'Be brave,' Mum said. 'Everything will be all right, you'll see. We'll talk tonight.'

*

I waved half-heartedly as she drove away, but she didn't glance back at me and make the little glove puppet bow. She was crouched over the wheel, the full force of her mind concentrated like a blowtorch on the problem the night had set her. Our quaint little routine had been shattered – we hadn't had breakfast together in the kitchen, we hadn't kissed each other in the hall, I hadn't told her to drive carefully like I always did. Everything had changed. Everything was changing: *should the worst happen and you are arrested . . .*

I was about to close the front door when I felt it. An eerie, cold sensation that crept over the left side of my face, a sudden self-consciousness, an acute awareness of myself in my own skin, my expression, the position of my hands, the way I was standing. *The feeling that someone was watching me.*

I scanned the trees and bushes in the island in the middle of the gravel drive, the yawning mouth of the garage with its stepladder and can of oil, the hedge to the right that bordered the farmer's field, but I couldn't see anyone. Away to the left were the plants and shrubs that separated the gravel drive from the front garden, and through their tangled foliage I could make out the close-cropped lawn.

And the sinister mound of the oval rose bed.

He's dead, for God's sake! He's dead!

I slammed the door shut and fumbled the chain across.

21

I still don't know how I got through that day.

After Mum left, I sat slumped at the dining-room table like a puppet whose strings have been cut. I must have sat there for nearly two hours, reliving the events of the previous night time after time, from the moment I woke up to the moment Mum shattered the burglar's skull with the chopping board.

It was as if my mind, unable to take in the enormity of the events while they'd actually been happening, had to go back over them obsessively in a desperate attempt to understand them now. I was powerless to resist and sat like a zombie, staring into space, watching the grisly drama unfolding in my mind's eye in agonizing close-up, hideous slow motion. And when it ended and the burglar was dead, the whole thing simply began all over again.

A loud knock at the front door jolted me back to the present.

The police! It's the police! How did they find us so quickly?

I sleepwalked my way slowly across the lounge, my

exhausted heart beating a frenetic tattoo in my chest once again.

I mustn't let them in, even if they've got a warrant, I mustn't let them in!

With a shaking hand I pulled back the curtain and peered out of the window. There were no police cars, no flashing blue lights, no black-uniformed officers with their pocket radios crackling. There was only Roger. Roger holding his battered satchel. Roger whistling to himself. Roger squinting up at the cloudless blue sky.

Roger was in extremely good spirits that morning. I'd never seen him so cheery and talkative, almost as if it were his birthday, not mine. He'd bought me a beautiful hardback edition of Daphne du Maurier's *Rebecca* and a birthday card with a cartoon dog in artist's beret and smock saying, *I want to paint something special for your birthday* – and inside, *SO LET'S PAINT THE TOWN RED!*

It took an enormous effort to feign the sort of girlish excitement Roger expected me to show when my mind felt on the point of fragmenting into a thousand tiny pieces. Just that word, birthday, with its terrible new associations (*What's this? It's my daughter's birthday present. What is it?*) made my face flush red-hot and tears well up in my eyes, so that I had to blink rapidly to dispel them.

I struggled to answer Roger's stream of cheery questions (*What did your mum get you? Are you going anywhere special tonight?*), stumbling over my words as if recovering from an anaesthetic or unused to speech, wearing a smile so forced that my face actually hurt with the effort. In case he detected something strained about my enthusiasm, I told him as soon as I could that Mum and I had drunk too much the night before and were both suffering for it this morning.

'Ye-es, I noticed your eyes were looking rather red, young lady,' he teased.

We went into the dining room and sat at our usual places, and Roger began to unpack his satchel. I watched him nervously, afraid of what his sharply observant eyes might notice as they glanced around the room. Hugely magnified, they darted this way and that behind his thick lenses like intelligent green fish. Would they notice something that we'd missed? A twist of the ragged rope he'd used to tie us up protruding from beneath the sofa? The white stump where the miniature cottage's chimney had been? A triangular shard of the broken vase lying next to his chair leg? What was the tiny thread that would unravel everything? I doodled manically in the margin of my notebook, not daring to look up in case something in my expression betrayed my anxiety.

To me, everything in the dining room was tainted, compromised, *impregnated* by the events of the previous night – the sideboard and the antique writing desk had been ransacked by the burglar just a few hours before; the wooden bowl of potpourri had been knocked to the floor in his frantic search; the ornaments on the sideboard had been scooped into the red sports bag he'd been holding when I'd stabbed him; his knife had been lying on the dining-room table (exactly where Roger now placed his pen case) when I'd snatched it up on my way out into the garden; the very chair Roger sat in, the one with the chipped back, was the one in which Mum had been bound hand and foot, meekly awaiting her fate.

I was convinced Roger would be able to see the traces these events had left behind them standing out as clearly as the vapour trails of jets in an azure sky. I expected him to cry out at any second: *What's happened here, Shelley? Something terrible's happened in this house!*

It seemed impossible to believe that for him the dining room was just as it had always been, that there was nothing different about the writing desk, the ornaments on the sideboard, the chair he was sitting in; that the sinister change that had come over everything was simply the projection of my guilty mind. I was convinced he'd notice something that Mum and I had missed, some tiny incriminating detail we'd been too tired to see. And if he did . . . what then? Mum hadn't told me what to do if Roger discovered our secret.

After a seemingly interminable period getting his notes in order, Roger began on the origins of the First World War, a subject he was fast on his way to becoming a genuine expert in. I nodded and uh-huhed and occasionally wrote something in my notebook while my mind, safe from detection in its impenetrable secret self, carried on obsessively playing back the events of the night before.

'You have to remember that Germany was tied to the Schlieffen plan, which called for France to be knocked out in a lightning attack so that all Germany's forces could then be concentrated on Russia – it was an absolute article of faith for them.'

Don't do anything or you'll get this!

'If the Russians completed their mobilization, they would be able to bring six million men under arms, and in spite of their defeat by Japan, there was still great fear in Germany of "the Russian steamroller".'

I gotta tie you up . . . That's why I brought the rope.

'Austria–Hungary's ultimatum to Serbia was so harsh it was nigh on impossible to comply with, although the Serbs did their very best – enough to satisfy Kaiser Wilhelm that the cause of war had evaporated . . .'

I shouldn't have had them eggs. Them eggs was off.

'There is evidence to suggest that Berchtold used a fabricated report of Serbian aggression on the Danube to force the emperor to sign the declaration of war . . .'

I know what I want, lady! I know what I want!

'Britain's reason for going to war was Germany's violation of Belgian neutrality, but Britain itself had plans to send troops into Belgium should that prove necessary. A truly neutral Belgium would have ruined Britain's plans to starve Germany via a naval blockade . . .'

He's going to kill us, Mum. I know it for sure.

'If France announced neutrality, Germany was going to ask for the fortresses of Verdun and Toul . . .'

Fancy a snog?

'France was to be forced into war whether she liked it or not . . .'

Mum, this rope's beginning to give. I think I can get my hands free . . .

When we'd finished the origins of the First World War and Roger had outlined the revision essay he wanted me to write (*The alliance system made the Great War inevitable. Discuss*), we moved on to an English comprehension exercise: a long passage from *Moby Dick* entitled 'Stubb kills a whale' that had been set for the exam the previous year.

As usual, I had half an hour to answer the ten questions on my own and then we'd work through the answers together.

I'd never read *Moby Dick* and I found the passage almost incomprehensible, full of nautical words I didn't know and strange names – Queequeg, Pequod, Daggoo, Tashtego. The questions on the text (*What literary role does Stubb's pipe play in this passage?*) seemed much harder than usual. Whole sentences seemed to make no sense to me at all. Waves of tiredness washed over me and I had to struggle to keep my eyelids from closing. I felt unbearably hot, the scarf around my neck suffocating, my mouth dry. I found it impossible to concentrate on the page of black ants that marched and swirled and span before my eyes.

I dimly understood that a crew of sailors in a rowing boat led by a man called Stubb were hunting down a whale, and that it was Stubb who actually killed the whale with his harpoon, but my ability to grasp the fine details was shattered every few minutes by powerful flashbacks triggered by the text. When Stubb sent his 'crooked lance' into the whale 'again and again' I saw myself chasing the burglar round and round the kitchen table, stabbing him over and over. (*We're playing musical chairs now! We're playing musical chairs now!*) When 'the red tide poured from all sides' of the dying whale, I saw that enormous lake of blood that had come trickling across the terracotta tiles towards me where I'd sat hunched and exhausted against the washing machine. When the whale sent up 'gush after gush of clotted red gore' from its spout hole, I saw the red jet that had spewed out of the burglar's neck when I'd nicked it with the tip of the knife. When Stubb 'stood thoughtfully eyeing the vast corpse he had made', I remembered that stillness, that silence in the kitchen after Mum's crushing blow, when the fact, the unbelievable fact that we'd killed someone, slowly began to sink in.

I became aware of Roger's voice, far, far away, barely audible. He was saying something for the second or third time.

'Sorry – did you say something?' I asked.

'You *are* out of it, aren't you?' He laughed. 'I was saying you've run out of time. It's over.'

It's over. Is that what the police would say if they came to the house today? *You've run out of time* . . . I finished the word I was writing and put my pen down. I'd only answered half the questions.

'Before we go through this,' Roger said, 'don't you think we should have a little tea break? We've normally had two or three cups by now . . .'

I hadn't offered him any tea because he had a habit of following me into the kitchen and chatting while the kettle boiled, and I was mindful of Mum's warning: *keep people out of the kitchen whatever you do.*

'I suppose because it's your birthday you want me to make it, is that right?' Roger joked. 'Well, as it's your special day – just this once—' And he started to get up.

'*No!*' I cried, jumping to my feet. 'I'll do it, Roger. I just forgot, that's all. Like I said, I had way too much wine yesterday. I'm still asleep, really.'

Roger sat back down, but as I went to pass behind him on my way to the kitchen, he leaned back in his chair and blocked my way.

'Is there any chance of a slice of your mum's lemon cake while you're out there, Shelley? I'm absolutely starving.'

'Yes, of course.' I smiled, and grinning cheekily, he let me pass. I felt sure he was going to follow me, and I desperately tried to think of some way to keep him in the dining room.

'Do you want to start looking through my answers now?' I said. 'I didn't get very far, I'm afraid.'

'Sure,' Roger said, reaching for my notebook. 'Sure.'

The smile vanished from my face as soon as I was on my own in the kitchen. I had to hurry. I knew he'd follow me in if I wasn't quick. I got the lemon cake out of the cake tin and dropped it on the table. I quickly filled the kettle, put two teabags in the pot, and snatched a plate from the cupboard. I took a fork from the cutlery drawer and then looked for a knife to cut the wretched lemon cake. I found the long sharp knife with the black plastic handle. As soon as I held it in my hand the flashbacks started again. *Thumping the knife into the gap between his shoulder blades. Slashing at him as he ran bent double towards the house. Nicking the side of his neck as I pursued him around the kitchen. 'We're playing musical chairs now! We're playing musical chairs now!'*

'You're finding it very difficult, aren't you, Shelley?' said a voice behind me.

I spun around, the knife in my hand.

Roger was in the kitchen, walking nonchalantly towards the back door.

What did he mean? What was I finding difficult? Did he mean pretending that nothing had happened in the house last night? Did he mean covering up the murder of the burglar?

'It's not easy,' he said, 'especially when there's so much blood.'

He knew! He knew! Somehow Roger knew!

I gripped the knife tightly in my hand, unsure what

I should do next. Should I stab him? Was that what Mum would have wanted me to do?

'It was a savage business, wasn't it?'

'What are you talking about?' I croaked hoarsely, barely able to give the words enough weight to reach him.

Roger looked surprised. 'The passage – the passage from *Moby Dick*. It's not only difficult technically, but also emotionally. Whaling was a savage, bloody business in those days. I'm surprised they set it for the exam last year. It upset a lot of students, there were lots of complaints. Why, what did you think I meant?'

I took the cake out of its greaseproof paper and tried to cut it with a trembling hand. My nerves were raw and jangling. I had a strange feeling in my head: a whirling vertigo, a craziness, and the sickening sensation that I was no longer in control of my own actions. I quite simply didn't know what I was going to do next, what I was capable of doing next. *I had to get him out of the kitchen!* This was the epicentre. This was where the killing had taken place. This was where all the blood had been. The knife wouldn't stop shaking, and I had to use two hands to steady it.

'It looks different in here,' Roger said.

I pretended not to hear, but his words made my heart race even faster.

'Where have the curtains gone?'

'Um – Mum's washing them,' I said, trying to make my voice sound breezy and unconcerned.

'And the doormat's gone, too.'

'Yes – uh, Mum hated it. She's thrown it out.'

Roger was leaning against the back door with his arms folded. His enormous green eyes panned this way and that around the kitchen like security cameras.

'There's something else . . .' he said, as though thinking aloud. 'Something else that's different . . .'

I could have told him: the heavy Italian marble chopping board that hung by the cooker was missing from its hook. It was upstairs in one of the bin bags, sticky with the burglar's blood and brain matter.

'What is it?' he pondered. 'What *is* it?'

I'd somehow managed to cut his slice of cake and put it on a plate. I held it up and smiled brightly but Roger was still scrutinizing the kitchen, tugging at the ends of his blond moustache.

And that's when I saw it. Mum had missed it. I'd missed it. Exactly level with the point of Roger's right elbow. Just above the handle on the door's sea-blue frame. A kidney shape with four vertical stripes hovering above it. Now more brown than red, but still unmistakable.

It was a handprint.

(*He tried to close the back door against me but I shoulder-barged my way inside.*)

It was a bloody handprint.

Roger only had to turn his head a fraction of an inch and he couldn't help but see it.

I didn't lose my nerve, much to my own amazement.

I fixed Roger's eyes with my own, held them so that those darting green fish were stilled, and began to talk non-stop, blurting out the first thing that came into my head.

'I thought the passage was impossible – the hardest comprehension exercise I've ever done and I didn't get number five at all, Roger, I didn't get it at all – "What's the literary role of Stubb's pipe?" What does "literary role" mean, for God's sake? I mean, it's just a pipe, isn't it? Maybe it's his trademark, maybe it's something that marks him out as a character, but I can't see that it's got any *literary role . . .*'

All the time I talked, I moved across the kitchen towards the dining room, holding the cake out in front of me. As Roger's gaze followed me, so his head turned slowly, slowly away from the bloodstain on the back door . . .

'No, that's very true, Shelley – the question isn't very well phrased at all, but I think what they're driving at is that the pipe isn't just a pipe, it's a symbol—'

'Come on,' I interrupted him, standing at the door to the dining room, 'let's sit down in here and you can have your cake.'

Obediently, like a dog whose master has taken down his lead ready for a walk, Roger smiled, pushed himself off the door without unfolding his arms, and followed me out of the kitchen.

22

When Roger had finally gone, I fell back against the front door and slid slowly down until I was sitting on the carpet with my legs stretched out in front of me. Those three hours had completely drained me. I'd never felt so exhausted in all my life.

My eyes felt swollen in their sockets, my vision strangely unequal, as if I were seeing more out of my right eye than my left. The spaghetti bolognese had started to come back, and every time I got the taste of it in my mouth I felt nauseous. It was as if all the horrors of the previous night were distilled into that taste of minced meat and tomato sauce. My stomach churned and groaned alarmingly. My head spun. I sat there in the hallway for a long time, holding my head in my hands, staring at the hall carpet, hoping that if I kept very still the nausea might pass, that I might still manage not to be sick.

Then I remembered the bloodstain. I had to get rid of the bloodstain before Mrs Harris arrived.

I dragged myself up and staggered to the kitchen and rubbed at the handprint with some damp kitchen towel.

It didn't come off easily – it had embedded itself in the cracks in the paintwork and I had to scrub hard. I had no strength in my wrists and the vigorous exertion made me feel even more nauseous. I began to have cold sweats and my mouth filled with bitter saliva, which I knew full well was the final stage before the sickness came. When I looked at the smear of clotted blood on the kitchen towel, it was the final straw.

I made it to the bathroom just in time.

I lay on the sofa in the lounge, but was too feverish to fall into a deep sleep. I tossed and turned in a kind of delirium, my mind racing at a million miles an hour, a train of confused, paranoid, guilty thoughts that went round and round the same tiny track at dizzying speed.

We hadn't buried the burglar properly; we'd left his right arm protruding stiffly out of the soil. Or if it wasn't his arm, it was his foot, the foot without a shoe in its threadbare green sock. I had to go out and cover him properly, I had to go out and bury him properly, or Mrs Harris would see him when she drove up to the house . . . Or we hadn't actually killed the burglar, somehow he'd regained consciousness and hauled himself out of the ooze of his temporary grave. Like a B-movie monster of mud and hacked flesh, he was calling me on his mobile phone as he limped towards the cottage, calling to torment me, to taunt me, to terrify me . . .

I sat up screaming when the phone rang. I stared at it in horror and let it ring, too scared to pick it up. But as my head cleared and the ridiculous thought that it was the burglar was slowly dispelled, my next thought was that it was the police. God knows how many times I let it ring before I finally snatched up the receiver.

It was Mum.

She was very guarded. She was working on the assumption that someone, somewhere, might be listening to our call, and so I did the same.

'Are you having a lovely birthday?' she asked cheerily.

'Yes, wonderful, Mum,' I replied without the slightest trace of irony in my voice. 'Roger bought me a beautiful edition of *Rebecca*.'

'Wonderful! How did your class go?'

'Fine, thanks – we did the origins of the First World War. It's Roger's special subject – you should hear him, there's nothing he doesn't know. He really should write a book.'

We talked without really saying anything for five minutes or so, but by the end of the conversation Mum had reassured herself that I was OK and that the police hadn't come to the cottage . . . yet.

She said she'd try to get home early.

I was sick again a little later, but there was hardly anything left in my stomach to bring up. I went upstairs and washed my face in cold water and brushed my teeth and gargled with some mouthwash to get rid of the acidic aftertaste. As I stood at the basin, the desire to sleep was overwhelming; sleep called to me like a siren, like the pipes of the Pied Piper, and I would have gone to bed (damning all the consequences to hell) if I hadn't heard Mrs Harris's car pull into the drive at just that moment.

Mrs Harris was far easier to cope with than Roger. She had no interest whatsoever in the fact that it was my birthday, and when she saw Roger's card and present she merely commented coldly that if she bought a present for every one of her pupils on their birthdays she'd be bankrupt by now. Unlike Roger, Mrs Harris had little curiosity in what was around her, and probably wouldn't have noticed if the entire sideboard had been removed from the dining room. Nor did she ever want a cup of tea, preferring to drink cups of black coffee from the small Thermos flask she always brought with her.

The dull flat surface of that lesson was only disturbed once, briefly, but with a violence that shocked us both.

Mrs Harris had poured herself a cup of coffee and was carefully unwrapping the cling film from her digestive biscuits.

'I've just taken on a new pupil who lives very close to here,' she remarked, 'a girl about your age. Her father's a farmer – his fields must come up to the rear of your property. Jade's her name. *Jade*, if you can believe it!'

I said nothing, merely glanced at my watch to see how much longer was left of the lesson.

'She's yet another so-called victim of bullying,'

Mrs Harris went on, dusting the biscuit crumbs from the tips of her fingers. 'In other words, she prefers to stay at home rather than be inconvenienced by the tiresome business of going to school.'

I'd let remarks like this pass several times before; I knew Mrs Harris's views on mice all too well. But this time, before I even realized what I was doing, I was speaking out.

'*How dare you?*' I hissed at her, unconsciously screwing up the piece of paper I'd been writing on.

Mrs Harris stared at me, completely stunned, as if her docile lapdog had suddenly bitten her finger right to the bone. I could feel my face twitching and contorting with uncontrollable anger.

'How dare you?' I shouted it right into her face. 'I suffered eight months of hell at the hands of bullies! I was attacked day in and day out. I was set on fire! I could have been killed! What do you mean, another so-called victim?'

My anger was so great that my words couldn't keep pace with it. I had so much pent-up rage to vent that now the floodgates were open it was impossible to know how to shape it all into words. My outburst fizzled out in tongue-tied incoherence.

Mrs Harris's reaction took me completely by surprise. I expected her to bridle with haughty indignation, to unleash a venomous, withering rebuke that would reduce me to tears in a matter of seconds. But instead of flaring up in self-righteous fury, she put her fingers to her lips as if she couldn't believe what had just escaped them.

'I'm sorry, Shelley. I – I'm so sorry!' Her freckled hand made an awkward, conciliatory move towards me across the table before retreating back to her lap. 'I didn't mean to belittle what you've been through. It was a stupid, tactless thing to say. I just forgot who I was talking to, honestly I did.'

My rage gradually subsided and we carried on with the lesson, but we were both distracted by what had happened and hugely relieved when four-thirty finally came around. At the door Mrs Harris apologized again, and wished me a very happy birthday.

I watched her driving away and even in the midst of all the trauma of that day there was room to feel pleased with myself for having stood up to her at long last, for having worsted such a tough old bird. I knew she'd probably only backed down because she was worried that her cynical view of the 'shirkers' and 'wimps' she taught might find its way back to the local authority and they'd stop her fat monthly pay cheques, but nevertheless I'd won the day. She'd left the field in disarray, in ignominious defeat; the imposing Mrs Harris had turned out to be just a paper tiger after all, I thought to myself, and smiled triumphantly – but as my gaze wandered towards the front garden the smile wilted on my lips.

23

It was only when I was on my own in the house again that I remembered the burglar's wallet.

The urge to know his name was irresistible. And it was more than just curiosity now. I felt that if I knew his name, the thought of him lying out there in our garden wouldn't fill me with so much terror.

A name, after all, would anchor the burglar in mundane reality. He'd be Joe Bloggs or David Smith, one person, one individual – and a pathetic one at that. Without a name it would be as if he had no boundaries; he'd be able to leak into all areas of my life like some poisonous fog, contaminating everything. He'd become a bogeyman, a repository for all the fears that would haunt me for the rest of my life. If I could just find out his name, I felt it would be like switching on all the lights in the middle of a scary movie.

I knew Mum wouldn't be home for hours, so I didn't have to hurry.

I went upstairs and into the spare room. I knew the bag with the dressing gowns, the one with the welling-ton boots and the one with the red sports bags. I was looking for the first one, the one with the broken dishes and the doormat. I soon found it, wedged behind the mop and bucket. Mum had tied one of her vicious little knots in it that took me ages to unpick. All the time my emptied stomach growled loudly. My appetite, which nine hours earlier I thought had been extinguished forever, was pacing hungrily back and forth inside its cage.

I had to move the doormat to see inside the bin bag. The wallet was there, right at the bottom. There was something on the doormat, a gelatinous grey goo that must have leaked from the back of the burglar's head as we'd dragged him out of the kitchen. I couldn't bear to look at it and turned my head away to the wall, reaching in for the wallet without looking, like a blind person. My fingers closed around it first time and I pulled it out.

It was a weird sensation to hold in my hands something that had belonged to the burglar – something that had been in his pocket when I'd stabbed him. It was like resurrecting him in a way. I could almost feel his presence in the air around me, and I was suddenly anxious to get out of the spare room as quickly as I could.

I clicked open the press stud with trembling fingers and a racing heart. There was a pocket lumpy with loose coins and another packed tightly with cards. I recognized the pinkish edge of one as a driver's licence, and tried to tease it out with my fingernails. As it worked loose, I found myself looking into the cold grey eyes of the burglar. Another queasy wave of nausea passed over me and I caught a faint taste of the spaghetti bolognese. The hair may have been a little shorter, the cheeks a little less gaunt, but there was no mistaking that face: it was the man Mum and I had killed in the kitchen the night before.

I looked for his name, and there it was.

Paul David Hannigan.

I slipped the driver's licence into my jeans' back pocket, snapped the wallet shut and tossed it back into the bin bag. I retied it, trying to replicate Mum's tight little knot as best I could. I couldn't see any stains on my hands or sleeve, but I washed my hands anyway and put on another top just to be on the safe side.

With my stomach gurgling and squeaking with hunger, I went to the kitchen and heated myself a small bowl of vegetable soup and sliced some baguette. I took it into the lounge on a tray and ate it in front of the TV, watching the cartoons. It was strange to watch Tom chasing Jerry round and round the kitchen (*'We're playing musical chairs now! We're playing musical chairs now!'*), bringing the frying pan down on his head and flattening Jerry like a pancake while the music raced jovially along and the comic sound effect – boing! – rang out again and again. Violence in bright colours. Violence without blood. Violence without death. It wasn't like that in real life. I remembered Mum lining up the blow with the chopping board, tightening her grip, taking a deep breath before she raised it high above her head like a diver about to submerge to the darkest depths. I remembered the sound the board had made when she'd brought it scything down . . . and it hadn't been boing.

I lay down on the sofa and examined the burglar's driver's licence in more detail. Paul Hannigan's driver's licence. I looked at the date of birth and worked out that he'd been twenty-four years old, older than I'd thought. Eight years older than me. There was his signature – a back-sloping child's hand with a ridiculous flourish as if he were a person of importance. His address on the licence was a city in the north with a reputation for high unemployment and drug-related gang crime. Just the month before, a fourteen-year-old boy working as a drug courier had been shot and killed there in broad daylight. So, I meditated drowsily, Paul Hannigan was a rat out of *that* rat hole. Or at least he had been. The licence was four years old; the chances were he'd been living locally when he came to burgle Honeysuckle Cottage.

I tried to think how the police would finally link his disappearance to Mum and me, I tried to think what invisible thread bound us together, but my eyes were heavy and I sleepily fumbled the driver's licence back into my jeans pocket. Someone had already missed him. Someone . . . was already . . . looking . . . for him . . .

24

I was woken up by a hand gently rocking my shoulder.

I opened my eyes to see Mum looking down at me. It was dark outside. The only light in the lounge was the orange glow from the standard lamp by the TV.

'Are the police here?' I asked, sitting up with a start.

'No, no,' Mum crooned soothingly. 'The police aren't here, Shelley. I've made you a nice cup of tea. It's half-past ten.'

'Half-past ten?' I'd been asleep for over five hours!

'You were sound asleep when I got in. I thought it was best to leave you. I went over the kitchen again with a fine-tooth comb, then I had a bath, came down here and sat in the armchair, and next thing I knew I was fast asleep too. I've only just woken up myself.'

I took the mug she was holding out to me. My mouth was dry and foul-tasting and I sucked thirstily at the tea, which was lukewarm and easy to drink.

'How's your neck?' Mum asked.

I swallowed. That scratchy feeling was still there.

'It still feels weird.'

'I bought you some throat sweets and linctus. Take

the linctus before you go to bed and we'll see how you are in the morning. With any luck it will make it feel better. I hope we don't have to take you to the doctor's – Dr Lyle's old, but he's no fool. He's bound to ask some awkward questions.'

'How was work, Mum?'

'Horrible. I had a flaming row with Blakely in front of Brenda and Sally.'

'A row?'

'He wanted me to work late and I said no and he didn't like it.'

I thought she was most likely exaggerating. I'd never known Mum to have a row with *anybody*.

'Did anyone notice your eye?'

'Sally asked me why I was wearing make-up.'

'What did you say?'

'I said I'd decided it was time I found a new man.'

'What did she say?'

'She said she'd heard there was a gorgeous criminal solicitor by the name of Blakely who was single.'

We both giggled. But our giggles faded away as we remembered the burden we lived with now.

We were silent for a long time, sipping our tea and staring into space the way you do when you've just woken up. The only sound was the occasional ghostly cry of an owl in one of the trees along the drive.

'Mum?'

'Yes, Shelley?'

'What's going to happen, Mum?'

She sank her face in her hands and dragged them back and forth across her features as if washing without water. When she turned to me again, she looked unspeakably tired.

'I don't know, Shelley. I don't know. I've been turning it over in my mind all day. I just don't know.'

The owl outside hooted again – a long, mournful vibrato – and I thought of the corpse lying out there in the oval rose bed.

I took Mum's hand and squeezed it tightly.

'Mum?'

'Yes, sweetheart?'

'Is it OK if I sleep with you tonight?'

'Of course it is, darling. Of course it is.'

That night I dreamt I was working with Roger at the dining-room table when the police came to the house. It was dark outside and when I opened the front door I was blinded by the flashing of their blue lights. 'Turn your lights off!' I cried. 'Can't you see I've got bloodshot eyes?' Mum and I were led out of Honeysuckle Cottage by policemen in gas masks carrying shotguns. Roger came to the doorway calling out weakly, 'You can't take her away – don't you realize she's got very important exams in two months' time?' Mum and I were wearing orange jumpsuits like American prisoners I'd seen on TV; our legs were chained at the ankles and our hands handcuffed behind our backs. 'Why are you wearing gas masks?' Mum asked one of the policemen.

He bellowed back at her, 'The stench! The stench of death! If you can't smell it, that proves you're guilty!'

I heard someone laughing and looked over to see the burglar standing up in the rose bed. He was uninjured, just as I'd first seen him standing at the top of the stairs, except that his olive-green bomber jacket was decorated with bright red bows and these bows streamed long red ribbons, which spooled on the ground at his feet. When he saw me his expression became hard, murderous. 'It was them eggs,' he said, 'you ugly, stuck-up bitch. Them eggs was off.' His mobile rang and he reached into his back pocket. 'Excuse me, I've got a call,' he said, and putting one finger to his ear to hear better, he wandered away in the direction of the house.

The policemen pushed us into an armoured van and it moved off down the drive. Out of the window I could just make out a car parked in the narrow lane and a shadowy figure seated behind the wheel, waiting. The car's headlights suddenly flashed on, its engine revved angrily and it began to follow us.

'Who's that?' Mum asked.

'It's the watcher,' I replied.

25

I was momentarily confused the next morning when I woke up in Mum's room. Mum had already got up, leaving just the ghost of her scent on the other side of the bed and a few corkscrew strands of hair on her pillow. I could hear the taps running in the kitchen, cupboard doors banging, the jocular burble of a radio presenter's voice.

When I tried to get up, I couldn't believe how stiff I was. All my muscles screamed with pain as if I'd run a marathon during the night, and it made me realize how ferociously I must have fought the burglar. I limped down the landing to the bathroom like a geriatric, wincing with discomfort at every step. When I sat on the loo my coccyx stung nastily where I'd fallen on the knife. My throat was still sore, but that strange scratchy sensation every time I swallowed had gone, and when I looked in the bathroom mirror I was relieved to see that my eyes were much less bloodshot. I brought my face close up to the glass so that my nose was almost touching it.

I asked my reflection, 'Will the police come today?'

I'd gone into my bedroom to get my slippers and an old dressing gown, when something outside – an un- familiar smudge of colour in the landscape – caught my eye. I went to the window and wiped away the condensation so that I could see better. And almost wished I hadn't.

Outside, in the narrow lane that ran along the side of Honeysuckle Cottage, was a car, a battered turquoise car. It had almost been driven into the thick hedge, its right front wheel halfway up the grassy bank and its back end jutting out, making it difficult for other cars to get past. On the other side of the hedge was our back garden – the cypresses marking the rear boundary, the vegetable patch, Mr Jenkins's compost heap, the rows of fruit trees.

I felt my blood run cold. It was Paul Hannigan's car. There was no doubt about that. Paul Hannigan's car parked right outside our house, pointing at Honeysuckle Cottage like a giant arrow, crying out to the police: *Want to solve the mystery of the missing driver? Enquire within.*

This was just the sort of clue, just the sort of loose end I'd dreaded! If Mum and I had stopped to think about it, we'd have realized that the burglar could only have got to Honeysuckle Cottage by car. No buses ran at that time of night, and it was highly unlikely that he'd walked – how was he planning to escape with all his loot? And if he'd come by car, then that car still had to be out there somewhere – for, as we well knew, once

the burglar had entered Honeysuckle Cottage he'd
never left it again. But in all the terror and confusion of
that night, something so stupidly obvious just hadn't
occurred to us.

Mum came stomping up the stairs when she heard
my frantic shouts.

'What is it?' she cried, lurching into my bedroom,
deathly pale and out of breath.

I didn't say anything. I just pointed outside.

She gasped when she saw the car and swore under
her breath. She stood behind me at the window, her
hands on my shoulders, her chin resting on the crown
of my head and I could feel her whole body trembling.

We went downstairs together in stunned silence and
went through the motions of having breakfast in the
dining room – neither of us was ready to return to
the kitchen to eat. I tried to force down some toast, but
Mum didn't want anything. She just drank cup after
cup of coffee. Black and very strong. She was horribly
pasty, her bruised eye tinged a dirty yellow round its
edges.

'We mustn't panic, Shelley. We've got to stay calm
and think this thing through logically,' she said. But
I could see that she wasn't finding it easy to stay calm
herself – she chewed her bottom lip distractedly and
dragged her hand through her hair over and over again.

'We've got to think this through,' she said, more to
herself than to me, 'we've got to think this through.'

'What is there to think through?' I cried in exaspera-
tion. 'The burglar's car is parked right outside our
house – it's going to draw the police to us like bees to a
honey pot!' I was overcome with a suffocating sense of
panic. 'It's going to lead them right to us! I *knew* something like this would happen! I knew it! I knew it!'

'Calm down, Shelley. Let me think. It might not be
his car. It could belong to someone who broke down in
the lane last night. It might have been abandoned by
joyriders. We don't know that it's definitely his car.'

'Oh, come on, Mum. It's a bit of a coincidence, don't
you think? It's parked right next to our house! That's
the corner of the garden he was heading towards when
I – when I caught up with him.'

'But we didn't see it yesterday. Maybe it wasn't there
yesterday.'

'Mum, we were too out of it to notice anything
yesterday – and anyway, it can only be seen from my
bedroom window and I hardly went in there all day
yesterday.'

Mum sat in gloomy silence, seemingly set on trying
to convince herself that the car wasn't the burglar's.

'Mum, we've got to move it! We've got to *get rid of it*!'

She looked at me as if I'd gone mad. 'Move it? How?'

'Don't you remember? There was a bunch of car
keys in his pocket, they're upstairs in one of the bin
bags now. We've got to drive the car away from here –
leave it somewhere. We've got to do it right now!'

'We can't do anything right now, Shelley. There isn't

time. I've got to get ready for work, and besides, it's too dangerous in broad daylight – someone might see us.'

I wanted to scream at her, to get hold of her and shake her out of her complacency. 'We can't leave it another day, Mum – it's blocking the road out there. Someone's going to report it to the police. They'll come here. They'll start asking questions!'

'We can't do it now, Shelley. It's too risky. We'll have to wait for it to get dark.'

I began to protest, but Mum interrupted me. 'I know it's a risk to leave it another day, but it's a risk we're just going to have to take. And now I've got to go and get ready for work.'

She got up as if she bore the weight of the world on her shoulders. At the door she stopped and said resignedly, 'Get the keys from the bin bag and – if it is his car – we'll move it as soon as I get in from work. It should be dark by then.'

'OK, Mum.'

'And Shelley,' she added over her shoulder, 'don't go near that car until I get home.'

The day passed in agony as I waited for Mum to finish work. I couldn't concentrate at all. I just went through the motions in my class with Roger like an automaton – glancing at my watch every few minutes and wondering how time had managed to slow down, to congeal, to no more than an excruciating trickle. As we sat at the dining-room table revising glacial drift and

French irregular verbs, all I could think about was the burglar's car.

Right at that moment, some busybody neighbour might be ringing the police to report a badly parked car obstructing one of the lanes. The police would come out and look the car over. They'd thread their way back along the lane and turn up the drive into Honeysuckle Cottage. They were bound to. It was parked right next to our back garden. There were no other houses around. They'd knock authoritatively at the front door and ask me if the car belonged to anyone in my family or if I knew anything about it. What would I say to them then? Would I be able to speak to them without saying something to make them suspicious?

Later in the day, they'd tow the car away and we would have lost our chance for good. When Paul Hannigan was reported missing the police records would show that his car had been found right outside our house. Surely they'd be able to put two and two together? And it was possible the car might contain clues to make it even easier for them – our address written on a scrap of paper, a map with our cottage marked on it. If Paul Hannigan had previous convictions for burglary, it wouldn't take a genius to work out that he'd come to Honeysuckle Cottage to rob it – and that he'd never been seen again.

The more I thought about it, the more anxious I became and the harder it was to concentrate. I felt Roger growing more and more irritated by my inattention and my incorrect answers, but he said nothing. When he'd finally gone, I raced upstairs to my bedroom to see if the car was still there and let out a squeal of relief when I glimpsed its turquoise roof through the roadside greenery. I spent the whole lunchtime up in my bedroom kneeling on my window seat, staring at the ugly car, thinking, thinking . . .

I thought about Mum that morning and how she'd tried to convince herself it wasn't the burglar's car. I was tempted to go out there right then and try the car keys, so I could say to her when she came in that it definitely was the burglar's car, so she'd stop clutching pathetically at straws. But I didn't. I didn't want to go against such a direct order from her. That would be like an open declaration of war.

In the hour or so that I sat up there, not a single car or tractor entered the lane, just a solitary cyclist in his skin-tight harlequin costume. He glanced at the car as he passed, but was more intent on getting something out of his back pocket with one hand as he steered the bike with the other.

Mrs Harris arrived with a birthday present for me – an expensive box of Belgian chocolates – but I hardly acknowledged it. While she droned on and on about prisms and the refraction of light, I had only one thought on my mind: *We have to move the car, we have to move the car!* I was convinced that if the police found it we'd be under arrest before the day was over. But if we were lucky, if it went unreported for just another few hours, and if Mum and I could safely get it away from the house without being seen, then we might have a chance, we might just have a chance.

The turquoise car was still there when Mrs Harris left. I stared at it from my bedroom window, drumming my fingers impatiently on the sill. Although it was only a quarter to five, I was pleased to see that the sky was already beginning to darken. In the west, long fingers of sunlight still pierced the banks of cloud here and there like theatrical spotlights, but over in the east black rain clouds were moving in fast, plunging the fields below them into premature night. It would be dark by seven.

A handful of rain suddenly spattered against the window, making me flinch. The dark rain clouds were spreading rapidly across the sky, extinguishing the luminous shafts one by one; the whole scene – the enormous sky divided almost equally between black and white reminded me of one of those nineteenth-century allegorical paintings with titles like *The Clash Between Good and Evil*.

I watched another delicate sunbeam become swallowed up in the swirling blackness. It looked as if the triumph of Evil would be absolute.

26

It was pitch dark when Mum got back at seven-thirty. The black rain clouds had strangled every last patch of light from the sky, but the storm they threatened had held off. Instead, a petulant, noisy wind had got up outside, roaring melodramatically in the chimney breast and rattling the windows in their frames.

Mum's first words as she came in through the front door were, 'Is it still there?'

'Yes.' I nodded excitedly. 'Yes it is!'

We sat at the kitchen table and hurriedly made our plans.

'I'm still not convinced it's the burglar's car,' she began, her chest visibly heaving beneath her suit jacket. I rolled my eyes and folded my arms in irritation, and seeing me, she went on quickly, 'But if it *is*, I don't think we should just leave it in another lane around here. I think we should get it as far away from here as we can – leave it somewhere in town.'

'Where?'

She pursed her lips before answering. 'I was thinking the Farmer's Harvest. The car park's enormous and with so many people coming and going all the time we can just leave it and walk away without being noticed.'

It was a clever idea. Hide the car in plain sight rather than in some back street, where a nosy neighbour might be watching through the net curtains.

'OK,' I said. 'Sounds good.'

Mum glanced at her watch and stood up. I did the same, and felt momentarily groggy, as if I were in a lift that had suddenly started to descend.

She began to walk away, then turned sharply back to me. 'And we mustn't forget to remove anything from the car that could lead the police back here – *before* we leave.'

I nodded emphatically.

'Now go and get dressed in the darkest clothes you have. And put some gloves on. I'll go and do the same.'

As I searched through my wardrobe for my black polo-neck jumper, my black cords and the old black coat I'd had since I was twelve, I found myself giggling with nervous anticipation – just as I used to do when we played hide-and-seek when I was a little girl and I could hear the seeker's breathing just inches away from my hiding place. How many times had I given the game away with my excited giggles? It was hard to believe that I was really dressing in black like a cat burglar so that I'd be less visible in the darkness, that I was really putting on gloves so that the police wouldn't be able to trace my fingerprints. It was all too much like something out of a movie to have anything to do with *my* reality.

When we stepped out of the kitchen into the back garden, the profundity of the darkness took us both by surprise. For a few seconds it was like being blind-folded, and we both hesitated, unsure of our bearings and frightened to take a step into the unknown. The moon was no more than a fingernail indentation, regularly blotted out by the scudding black clouds that the blustery wind drove across the sky like a fleet of phantom galleons. The night was so dark I couldn't make out a single star.

I set off cautiously in the direction of the car but hadn't gone very far before I heard Mum's anxious voice.

'Shelley! Shelley! I can't see anything! Wait for me!'

I stopped and waited for Mum to grab on to me. I led the way, but I could hardly see anything myself and shuffled forward hesitantly. *The blind leading the blind*, I thought. Disorientated, I veered too close to the fruit trees and walked straight into a branch. It dug sharply into my temple, just missing my eye, and I jumped back with a yelp of pain, stepping heavily on Mum's toe.

'It's no good! It's too dangerous!' she said, having to raise her voice to be heard over the gale. 'Go back into the house and get the torch! It's in the second drawer down under the sink!'

I was back in a few minutes. Mum hadn't moved from the spot where I'd left her. She put up her hand to shield her eyes from the glare of the torch.

'Turn it off if you hear a car,' she said. She held on to me and I took the lead again.

The torch was a good one, bought in case of power cuts, but it wasn't very effective outside in the all-pervading darkness. Its beam illuminated an area no bigger than a dinner plate and our progress was still very slow. The grass looked strange in the torchlight, not green but silvery, ghostly, and the fallen branches were like skeletal hands reaching up through the soil. I thought about the burglar lying buried under the oval rose bed behind us. And I found myself thinking: *What if the dead don't stay dead? What if the dead don't really die?*

I imagined him coming towards us through the murky darkness. I saw his dead face, the Neanderthal brow, the glassy eyes, the fractured jaw, the gaping wound in his neck. I expected his cadaverous hand to reach out and seize hold of me at any moment. I tried to walk faster, but it was impossible with Mum holding on to me so tightly. I tried to drive away my morbid thoughts, telling myself that there was no such thing as ghosts, that the burglar was Paul David Hannigan, a weedy twenty-four-year-old crook and he was *dead, dead, dead!* But his name wasn't the talisman against fear that I'd hoped it would be.

At last we reached the hedge and I peered over it. The lane seemed to be completely deserted, but I could make out a strange sound when the gusts died down, an intermittent clacking and hissing coming from somewhere nearby and I held back. It took me a while to figure out what it was: a water sprinkler in the field across the road. There'd be little need for that when this storm broke, I thought.

I squeezed through the hedge and out onto the grassy bank, and Mum followed me. She went around to the driver's side of the car and tried the key. I heard it slide home and unlock the door first time. I felt the childish urge to say something – *I told you so! I told you so!* – but managed to gag the impulse. When Mum yanked the door open, the interior light came on, taking us both by surprise. We scrambled into the car as if we'd been caught in the beam of a powerful searchlight, and quickly slammed the doors shut.

We sat for a moment in the dark car without speaking. I listened to Mum struggling to control her rapid breathing, and wrinkled my nose at the overpowering stench of stale tobacco.

'OK,' she whispered, 'let's see what's in here.' She began groping desperately around for the interior light switch. 'Where's that bloody—!'

'It's all right, Mum,' I said. 'I've still got the torch. We can use that.'

I flicked the torch on and we hurriedly began to search the inside of the car. In my feverish paranoia I expected another car to turn into the lane at any moment. I took a secretary's notepad, full of what looked like calculations, from the glove box, but I left the sweet wrappers, cigarettes, parking tickets and

the cellophane bag of what I took to be cannabis –
a tobacco-coloured half-brick with a pungent aroma.
Mum found a road atlas in the driver's door and took
that, just in case there was something incriminating
scribbled inside. There was a big khaki trench coat on
the back seat, and I rolled it into a bundle and brought
it into the front with me. I shone the torch around the
floors, but there was nothing apart from chocolate bar
wrappers and an empty vodka bottle.

'Shall I take all this back into the house?'

'No,' Mum said, her anxious face stained an ugly
yellow in the torchlight and criss-crossed with deep
black shadows. 'It'll take too long. Just put them in
the garden behind the hedge. We'll take them into the
house when we get back.'

I let myself out and wriggled back through the hedge,
dropping the notepad and atlas on the grass and putting the heavy trench coat on top to weigh them down.
I didn't want to risk anything blowing away in the wind.

As soon as I was back inside the car Mum tried to
start the engine, but her hands were shaking so much
she couldn't get the key in the ignition. The other keys
in the bunch jangled together noisily as she struggled to
wriggle the key home. Then I remembered something
and gently touched her shoulder. She jumped and glared
at me.

'Mum – Mum, *wait*. We haven't looked in the boot!'

She didn't say anything. She got out of the car and
went round to the back. After another age of fumbling

with the keys, I heard the boot spring open and a moment later slam shut again. I tried to look for her in the rear-view mirror but I couldn't see her. It was as if she'd just disappeared, swallowed up by the night. *Where is she?* I wondered with growing anxiety. *Where's she gone?* I heard something heavy crashing through the bushes on the other side of the hedge, in our back garden, and glanced around nervously, feeling my eyes grow enormous with fear. *What the hell was that?*

Mum's door was suddenly wrenched open and she slipped back into the driver's seat.

'What was that noise?' I gasped.

'That was the bag of tools,' she said, a little out of breath.

'Tools?'

'There was a bag of tools in the boot. I threw them over the hedge into our garden. If we have them, then they can't be of any help to the police. Why take chances?'

'It sounded like someone—' but my voice was drowned out by the engine exploding into life. We lurched into motion and bumped off the grassy bank. The gears whined and groaned as Mum struggled to find second, and the engine over-revved deafeningly.

'Change gear, Mum! Change gear, for Christ's sake!'

'I'm *trying*, Shelley!'

'Your lights! You haven't got your lights on!'

We were driving into a darkness as unrelieved as deep space; it was impossible to see where we were going. Mum slapped at the dashboard, searching for the lights, but instead the windscreen wipers began scraping frenetically back and forth across the glass. Mum killed them with a curse and tried again. Now the left indicator came on, flashing impatiently on the dashboard like a nervous tic. I was praying: *Please don't let another car come now, please don't let another car come now. They'll plough straight into us!*

And then she found them, and a swathe of yellow light illuminated the terrible danger we were in. We'd left the lane altogether and were on the point of going into the ditch that ran along the side of the road. I screamed out, and she jerked the steering wheel round hard. I waited for the front of the car to drop into empty space, but somehow all four wheels stayed on the road. We clipped the opposite bank as Mum counteracted the sharp turn she'd made, and then we were back on the tarmac. She found second gear at last and the anxious moaning of the engine abated, like a starving animal finally thrown some food.

We negotiated the twisting lanes at a crawl, Mum still battling with the unfamiliar gears. Fifteen minutes or so later we emerged onto the B road that eventually joined up with the main road into town. I felt exposed and vulnerable as we left the darkness of the lanes behind us and joined the stream of traffic under the bright glare of the street lights. I sank down in my seat and put a hand up to cover my face. What if a friend of Paul Hannigan's was in one of the cars behind us and recognized the car? What would he do if he saw two strangers driving his friend's car? I tried not to think about it . . .

'Can't you go any faster, Mum?' I groaned.

'It's thirty here, Shelley. The last thing we want is to get pulled over by the police.'

I hunkered lower.

After fifteen agonizing minutes, the garish lights of the Farmer's Harvest loomed up ahead on our left.

The Farmer's Harvest was a chain of restaurants with an olde-worlde theme, where the waitresses dressed like characters from a Thomas Hardy novel; the walls were decorated with horse brasses and antique farm implements and the 'chicken' came in perfect rectangles, the tomato sauce in little sachets that you had to pay extra for. Yet in spite of its hideousness, the Farmer's Harvest was always packed. When we passed it Mum often used to say it was 'the living proof' of a remark some wit had once made. *The public taste? The public taste is awful!*

Mum slowed down, indicated left and turned into the Farmer's Harvest's car park with all the prissy precision of a learner driver on their test, anxious not to do anything that might attract attention to us. She drove through the rows of parked cars towards the rear where there were bushes and trees and it was less well lit. We went to the very end, but there were no free spaces.

'Don't tell me,' Mum said under her breath. '*Don't tell me!*'

We did an entire circuit of the car park, but there was nothing. Soon we were in front of the brightly lit restaurant again.

'Go round again, Mum, go round again! Maybe we missed one!'

We had to wait while a large group of diners crossed in front of us. They looked like wedding guests – the women in tight fishtail dresses and high heels, the men in suits, some with carnations in their lapels. In spite of all their finery, there was something rough, something threatening, about them. I noticed the men's tattooed knuckles, the ponytails, the obligatory earrings. They seemed drunk already, grinning inanely into the car at us.

I thought they were just the sort of people that Paul Hannigan would have known. His greasy long hair and weasel face would have fitted in perfectly among them. I covered my eyes with my hand and prayed that none of them would recognize the car. A youth with a shaven head and jug ears, a fag see-sawing between his lips, hit the bonnet of the car hard with his fist and shouted something at us that I couldn't make out. I squirmed in my seat and wished I was anywhere, *anywhere*, but where I was. At last I felt the car rolling slowly forward again, and when I looked up the wedding guests were in a scrum around the restaurant door, shouting and gesticulating, the jug-eared youth's head thrown back in raucous laughter – a laughter full of brutal malice and devoid of human warmth.

We headed to the back of the car park again, passing other cars also circling, looking for spaces. Then I saw one – in the middle of the second to last row – and cried out to Mum to back up.

'I don't know, Shelley,' she said. 'I don't know if I'll fit.'

Mum was a terrible parker and never reversed into a parking spot if she could avoid it.

'It doesn't have to be perfect, Mum. Just put it in there and let's get out of here!'

Mum ground the gear stick into reverse and edged her way slowly back into the space. She hadn't steered enough, however, and had to come forward for another attempt. There was a car on either side of the space, the one on my side a very new-looking four-wheel drive. Mum got it wrong again and had to move forward for the second time. Her face was contorted with concentration, her jaw tightly clenched. Another car appeared now, wanting to get past, their way blocked by our manoeuvre. Mum crunched the gears and tried once more. This time the angles worked and we could at least move far enough into the gap to let the other car pass. She drove forward one more time and then we were able to ease slowly into the space.

She turned off the engine and let out a huge sigh of relief.

'Well done, Mum,' I said, and she looked at me and shook her head as if to say: *What a nightmare!*

There was hardly any room to get out of the door on

my side; Mum had even less on hers, and I could see
the door cutting into her waist as she squeezed herself
out. I'd managed to ease myself halfway out and was
just swivelling round to free my right leg when the world
around me suddenly exploded.

There was an ear-splitting noise and a flashing of
orange lights. I looked around, expecting to see police
cars closing in on all sides, but there was nothing. I
stood in a daze, dumbfounded by the noise, blinking
stupidly. Only slowly did it dawn on me that the four-
wheel drive's alarm had gone off.

Mum was suddenly beside me, leading me away by
the arm. I could just hear what she was saying under
the deafening wail of the alarm.

'Don't panic, Shelley. Just keep walking.'

I did as I was told, convinced that the alarm was
going to bring all the diners out of the restaurant to see
what was going on. Then suddenly it stopped.

We feigned indifference and kept walking quickly
away. And then a man's voice behind us called out.

'Oi! Where d'you think you're going?'

We stopped and looked around.

The owner of the four-wheel drive was standing
there, his car key in his hand after deactivating the
alarm. He was heavily built with a shaved head and
dark goatee.

'You don't just walk off when you've damaged someone's car,' he snarled.

I tensed myself to run. We were meant to leave the

car without being noticed, *without attracting attention to ourselves*. If we stopped now, this man would be able to describe us to the police. But Mum, who still held me firmly by the arm, didn't move.

'What do you mean?' she said. 'We haven't damaged your car.'

'Yes, you did,' he grunted. 'I was watching you. She hit it with her door.' He indicated me with a brutal butt of his bony head and bent to examine his car, running his hands over it like a vet stroking the flanks of an injured thoroughbred horse.

'No, I didn't,' I said. 'The door never touched your car. I must have bumped it with my backside.'

'I can't see any damage,' he said, almost with disappointment, 'but then there's not much light here. Let me take your details.'

We couldn't let this happen. This was insane. We had to leave the car without being noticed. I suddenly remembered the torch in my pocket.

'Use this,' I said. 'I didn't touch your door.'

As he took the torch from me, he stared hard at my face and I saw a wrinkle of disgust pass across his features. My first thought was that he'd noticed my scars, so I was confused when he pointed to my left eye and said, 'You're bleeding.'

I put my hand up to my temple and sure enough, there was a small dark stain on the woollen tip of my glove. *The branch! The branch I'd walked into when I was crossing the back garden in the dark!*

He went back to his car and began running the beam over the driver's door, meticulously examining the paint-work. He made no effort to hurry himself while Mum and I stood in the car park, battered by the capricious gusts of wind, completely at a loss what to do next.

Without looking up from the door, he said, 'D'you always carry a torch around with you?'

My face burned as the magnitude of my mistake dawned on me. I'd given him the torch without think-ing! What girl carries a torch like that around with her in her pocket? And when she's meant to be going out to dinner! I looked at Mum in horror, but she just pressed my arm firmly as if to say, *it's OK, Shelley, it's OK.*

When he started moving towards the back of his car, Mum – to my astonishment – suddenly broke away from me and strode boldly towards him.

'This is ridiculous!' she exclaimed. 'The car door's up here, not down there! Give me the torch! We haven't got time for this nonsense!'

He gave her back the torch, eyeing her contemptu-ously, an arrogant half-smile on his lips.

'There's no damage to your precious car! Maybe your alarm shouldn't be so sensitive.' She took my arm again and we started off towards the restaurant.

'Hey!' he shouted. 'Where are you going? I still want to exchange details!'

Mum spun on her heel. 'We haven't damaged your stupid car! And that's an end to it!'

We strode on purposefully until we were almost at

the door to the restaurant. I could see the queue of
people inside waiting to be seated, a girl who I thought
I recognized from school offering a basket of bread to
a group of Japanese businessmen wearing paper hats.
We didn't want to go inside the restaurant – that would
only increase our chances of being noticed and remembered. I glanced back. The man had his back to us and
seemed to be examining his car door again, his hands
bunched on his hips.

'Is he watching us?' Mum asked.

'No, he's not.'

Mum looked to make sure for herself and then
tugged me into the dark alley beside the restaurant. We
only had to follow this alley to the end, and it would
bring us out onto another main road. About half a mile
along was the train station, where we'd be able to catch
a taxi home.

27

Mum and I were wired when we got back to Honeysuckle Cottage, euphoric that we were free of the burglar's car at last, and that it no longer squatted beside the house like a terrifying bird of ill omen.

We sat in the lounge going over our adventure again and again – not being able to find the car's headlights, nearly going into the ditch, setting off the alarm in the car park, the confrontation with 'Four-wheel-drive Man', as we'd christened him.

'You were amazing, Mum,' I said. 'The way you stood up to him! I've never seen you so – so fearless. You were like a completely different person!'

Mum didn't say anything, but I could tell she was proud – and maybe a little surprised too – at the way she'd got us out of such a difficult situation.

'I mean,' I went on, 'he was a really scary guy! He was like a gangster or something. I was getting ready to run!'

'Well, this calls for a celebration,' Mum said, and went to the kitchen, returning with a bottle of wine. She drank three glasses while I was still on my first, and before I could protest went off to open another bottle.

We were like players on a winning team or actors after a performance; we couldn't come down after the intense excitement we'd just lived through. I had Mum in fits doing impressions of her confronting Four-wheel-drive Man – outrageously exaggerating her posh accent for effect – 'I haven't got time for this *nonsense*! We haven't damaged your *stupid* little car, you *stupid* little man!'

'But your line was best of all,' Mum said.

'What do you mean?'

'What you said to him – *I must have bumped it with my backside*!'

I'd forgotten that I'd actually said that. It sent me off into hysterics, and the more I cracked up, the more Mum screamed with laughter too. We laughed and laughed until the tears streamed down our faces. At that moment, *I must have bumped it with my backside* was the funniest thing I'd ever heard in my life.

We talked for so long that it was nearly eleven before we got round to going through the items we'd brought in from the back garden. The tools in the canvas bag looked like ordinary work tools, but we assumed the burglar regularly put them to other uses. In the pockets of an anorak, which Mum had also taken from the boot, there was a Stanley knife, a filthy handkerchief, a disintegrated cigarette and a cinema ticket. We flicked through the road atlas, but there was nothing marked or written on any of the maps, just a few telephone numbers on the inside front cover. As I'd thought, the notepad was full of mathematical calculations. Mum sat back in her chair and flicked through the pages.

'Drug calculations,' she said. 'Quarters, eighths, sixteenths. He wasn't just a user, it looks like he was a pusher too. I don't think he's a great loss to the human race.'

Her face became thoughtful. She struggled to sit back up, and I could tell she was already quite drunk.

'You know, Shelley, this could work out well for us.'

'What do you mean?'

'Well, think about it. The management of the Farmer's Harvest will report the abandoned car to the police. The police will try to contact the driver – without any luck – and they'll end up impounding it. They'll search the car eventually and they'll find the drugs.'

I wasn't sure how this helped us, and my confusion must have shown.

'Well, how hard are the police going to try to find a missing drug dealer? They're not going to make the same sort of effort they would if a young child had gone missing, are they? I'd imagine that drug dealers disappear all the time. Just up sticks and vanish if they think the police are about to arrest them.'

'What if they think he's been –' the word stuck in my throat for a second and wouldn't come out – '*murdered*?'

'They're most likely to suspect other drug dealers, aren't they? Why would they suspect us? There's nothing in the car that could lead them to us, and the car's their only clue.'

'But what about Four-wheel-drive Man? He saw us leaving the car. He won't forget us after what happened with the alarm and everything. He got a good look at my face. He's bound to remember me.' (*He's bound to remember my scars.*)

'You're missing my point, Shelley – I don't think the police are going to look very hard for a drug dealer. They'll have his drugs. He'd have every incentive to make sure the police never find him.'

'But *someone's* looking for him, Mum. They'll report him missing.'

(*I heard those eight cheery musical notes in my head again, the terrifying music the dead could still play.*)

'OK,' said Mum, visibly warming to her theme, 'let's say the police decide he hasn't just skipped town because things were getting too hot for him, but that he really is a missing person. Then let's say that – in the worst-case scenario – Four-wheel-drive Man reads about the car abandoned at the Farmer's Harvest and remembers that that was the car he saw us getting out of – do you really think he's the type to come bounding forward to help the police with their enquiries?'

I shrugged.

'I mean, you saw him,' she went on. 'You said yourself he looked like a gangster, and you're probably not far wrong. I know these sort of people, Shelley. I've had them as clients for the last two years. They don't talk to the police about anything. *Full stop.*'

It seemed to me a very weak foundation on which to build with so much confidence, and I wondered if it was the wine talking.

Mum tossed the notepad onto the pile on the floor and leaned forward and stroked my hand.

'I think we're going to be all right, Shelley.' She smiled. 'I think we're going to get away with this.'

I couldn't help cringing a little. It was partly super-stition, it was partly a habit of fearing the worst, but talk like that always made me feel uncomfortable – it felt too much like a direct challenge to the gods.

'I don't know,' I said. 'You shouldn't speak too soon, Mum, you're assuming too much – there's so many things we don't know . . .'

Mum laughed. 'Your problem is that you've seen too many movies. You *expect* to get caught, you *expect* something to go wrong. No one ever gets away with anything in the movies because they can't have an audience thinking that crime pays. But this isn't a movie – this is real life. And people get away with things all the time in real life.'

I hoped she was right, but I didn't want to tempt fate by saying anything. I didn't think we'd really know we were safe until months, maybe even years, had passed. It was still too early to say. There were too many imponderables. I still couldn't help thinking that this would all end in flashing blue lights and that sickening knock at the door. I preferred to change the subject.

'The trench coat,' I said. 'We haven't looked in the trench coat that was on the back seat.'

The khaki trench coat was on the floor by the TV. I went over and picked it up. 'It weighs a ton!' I exclaimed, walking over to Mum.

And then the material slipped through my tipsy fingers and the coat, which I'd picked up by the bottom instead of the collar, unrolled in my arms, and something heavy birthed through the lining of the pocket. It struck my stockinged foot a glancing blow, flooding me with searing pain, and clattered, spinning, across the wooden floorboards.

Normally I'd have screamed the house down, but my surprise acted as a sort of anaesthetic. I merely flumped back onto the sofa, holding my injured toes, my bottom lip clamped under my top teeth, and stared stupidly at the gun that lay in the middle of the lounge floor.

The storm broke in the middle of the night and I lay awake for a long time listening to it. I'd never heard it rain so hard; when I thought it had reached the fiercest intensity possible, it would rain even harder, even louder. It felt as if the entire world outside my bedroom window had been turned to liquid – everything ran, everything dripped, trickled, spattered, *bled*.

The gusts of wind were so violent that they were like lunatic hands beating against the windows, and there were moments when I really thought the glass was about to break and let all that howling, screeching chaos inside. It was as if something dangerous and obscene had escaped from its prison and was running amok. And now it was loose, it would only be subdued again after a titanic struggle.

As I lay there listening to the deafening torrents of rain drumming on the roof, I imagined the garden and all the surrounding fields flooding, the rising waters slowly loosening Paul Hannigan's body from its muddy mooring and floating it away on the current for all the world to see. I saw the police in a landscape transformed into one vast lake, leaning from their dinghy and trying to gaff the bloated corpse from the branches of a tree where it had become entangled . . .

Forty days and forty nights of rain like this would be enough to drown a world, I thought. And I was so full of foreboding about the future that part of me felt that mightn't be such a bad thing.

28

Every day, my first thought on waking up was the same: *Today's the day the police will come.*

I could see it all so clearly: the forensic experts in their white overalls swarming over the kitchen and the patio; the police cadets working their way meticulously across the garden on their hands and knees; the tent they'd erect over the oval rose bed when they found the body; Mum and me pushing our way through the scrum of journalists gathered on the gravel drive; entering the doubtful sanctuary of the waiting police car . . .

In those days I endowed the police with almost supernatural powers. I didn't stop to analyse the situation, to see what pieces of the jigsaw they actually had in their hands (*a missing man, an abandoned car*), I simply felt that they knew what we'd done, that, like the all-seeing eye of God whose penetrating vision no walls could obstruct, they'd seen everything that had gone on inside Honeysuckle Cottage that night.

Yet, to my continuing surprise, nothing happened. The flashing blue lights, the sickening knock at the front door, still didn't come. The next few days passed

– ostensibly at least – just as they had before. Roger came to teach me in the mornings, Mrs Harris came in the afternoons, I worked on my homework at the dining-room table till Mum came home, practised my flute, prepared dinner with Mum, read my novels and listened to Puccini; Mum went to work and tended each of her cases 'little and often' like a careful gardener, and did her best to avoid Blakely's wandering hands and ugly temper.

A new week began . . . and still nothing happened.

The struggle in the kitchen with Paul Hannigan left me feeling physically exhausted for days. At first I slept at any and every opportunity, like a cat – deep, deep sleeps from which I'd wake with a dry mouth and gummy eyes. But once I'd slept the exhaustion off, I started to have serious problems sleeping. I'd had insomnia before, especially when the bullying was at its worst, but those intermittent episodes were nothing compared to the bleak white nights I suffered now.

When I went up to bed and closed my eyes, I would see Paul Hannigan's face with astonishing clarity, as if he were standing right in front of me again. The chalky pallor of his skin, the lank, greasy, black hair leaking like oil over his ears and shoulders, the barely visible fuzz of immature beard around his mouth, the way his eyelids flickered wildly as they struggled to stay open, and his eyes rolled back into his head like a medium who's just made contact with the spirit world. I would hear his voice, the twisted vowels of his ugly accent, his slurred arrogant cocksureness (*I know what I want, lady! I know what I want!*). Sometimes his voice sounded so real in my head that I became convinced he was actually in the bedroom with me – I even thought I could smell him there, that fetid mixture of alcohol, cigarettes and sweat that enveloped him like a mist. I'd sit up in bed and peer terrified into the darkest corners of my bedroom, expecting to see his silhouette detach itself from the surrounding shadows and walk towards me.

I tossed and turned, but that malicious weasel face wouldn't let me sleep. After three nights of this I told Mum, and asked if I could sleep with her until it passed. She readily agreed, giving me one of those reassuring *everything will be all right* smiles. Enfolded in Mum's arms that night, snug in her warmth, the shadow of the burglar's face vanished completely from my mind as if within that magic maternal circle nothing whatsoever could hurt me.

But what Mum hadn't told me was that she was suffering from insomnia as well, and although I could fall asleep in her bed easily enough, her own agonized efforts to get to sleep would soon wake me up. After a few nights I went back to my own bed, hoping I might have broken the cycle, but found insomnia still waiting for me there. I was back to square one.

Reluctantly, we decided to try sleeping pills. Mum had always been strongly against them in the past, fearing they could be addictive. But the little mauve pills she got from Dr Lyle worked wonderfully for me. I took one, half an hour before going to bed and fell into a deep dreamless sleep almost straight away. I cut it down to half a pill, and then to a quarter, and in a week or so I was able to fall asleep within ten minutes of my head hitting the pillow without taking any medication at all.

That was when the nightmares started.

The first nightmares were confused, fragmentary affairs. They jumped rapidly from one chamber of horrors to another, like restless flies, unable to settle anywhere for very long. When I woke up I could remember little about them, just the general impression of being pursued the whole night long by some unseen horror (I didn't have to see it, I knew what – or rather *who* – it was).

I only remember two from that time with any clarity. In one, I was in the lounge practising my flute when I looked up to see Paul Hannigan staring at me through the window, his horribly dislocated lower jaw hanging open like a ghost-train ghoul. In the other, Mum and I pulled the body of the burglar out by his feet from under the kitchen table, only to find that it wasn't Paul Hannigan we'd killed after all, *but my dad.*

This nightmare tortured me for days, and not only because the image of Dad face-down in all that blood was so graphic. It was more than that. It gnawed at me like an accusation. Was that what the killing of Paul

Hannigan had really been about? I refused to believe it – I couldn't even kill my feelings for my dad, so how could I possibly want to kill him?

Gradually, instead of countless confused and disjointed nightmares, I started to have the same one night after night, as if my brain had finally distilled all the horrors I'd lived through into a perfect script that wasn't to be altered in even the tiniest detail.

It always began with Mum and me playing croquet in the front garden on an idyllic summer's day. I was about eight years old, wearing the blue-and-white striped dress that had been my favourite when I was a little girl (there was a period, Mum told me, when I wouldn't wear anything else). Mum was different too. She looked as if she'd just stepped out of the framed wedding photograph that used to stand on the mantelpiece in the *matrimonial home*; she wore a flowing white wedding dress and was still young and fresh-faced – the streaks of grey in her hair and the crow's feet around her eyes were yet to arrive.

Mum croqueted me and sent my ball racing away across the short grass. I went running after it, calling over my shoulder that she was playing really well – better than I'd ever seen her play before. The croquet ball raced on and on and came to rest in the oval rose bed. I stopped running. I stopped smiling. I didn't want to go any closer. I knew that the burglar's body was buried there. I looked round for Mum, hoping she'd say that I could leave it where it was, but she was suddenly an immense distance away, at the far end of a garden that was now enormous. I called out to her, but I knew she wouldn't be able to hear me. I made up my mind to make a quick grab for the ball, then turn on my heels and run as fast as I could back to her. But when I looked back at the oval rose bed, I saw that right next to the croquet ball, actually touching it, the burglar's green decomposing hand protruded through the soil.

I knew I had to cover the hand up or someone would see it and call the police and all would be lost. I was now my real age and wearing my dressing gown and nightie. I took off my dressing gown and threw it over the hand. I realized it was only a temporary solution, but it would do until I could tell Mum. I knelt down in the grass and reached for the croquet ball, but the instant I touched it, my wrist was seized by the burglar's other hand, which suddenly came snaking up out of the shallow grave.

This hand was immensely strong. It dragged me down into the thick mud until my face was pressed right up against Paul Hannigan's and I could smell his nauseating corpse breath.

'I've been trying to ring you,' he said, 'but you won't answer the phone.' A sudden jump-cut transported us to the bottom of a real grave. Paul Hannigan was on top of me, with both his hands clamped around my throat – hands that sometimes changed into snakes or the roots of trees, but with the weird logic of dreams somehow always remained hands as well. Above me, the sky was just as it had been on the night we'd moved the car: the clouds' dirty thumbprints grubbily obscuring the stars, the moon a thin silver scimitar in the blackness. I struggled ferociously, but he pinned me down with ease.

'I'm gonna do it *right* this time,' he leered, and tightened his grip around my throat. I couldn't breathe. I started to lose consciousness. I made one final maniacal effort to free myself but it was useless. The grotesque Halloween-mask face above me was grinning triumphantly. And then I saw Mum loom over his left shoulder, holding the chopping board in her hands. She wasn't her young self any more; her face was now exaggeratedly haggard and drawn and the white wedding dress had been replaced by her blood-soaked dressing gown. I knew what she was going to do. I was willing her to do it: *Hit him! Hit him!* But instead of raising the chopping board high above her head as I expected, she drew away, saying, *I don't want to go to prison*, over and over again, until I couldn't see her any more . . .

I'd wake up soaked in sweat, my heart thumping so violently in my chest that I could scarcely draw breath, the quilt kicked into a lump at the bottom of the bed, its empty cover twisted in knots around my body.

29

We put the gun and everything else we'd taken out of Paul Hannigan's car into bin bags and stored them upstairs with all the others. If the police had come to the house then, they'd have found the entire case against us piled up neatly in the corner of the spare room just waiting to be tagged as exhibits for our trial. In spite of this, it was six days before we finally got rid of them.

This wasn't because Mum was somehow ignorant of the danger – it was the very opposite. She was so aware of the need to make all the evidence disappear *forever* – so acutely aware that this was the most important move we would make in our deadly game with the police, that she was terrified of getting it wrong. She knew that if the police ever found the bin bags – if they ever discovered the bloodstained nightclothes, the tea towels, the bloody knife – it would unleash an investigative frenzy. The police would come bearing down on us like a pack of hunting dogs that had picked up the scent of their quarry. If they ever found the bin bags, they'd have an abundance of clues, any one of which could lead them back to Honeysuckle Cottage and the body buried in the oval rose bed. And while she agonized over her decision, the bin bags festered away in the spare room, the smell of stale blood growing stronger every day.

Mum's first idea was to dump them one at a time in municipal refuse bins – miles away from Honeysuckle Cottage and miles apart from each other. This way, she said, the police would be unlikely to link the eight bags together or trace them back to us.

But on reflection, she decided this plan was too risky. It all seemed too public for her. Someone might see her getting rid of one of the bags and be able to describe her to the police later. And even if there weren't any eyewitnesses, she might be picked up on one of those CCTV cameras, which she said were everywhere nowadays – if it didn't get a clear image of her face, it might record the Escort's number plate and the police would be able to trace her easily enough from that.

On top of this, neither of us really knew what happened to rubbish after it was collected – it wasn't something we'd ever needed to think about before. It was possible that it was crushed and buried or dumped at sea straight away, but Mum was haunted by the possibility that the bags would end up on a council tip, where they'd lie around in the open air, possibly for months. It only needed one of the bags to split open and a refuse worker to notice the bloody rags spilling out – bloody rags full of invisible traces of DNA – and the police would have the piece of thread that could eventually unravel all the way back to us.

I suggested we have a big bonfire in the back garden and burn everything. The bloody nighties, the dressing gowns, the kitchen curtains and trench coat would all be reduced to an innocent pile of ash. But Mum wasn't keen on this idea at all. There were too many things that wouldn't burn down to ash – the wellington boots, the mobile phone, the tools, and of course the gun, the hideous gun. So at best it only half solved the problem. Besides, she said, she'd never made a bonfire before – a bonfire was a man's thing – and she was worried it might get out of control. If the fire service had to be called, they'd discover everything. And even if the bonfire didn't get out of control, the neighbouring farmer, seeing the smoke so near to his crops, might come down to see what was going on. He might start asking questions, interfering, trying to show us how it should be done . . .

My other suggestion was to seal everything up in the metal trunk we had in the attic, tie weights to it and then sink it in the huge reservoir in the Morsely National Park about eighty miles to the north. To my surprise, this idea didn't excite any interest in Mum either. I said that if she was unhappy with the reservoir, we could always drive to the coast and dump the trunk at sea. 'It's not that,' she said. 'I just don't trust the water. The water always gives up its secrets in the end.'

MICE

Mum said it with such conviction that I thought she might have been referring to some experience of her own, but then I remembered she had borrowed my copy of *Rebecca* when she couldn't sleep one night. So much of what Mum was was made up of what she'd read. Is that what our middle-class culture created? People formed more by the books they'd read than the lives they'd lived? But maybe that had all changed for Mum after Paul Hannigan had pushed open her bedroom door. Maybe we'd both begun to live real lives after the chopping board had fallen.

Mum toyed with the idea of using acid, but like the bonfire it would only half solve the problem, as it was unlikely that even the strongest acid would be able to dissolve the metal tools or the marble chopping board. Moreover, acid was highly dangerous, and just purchasing it and the protective gloves and aprons we'd need would be enough to arouse suspicions.

Eventually, she decided to bury everything in the vegetable patch in the back garden, in the extension we'd dug ourselves in happier times. She wasn't entirely satisfied with this solution, but at least it would get the bags out of the house, and compared to the other schemes it carried much less risk of detection. It would be a lot of work – we'd have to dig quite a substantial hole to fit the contents of the eight bin bags – but it could certainly be done.

Mum thought she could make some of the more awkwardly shaped objects easier to bury if she sawed them into smaller pieces. So one night, as soon as she got home from work, we took the mop and the bucket and the plastic bowl to the bigger of the two sheds, which Mr Jenkins had equipped with buzzing fluorescent strip lights and where Mum kept her small collection of tools. We sawed the mop handle into several sausage-sized sticks, and after an hour of slapstick bumbling worthy of Laurel and Hardy – it was a miracle we didn't lose any of our fingers – we finally succeeded in sawing the hard moulded-plastic bucket in half. After that, neither of us could face making an attempt on the plastic bowl.

My heart started racing when Mum took Paul Hannigan's mobile out of her pocket; I knew it had been in the same bin bag as his wallet. But I quickly reasoned my guilty panic away: *She'd never looked inside the wallet, she had no way of knowing that the driver's licence was missing.*

Sure enough, she didn't even glance over at me as she put the mobile down on the work bench and began rummaging through the tool box until she found the hammer. She said she was worried the police might still be able to trace the mobile phone even if it was turned off, and insisted on smashing it to smithereens before we buried it, 'just to be on the safe side'. She put the mobile on the concrete floor, knelt down beside it, and with a strange grimace on her sweating face, somewhere between destructive glee and pained disgust, she beat it into a masticated pulp. Remembering other blows I'd seen her strike, I looked away uncomfortably into the cobwebby corners of the shed.

But we never did bury the bin bags in the vegetable patch. On the night we'd set aside to do it, Mum came home from work ready to put a completely new plan into action.

30

Mum had seen a client that day whose twelve-year-old son had been injured while his class photograph was being taken. The stack of benches he'd been standing on had collapsed and although he'd only fallen four feet or so, he'd landed awkwardly and suffered a serious fracture of the left ankle.

As Mum flicked through the medical reports that lunchtime, she'd been reminded of another case she'd had not long after she joined Everson's. Another twelve-year-old boy had badly fractured his left ankle in a fall, but she couldn't for the life of her remember the boy's name or the circumstances of the accident. She would have liked to check through the old file to compare the doctor's prognosis and see how much the case had settled for, but she knew Everson's would have destroyed it years ago.

It was only later that day, while she was taking instructions from a new client in the interview room, that it suddenly all came back to her. Pugh. Thomas Pugh. A smiling, tubby little boy with a butter-blond fringe. He'd been on a camping holiday with his family in the Morsely National Park and had decided to go exploring early one morning with his younger brother while their parents were still asleep. They'd come across some wooden structures in the forest that they'd taken to be an assault course and they'd been racing each other to them when Thomas had suddenly disappeared into thin air. His little brother's first thought was that Thomas had been zapped by an alien death ray. In fact, he'd fallen into one of the abandoned copper mines that honeycomb the national park's mountains. The wooden structures were all that was left of the old pithead.

And that's when Mum had the inspiration: the abandoned mines were the perfect place to get rid of the pile of incriminating evidence in the spare room.

She made an excuse to slip out of the office and went across town to the public records office, deep in the basement of the grandiose council building that dominated the town square. There she requested copies of the National Park Authority's plans of all the old copper mines in the Morsely National Park. Half an hour later five A3 sheets were handed over to her.

'It's absolutely perfect!' Mum exclaimed excitedly that night as we sat in the lounge after dinner. 'The mine shafts are deep inside the national park and they're fenced off to the general public now. The authority was forced to do that after the Pugh case. Some of the shafts are extremely deep – the one I've got in mind is over *one thousand feet*. Tommy Pugh only fell into an eight-foot service shaft – if he'd fallen into one of the main shafts he'd never have been seen again.'

'But how will you find it, Mum?' I asked. 'The national park's vast.'

'I've been there before,' she said, leaning towards me, right on the very edge of her seat, her coffee cup hanging loosely in her large hands. 'During the Pugh case I made a site visit to the mines. I was there all day. The park rangers took me all over the mountain in their Jeep. It's not going to be easy, but I'm sure it'll all come back to me when I'm up there – and I've got the maps, don't forget. They show everything – every main shaft, ventilation shaft, every adit, every stope.'

I still wanted to grill her about her new plan; I still wanted to find some flaw that hadn't occurred to her, probably for the simple reason that she'd rejected all my suggestions so brusquely.

'What if they decide to reopen the mines in the future as some sort of tourist attraction? They'll find everything then.'

Mum was clearly delighted I'd asked this question. 'They won't be opening these mines to tourists, I can promise you that.'

'Why not?'

'Because they're poisoned, Shelley. That's the reason they abandoned the mines back in the 1840s – naturally occurring hydrogen sulphide. In the twenty years the mines were open, more than fifty miners died from exposure to the gas. Their relatives tried to bring an action against the mining company – and failed, need-less to say. The mines are a death trap!'

I had to admit I liked the sound of this plan much more than anything else we'd come up with, and it was infinitely preferable to burying everything in the garden. With Paul Hannigan's corpse mouldering under the oval rose bed, I felt the garden was already harbour-ing enough of our secret history.

Mum didn't want me to go with her to the national park; it was already nine by the time she was ready to leave and she said she had no idea what time she'd get back. The park was about an hour and a half's drive away and she then had to find the specific shaft she was looking for, armed only with the five maps and the torch.

I helped her carry the bin bags out to the car. We couldn't fit all of them in the boot and I had to put three on the back seat of the Escort.

'Be careful,' I begged, taking her by the hands.

I hated the thought of Mum in that immense forest in the middle of the night with just the feeble light of the torch to guide her. I'd seen for myself how bad her eyes were in the dark. I kept imagining the ground suddenly giving way beneath her feet, the terrifying fall into one of those poisoned mine shafts.

What would I do then? What would I do then?

'Please, please, be careful, Mum.'

She hugged me tightly and told me not to worry, she'd be OK.

I watched her drive slowly away, her face set in grim determination, the torch and the roll of maps beside her on the passenger seat. I hurried back into the house, keeping my eyes fixed firmly on the ground before me so that I wouldn't catch even an accidental sight of the oval rose bed.

I sat at the dining-room table and tried to catch up on all the homework I was falling horribly behind with. I'd only just finished the essay on the First World War that Roger had set me, and there was already another piece of history coursework due, plus two English essays and a geography question, not to mention the maths revision papers Mrs Harris had been setting.

Since the night we'd killed Paul Hannigan, my concentration had been pathetic – shattered every ten minutes or so by flashbacks that dragged me into that kitchen-turned-charnel-house and forced me to dance the dance of death with the burglar all over again. When I came around I hardly knew where I was, as if I'd just snapped out of a hypnotic trance. Interrupted again and again in this way, an essay that would have taken me two hours to write before was now taking me four or five.

I started to plan out one of Roger's English essays (*Macbeth goes from a man 'too full o' the milk of human kindness' to a 'butcher' and 'tyrant' in five Acts. How?*), but even though I drank almost a whole pot of coffee, I only managed to write one side in an hour, and even then I knew what I'd written wasn't very good. My mind kept wandering from my dog-eared paperback copy of *Macbeth* to Mum. Where was she? What was she doing right at that moment? I prayed that she'd be OK. I prayed that she'd get back safely.

Eventually I pushed the essay to one side (it really was rubbish – 'Macbeth is a good man when the play starts . . .') and began doodling idly on a scrap of paper. Without really thinking about what I was doing, I drew the Escort winding its way up through the mountains, jagged pine forests on either side, its headlights sending out two elongated teardrops of light into the surrounding darkness. A strange groan came from somewhere upstairs and I stopped drawing and looked up. I remembered the nightmare where Paul Hannigan's ruined face had suddenly appeared at the window. I quickly went into the lounge and drew the curtains, fussing until I was absolutely sure that every gap was closed and no one could see in from outside.

I poured myself a glass of wine (there was always wine in the house now) and sat on the sofa to try to read, but the house was alive with ambiguous sounds: the floorboards upstairs creaked arthritically as though someone were moving stealthily around in the spare room; there were intermittent rustlings just beyond the lounge window that could have been footsteps or merely the breeze scuffing fallen twigs across the gravel.

It was nearly eleven but I was too frightened to go upstairs to bed. I kidded myself that I'd decided to wait up for Mum, and put the television on to drown out the unsettling noises. With a sensation like cold fingers on the back of my neck, I realized that this was the first time I'd been alone in the house late at night since we'd killed Paul Hannigan. It was no wonder that I felt more afraid than usual. *Why had Mum left me behind?*

I curled up on the sofa and sipped my wine, struggling to shut out the thoughts that tried to terrify me (*he could be outside the house now – risen from his shallow grave, about to beat at the front door with his maggoty fists . . . or, worse, he could be inside the house already . . .*)

I flicked up and down the TV channels, but there was nothing that interested me – celebrities on a desert island, a competition to find the world's strongest man, a sitcom set in a hospital where every remark, every expression or gesture of the actors released helpless peals of canned laughter.

There was a programme about a tribe in Africa (or the Amazon, I wasn't sure which) that I half-watched for want of anything better. Their village was on the banks of a river, slimy with yellow-ochre mud, which the children dived into and swam about in as happily as if it had been the chlorinated water of an English swimming pool. The documentary showed the men hunting wild pigs with home-made bows and arrows and decorating their bodies with a tool that seemed to slice into their skin and fill the groove with pigment at the same time. I would normally have changed the channel when they prepared to sacrifice one of their goats as a religious offering because I hated seeing cruelty to animals (as a little girl if I ever saw a bullfight or a fox hunt on TV it would send me into hysterics), but that night it didn't seem to bother me as much as usual.

It's just an animal, after all, I found myself thinking, as a tribesman knelt on the goat's chest and nonchalantly cut its throat. *It's just a stupid goat.* Its intelligence was so low it had no awareness of what was happening to it, no understanding of cruelty, no understanding of death – no understanding of life, for that matter. Only if there was intelligence, real intelligence, could there be any sympathy for the victim . . .

I dropped off to sleep for a few minutes and when I opened my eyes again one of the elders was talking about the tribe's religious beliefs. His words came up in subtitles that were white against a pale background and hard to read. He was saying that the tribe lived closely with the animals of the forest and knew their different characters well.

They respected certain animals for their good qualities; they reviled others for their bad. One of their fundamental religious beliefs, he said, was that a man took on the qualities of any animal he killed. So a hunter who killed lots of monkeys would become an ingenious and clever man who'd always be making people laugh with his clownish antics. A man who killed lots of wild pigs would become an exemplary family man, a devoted father who'd fight to the death to protect his loved ones.

He mentioned an animal I'd never heard of and said they didn't kill this particular animal because it was thought to be untrustworthy and cowardly, and they were afraid of contracting these bad qualities. They believed that in the spirit world the spirits of animals and men intermingled and sometimes even fused together. In fact, many of the gods they worshipped were spirit-world fusions of humans and animals, such as the monkey-man and the inexhaustibly fertile chicken-woman.

I finished my wine and stretched out full-length on the sofa. I'd heard about this sort of idea before, probably at school – tribesmen who thought that killing a lion would make them as brave as a lion. Something about the idea intrigued me. I wondered if there'd ever been a time thousands of years ago (before police and prisons and documentary crews), when the tribe had believed that they took on the qualities, not just of the animals they killed, but of the men they killed too. Were the forests filled with ancient graves of people murdered for their good looks, their intelligence or their witty sense of humour? And what if it was true, I wondered drowsily, what if you really did take on the qualities of the person you'd killed? Would Mum and I then become like Paul Hannigan? Would we contract his savage thuggery like some horrible disfiguring disease?

I must have drifted off to sleep again because the next thing I remember was being woken up by the sound of Mum's car rolling heavily over the gravel outside. The channel's programming had finished for the night and the screen showed a wallpaper of white clouds in a blue sky and played banal muzak. The clock on the DVD player said 1:53.

I was standing in the kitchen in the middle of an enormous yawn when Mum put her key in the door.

'What are you doing up?' she said in a whisper, as if it was too late at night to speak any louder.

'I fell asleep watching TV,' I said, rubbing a watery eye with the knuckle of my index finger. 'Did you find it OK?'

Mum looked wide awake. Her cheeks were rosy from being out in the fresh air. Her eyes shone.

'Yes, I did. But it was a hell of a job in the dark, I can tell you. I thought the car was going to give up the ghost struggling up those forestry tracks. It's absolutely covered in mud – I'll have to take it to the carwash first thing tomorrow. Thank God for the radio mast up there – it's lit up at night. It really helped me get my bearings.'

Her nose had started to run now she was back in the warm house, and she loudly sniffed back a droplet and frisked her pockets for a hanky.

'I had some luck too,' she went on between soft blows into the tissue she'd found. 'Part of the fence near the shaft has been broken down, and I was able to drive the car almost up to the pithead.'

Fighting back the tears, I threw my arms around her and hugged her as hard as I could.

'I'm so glad you're OK! I was so worried!'

She held me tightly and I smelled the outdoors in the folds of her coat. 'It's all gone, Shelley,' she whispered, her lips almost touching my ear, making the hairs on the back of my neck stand up. 'It's all gone! Gone forever. They'll *never* find it!'

She cupped my face in her hands and contemplated me intently. I could hardly keep my eyes open and broke into another enormous yawn.

'You go on up to bed now, sleepy-head.' She smiled. 'I need to eat something and unwind a bit before I come up.'

I kissed her goodnight and trudged sleepily up the stairs. I heard her take a bottle of wine from the fridge, and the glugging sound it made as she generously filled her glass. As I passed the spare room I was shocked by how empty it looked without the bin bags.

I lay in bed waiting for sleep, knowing it wouldn't be long in coming and hoping that I might be spared the now-familiar nightmare. It was a great relief to have that mountain of evidence gone from under our roof at last. The police could come tomorrow and they'd find nothing incriminating in the house. Everything that connected Paul Hannigan to us was sunk one thousand feet underground in a labyrinth of dark chambers.

Or rather, *almost* everything.

I'd kept Paul Hannigan's driver's licence. It was hidden in my secrets box in the bottom drawer of my dressing table, along with some photos of my dad that Mum didn't know I'd kept, my hospital ID bracelet and my drawing of the mouse with the noose around its neck.

I'm not exactly sure why I was so determined to keep the licence in spite of the risk, in spite of how crazy Mum would go if she knew what I'd done. All I knew was that I wanted something to show that what had happened that night had really happened. I wanted *proof*. Proof that a man really had broken into our house on my sixteenth birthday and that Mum and I really had killed him.

I suppose I wanted a trophy.

31

May arrived, bringing day after day of fierce dry heat and cloudless blue skies. After an unnaturally mild winter, it was one of the hottest springs in living memory, with temperatures regularly rising into the thirties. There was endless talk on the news about global warming and how the world's weather was changing beyond recognition, with footage of heavy snowfalls in Turkey, dust storms in Australia, and catastrophic floods in central Europe. One of the celebrity TV weathermen, darting back and forth in front of his computerized maps, exclaimed, 'You can throw your geography textbooks out the window! All bets are off as of today! The world's weather has gone absolutely mad! Everywhere something unprecedented is happening! *Everything* is changing . . .'

As if it had received a secret coded message, the front garden suddenly exploded into bloom, and although I hadn't liked Mr Jenkins, I couldn't help but admire his Godlike eye for colour. The white flowers of the mock orange superbly set off the vibrant blue of the ceanothus, the golden poppies threaded their way through the red

valerian like delicate embroidery, the creamy white of
the mountain avens answered the bright yellow of the
tree peony like a half-rhyme – almost its mirror image,
but not quite. The most eye-catching of all was the bed
of lupins, a great swirling chaos of colour that reminded
me of the coloured-glass kaleidoscopes we used to play
with at kindergarten.

I admired Mr Jenkins's mastery, but I admired it
from afar. I tried to keep away from the front garden
as much as I could. Even though the roses in the oval
rose bed had blossomed into exquisite pink flowers, the
bushes forming one huge bouquet that touched the grass
like the hem of a luxuriant gown, the sight of it still terrified me. Those Valentine's day blooms filled my head
with macabre thoughts. *What would Paul Hannigan's
face look like now after two weeks, three weeks, underground? Were the nutrients from his corpse responsible
for such fat pink petals?*

The house grew stiflingly hot, but when we opened
the windows to let in fresh air we were plagued with
flies. Even when we didn't have the windows open some
still seemed to find their way in. I became adept at killing them with a twisted tea towel and delighted in the
pile of tiny black corpses that lay beneath the lounge
window at the end of every day.

The heatwave went on and on, breaking all records.
I walked around the house in shorts and the skimpiest
tops I could find. I hated wearing so little – I hated
exposing my thighs and the fat on my stomach which,

if I didn't concentrate hard on holding it in, would swell over the belt of my shorts. But it was impossible even to think of wearing jeans or a shirt in that sticky, suffocating heat.

I bought a little hand-held propeller fan, which I kept close to my face on those days when it seemed as if all the oxygen had been sucked out of the house, when even the deepest breath seemed to bring no relief at all. The waspy buzzing of the fan irritated Mrs Harris intensely, but she was wary of saying anything to me now and tried her best to pretend it didn't bother her. I put it on in her lessons, even when I didn't need it, just to annoy her.

The heatwave triggered the worst attack of hay fever I'd ever had. I couldn't breathe through my nose and my eyes streamed constantly. I had a pounding headache by lunchtime every day. It was right at this time, when the heatwave and my hay fever were at their worst, that Roger and Mrs Harris decided to set me a week of mock exams.

I tried to wriggle my way out of them, pleading my obvious symptoms, but they were both firm: my exams began on June the fifteenth and I needed to be tested under strict exam conditions. I didn't give up easily – I felt sure that if I could hold them off for a week my concentration might start to improve, but Roger poohpoohed my concerns. 'You're an A student, Shelley. You'll get As in everything standing on your head. A runny nose shouldn't prove a major obstacle.'

But as I'd feared, my results were disappointing. The flashbacks plagued me horribly during the week of tests, toppling my thoughts like a tower of children's building blocks and forcing me to start constructing them all over again. Although I managed As in English language and history, I got Cs in maths and physics and Bs in everything else.

Roger was surprised by my low grades for Mrs Harris, but as I'd earned either As or Bs in the subjects he taught me he wasn't unduly concerned. In fact, he was thrilled by my answer to the question about Macbeth's character on the literature paper.

Pacing around the dining-room table, he excitedly read parts of my essay aloud:

' "Perhaps the most brilliant thing about Macbeth is that, in a way, he doesn't *have* a character. He is loyal, he is treacherous; he loves his wife, he's unconcerned when she dies; he's fearless in battle, he's a coward the night of the murder; he kills a defenceless woman and child, he dies like a hero . . . Shakespeare seems to be saying that real people are not *characters*, we are our *actions*. The brave turn out to be cowards, cowards turn out to be brave, the cruel can be kind, the kind cruel . . ." This is university level, Shelley, *university level!*' he exclaimed, slapping the table with the flat of his hand.

I felt his enlarged green eyes staring at me. And when he spoke again his tone was different, intimate. 'How did you get such profound psychological insight so young?'

I saw Mum dump a dark shovelful of soil over Paul Hannigan's face and shifted uncomfortably in my seat.

'I think I know,' he said.

I felt myself starting to blush and my chest cramp. *What was he trying to say?* I only exhaled the breath I was holding when he added softly, 'The JETS.'

Trying not to show my relief, I nodded and looked away, twisting the corner of my notebook.

Apart from that one bright spot, there wasn't much to celebrate. Mrs Harris was completely demoralized by my poor results. She seemed to think I'd done it deliberately to spite her and make her look incompetent. Fussily wiping the drips from the lid of her Thermos flask, she looked at me reproachfully and said, 'I thought we were making progress, Shelley, in our work – *and* personally.'

I left her comment hanging in the air without answering.

Mum was disappointed too, very disappointed, but she did her best not to show it – she even tried to cheer me up, joking darkly, 'The exam board gives students an extra half-hour if they have dyslexia – I wonder what they give you if you're suffering from post-traumatic stress disorder after killing someone?'

I brooded on my poor results and even shed a few tears when I was alone in my bedroom. I was furious that Paul Hannigan – that worthless *nothing!* – was spoiling what should have been my moment of glory, the well-earned exam success that would brilliantly round off my time at school and propel me on my way to university. After all, if I wasn't good at schoolwork, *what was I good at?*

Yet at the same time, there was another part of me that thought: *What the hell does it matter?* The police will come any day now and it will all be over. There won't be any more revision, there won't be any exams – instead, there'll be the forensic experts in the kitchen, the police cadets on their hands and knees searching every inch of the lawn, the scrum of shouting journalists, the hand on my head ducking me into the back seat of the police car . . .

But the weeks went by and still the police didn't come.

Every weekend I scoured the papers to see if there was an article about Paul Hannigan. I knew exactly what I expected to come across; I'd almost written the article in my own mind. Under a headline like police hunt for missing man it would begin:

> Police are increasingly concerned by the mysterious disappearance of twenty-four-year-old Paul Hannigan. Mr Hannigan was last seen on Monday the tenth of April. His car was later found abandoned in the car park of the Farmer's Harvest eatery . . .

There'd be a quote from a relative (his mother? his wife?) asking him to make contact as they were 'worried sick about him', and adding, 'It's not like Paul to disappear without telling anyone where he was going.' And then would come the devastating sentence that would make my blood run cold, the sentence that would spell the beginning of the end for Mum and me: 'Mr Hannigan's car was seen badly parked in a country lane on the twelfth of April and reported to the police by a local farmer . . .'

Or even worse:

Police are looking for two women, possibly a mother and daughter, who were seen leaving Mr Hannigan's car in the car park of the Farmer's Harvest two days after his disappearance; an eyewitness who spoke to them has given police a detailed description of the women . . . the police investigation is continuing.

They'd only have to interview the taxi driver who brought us home that night to know exactly where to find us.

But there was nothing in the papers about Paul Hannigan, absolutely nothing.

I was relieved, of course. I didn't want to see that weasel face smiling back at me from some blurry family snapshot, I didn't want to be caught. Yet, at the same time, I found the silence strangely disconcerting.

It was as if a terrible earthquake had struck Honeysuckle Cottage in the early hours of my sixteenth birthday, collapsing the ceiling and bringing the walls down on top of us. But when we'd staggered shell-shocked from the house, we'd found the rest of the world completely unaffected, everyone going about their business as usual. It was impossible to accept that the shockwaves from that night hadn't been felt anywhere else, that it had only been our earthquake – our secret earthquake.

And there was something else about this silence that was even more disturbing. That Paul Hannigan could disappear from the face of the earth without apparently arousing the slightest interest or concern seemed to go against everything I'd been taught to believe about the sanctity of human life.

Surely it wasn't meant to be like that? The loss of just one person, one individual, no matter how worthless their existence had been, was meant to matter. Our religious education teacher had asked us once: *Imagine that you could end the life of some stranger by simply pressing a button on your armchair. You could never be found out, never punished. Would you do it? Would you press the button?* I'd answered with an emphatic 'no' because I was convinced that the loss of just one individual mattered, that in some subtle but profound way the fabric of the universe would be changed for the worse if that hypothetical stranger died.

Yet Paul Hannigan had vanished off the face of the earth, and, as far as I could see, nothing whatsoever had changed. Life carried on just as it always had. His disappearance hadn't been reported in the national papers. It hadn't even been reported in the local paper – Paul Hannigan hadn't merited so much as two lines amid the council's plans to extend the local library or the success of the Rotary Club raffle or the opening of two high-class takeaway outlets in the shopping precinct.

For the first time in my life I began to think that perhaps the loss of an individual wasn't of very much significance after all. Perhaps it was as meaningless as the casual crushing of a fly against a windowpane. Perhaps the fabric of the universe didn't change one iota.

When I thought about the religious education teacher's question now, I found myself thinking: *Why not press the button? What difference would it really make?*

32

Time lived up to its reputation as the great healer, and our life in Honeysuckle Cottage slowly returned to normal.

It began with small things, such as going back to eating our meals on the pine table in the kitchen, and re-establishing our old morning routine – two kisses in the hallway and the reminder to drive carefully, Mum's glance back and wave as she drove away. We took the garden furniture out of the shed and sat out on the patio again. Over our evening meals we – cautiously at first – started to describe our daily highs and lows to one another like we used to. We ate spaghetti bolognese again. One Sunday morning we picked cherries in the back garden and made a gorgeous pie, which we ate with vanilla ice-cream – just as we'd planned to do before our uninvited guest arrived. We began to rent DVDs again and one Saturday night watched two George Clooney movies (*O Brother, Where Art Thou?* and *Leatherheads*) back to back as we munched our way through an enormous bowl of buttered popcorn.

On our weekly shopping trips into town, we

gradually replaced everything that had been tainted that night and had ended up at the bottom of the mine shaft: we bought new curtains for the kitchen, new tea towels, a new mop and bucket. In response to an instinct too strong to resist, we often sought replacements that were markedly different from what we'd had before: a thin rubber doormat instead of another coir fibre one: brightly coloured – almost garish – wellington boots instead of black ones. And Mum didn't look for another marble chopping board – she insisted on getting a cheap plastic one from a discount store.

As each tiny gap in the jigsaw was filled in – new bath towels, new nighties, new dressing gowns – I felt as if our home was being reconstituted, made whole again, and it surprised me how much this made *me* feel whole again. I'd never realized until then how important these small things were in our lives. The puzzle was finally complete when Mum found the miniature thatched cottage's chimney in the bowl of potpourri and sat at the dining-room table one night and patiently super-glued it back in place.

The bruises on my neck gradually faded away to nothing, and at last I was able to put away the scarves I'd had to wear whenever I was with Roger and Mrs Harris. The bruise on my coccyx also lost its angry red halo and shrank in size until it was no bigger than a charcoal-grey coin, and eventually disappeared alto-gether. Strangely, as my bruises went, my scars started to show real signs of improvement too. The burns to my left hand and right ear were invisible in all but the brightest lights, and even then showed as nothing more than sheeny patches on the skin. And the scars on my forehead and neck lightened from a dirty coffee colour to more of a honey tone, and were far less noticeable than before.

As my physical injuries healed, so too did my mental wounds. The flashbacks' grip on me grew weaker and weaker. They didn't stop (they've never stopped altogether), but they became less frequent. It was as if my mind had slowly begun to absorb, to accept, what had happened. The periods when I didn't think about that night grew longer and longer – ten minutes, twenty minutes, half an hour, a whole hour. My ability to concentrate began to return. I could write a good essay at one sitting rather than in broken snatches over several days; I could lose myself in a movie; for long periods of time I could actually forget who I was, where I was and – miracle of miracles – *what I'd done*.

To my immense relief, the recurring nightmare eventually stopped too. After one final chilling performance it never came back again. I still had dark dreams (sitting astride Emma Townley on the floor of the school toilets, pounding her head into a red jelly with the marble chopping board), but the important thing was that I began to have normal dreams as well. I had anxiety dreams about my approaching exams (I couldn't read the exam questions because the print was so minuscule; I'd been set the medieval history paper instead of the

modern history paper I'd revised for); comic, surreal
dreams (walking across the desert on stilts with a litter
of baby hamsters squirming around down my shirt
front; Mum turning into a giant hen able to lay eggs the
size of cars). I had romantic dreams again too: flirting
with George Clooney on the back seat of a New York
cab after Mum and I had watched *One Fine Day* for
the fifth time. (We were both talking on mobiles –
ostensibly to other people, but really to each other.
He said into his phone, 'Do you want me to kiss
you?' and I said into mine, 'I'd like that very much.')
I even had a romantic dream – I suppose erotic would
be more honest – about Roger, of all people, a dream
whose explicitness shocked me and left me feeling a
little shamefaced around him for several days.

Another sign of my recovery was that my interest in
the laptop began to reawaken.

I hadn't gone near it since that night. I hadn't wanted
to touch it; I hadn't even wanted to look at it. It was so
caught up in all the horror (in some ways I even blamed
it for everything that had happened) that the thought of
taking it out of the sideboard was almost as repulsive as
the thought of disinterring the burglar's body.

As the weeks passed, however, I slowly started to
overcome my aversion. I began to feel excited again by
the thought of writing my essays on it, and being able
to use the Internet without all the torturous delays and
inexplicable glitches I had to endure with the beast. I
was convinced the laptop would help drag my work out

of the malaise it had fallen into. And my writing ambition, which had become so caught up with the whole idea of the computer, started to twitch back into life. I caught myself thinking with a callous egoism that even I found shocking: *After everything I've lived through, surely I'll be able to write something truly great? After all, how many writers actually know what it's like to kill somebody?*

Eventually I took the laptop out of the sideboard, where it had lain untouched since my birthday, and with Mum's help, set it up on the dining-room table. At first I was worried it wouldn't work, remembering how heavily it had fallen to the ground when I'd struck the knife between Paul Hannigan's shoulder blades, but it flickered into electronic life at the first click of the switch on its side.

As I'd hoped, the laptop gave my revision a much-needed boost. I stopped writing in longhand altogether and wrote notes, essays, everything, on it. I think I was actually able to type faster than I could write with the swirly girly hand I'd developed over the years at school. When Mum's printer went on the blink, Roger was happy to take my memory stick home each day and print everything out for me on his computer. He refused to take any money for the paper or the ink that he used and I felt a huge gratitude towards him – more than gratitude, in fact, more like a *warmth* – and it reassured me to think that my capacity for friendship hadn't been poisoned by what had happened with the JETS.

33

On the surface, Mum seemed to be making an excellent recovery too. Her eye healed up quickly and she was delighted when she didn't have to wear make-up to work any more to camouflage the bruising.

She carried on in the office as if nothing had happened; she settled several small claims and even won a case that unexpectedly went to trial. This win gave her an enormous amount of pleasure, partly because the circumstances of the accident – a fall on some stairs in a restaurant – had been difficult to prove, but mainly because the losing defendant, the Love Shack Rib House, was represented by Everson's, her old employer. It was the closest she'd ever come to scoring a victory over Dad and she was absolutely ecstatic about it.

But there were signs that, behind the facade, Mum wasn't finding things anywhere near as easy as she made out.

The sleeping pills that cured my insomnia had little effect on Mum's. Although she still went up to bed at around eleven, she was rarely able to fall asleep. She tossed and turned for hours, but sleep evaded her desperate pursuit. Eventually, unable to bear the futility of it any more, she'd get up and go downstairs. I often heard the sound of the television drifting faintly up the stairwell when I got up to go to the bathroom in the night, as she whiled away the long sleepless hours. For someone like Mum, insomnia was the worst type of problem she could face because it couldn't be solved intellectually: the harder you try to sleep, the less likely you are to sleep. She tried to out-think it instead of just not thinking about it at all. And so the insomnia utterly defeated her.

She'd go back up to bed around three o'clock in the morning and finally succeed in falling asleep as dawn was breaking. When her alarm beeped urgently an hour later, she'd wake up more exhausted than if she'd had no sleep at all. At breakfast her eyes would be puffy and watery, her face pale, her brow furrowed – a furrow that didn't disappear even when she smiled. I'd ask if she'd slept badly again and she'd just shrug it off. 'It'll pass,' she'd say, 'it'll pass,' or else she'd quote a line from Dorothy Parker – 'How do people sleep? I seem to have lost the knack.' But she didn't want to talk about it, and if I kept on, she'd quickly grow short-tempered and snappy.

Mum drank every night now, something she never used to do. Often the very first thing she did when she got in from work was to pour herself a glass of wine, before she'd even taken off her jacket or kicked off her shoes. I don't think she drank because she liked it. She drank, at first, to anaesthetize herself. The wine dispelled the demons that were haunting her, or at least rendered them more manageable. After all, she was the one who had actually killed Paul Hannigan with that second deadly blow of the chopping board; she was the one who had dug up his corpse and searched through his blood-soaked pockets. Later on, I think she drank in the hope that the alcohol would bring her the undisturbed night's rest she craved so much; and which, of course, that false friend never did.

While I'd gone back to playing my flute almost immediately after that night, Mum wouldn't *touch* the piano. When I asked her to play a duet with me now, she always had an excuse – she was too tired or she had too much work to do. But I knew full well what the truth was. I knew she avoided going near the piano for exactly the same reason that I avoided going near the oval rose bed. (*Was* The Gypsy Wedding *still playing in her head when Paul Hannigan marched us down the stairs?*)

Mum became obsessed with security, and regularly came home with new locks that she'd bought in the hardware shop in town. She installed two new heavy-duty chains on the front door and two on the back, and put sturdy locks on her bedroom door and mine. She bought a decoy alarm system (the packet boasted that a burglar won't be able to tell the difference), since the real thing was prohibitively expensive, and fitted it in a prominent position at the front of the house. She bought

clever clip-on locks for every window, as she'd con-
cluded that Paul Hannigan had probably got in by
forcing the one in the downstairs toilet.

I watched her going up and down the stairs with her
screwdriver, climbing up and down the stepladder outside the front door, and managed not to say what I was
thinking: *The lock hasn't been invented that can keep
our own fears out.*

But the most worrying change I noticed in Mum was
in her relationship with Graham Blakely. When she
talked about her run-ins with him now, she appeared
less the victim and more an equal and willing belligerent in their office wars. She backed down less readily
when he lost his temper with her, and – to Brenda and
Sally's amazement – often gave as good as she got in
their exchanges. If this had been all, I wouldn't have
been concerned. I was sick and tired of hearing about
how this office Hitler intimidated her. But it was more
than just standing up for herself. Ever since she'd had
that first row with him on my birthday, it was as if Mum
had actually begun to *relish* her confrontations with
Blakely. Sometimes it seemed to me that she actually
went out of her way to provoke them. And if she got
the better of him in an altercation, she would recount
it with breathless enthusiasm over dinner, her hands
swooping wildly around her as if they had a life of their
own, brushing blindly against her glass and threatening
to knock it to the floor.

One night during dinner we were playing highs and

lows when Mum, with an anticipatory giggle, announced that her high that day had been *slapping Blakely's face*.

'You did *what?*' I asked incredulously.

'I slapped Blakely's face!' she repeated with a self-satisfied grin, like a child who's proud of a naughty prank.

'What – what happened?'

'Well,' she said, matter-of-factly, as if it were just another piece of office gossip, 'he came into my office when he saw that I was on my own and started to talk to me about holiday dates for August. As we were talking he came round behind my chair and I thought he was going to touch my breast. I didn't even think about it, I just hit him hard across his cheek!'

'*Mum!* Did anyone see?'

'No, I don't think so.'

'What did he do?'

'Nothing! Nothing at all. He just walked out holding his cheek. You should have seen the look on his face!'

I didn't know what to say. The recollection clearly exhilarated her. She couldn't stop talking about it, bursting into laughter every time she remembered the look on Blakely's face.

'He didn't say a word!' she cried. 'He couldn't believe it! He was in total shock! It was the last thing he expected me to do!'

I laughed along with her as best I could, but there was something about the whole thing that I found deeply disturbing; it left me feeling unsettled for days afterwards. Mum had always been the calm hand on the tiller and I didn't want her to change. This new recklessness of hers scared me. I wasn't sure I wanted to follow her into the uncharted waters she seemed set on exploring. I was worried that in this mood she'd say something in front of Sally and Brenda that could be our undoing. And it irked me that after everything that had happened *I'd* managed to find some balance, some equilibrium – so why the hell couldn't *she*?

34

On Monday, May the twenty-second, with just three weeks before my exams started, I began my intensive revision programme, long marked off on my bedroom wall calendar in a frenzy of red biro crosshatching.

This programme involved getting up at seven in the morning and putting in at least two good hours before Roger came at ten. In the evenings, instead of stopping when Mum got home, I worked from about five through to nine, when I'd finally stop and have a late dinner with her. I'd planned to work over the weekends too, but Mum insisted I have at least one complete day off a week. So I worked all day Saturday and left Sunday free.

Since the majority of the work I had to do was memorizing – dry labour that would require my very best concentration – I decided to move all my books and papers from the dining room and revise upstairs in my bedroom. I figured there'd be fewer distractions – no telephone ringing, no Mum going backwards and forwards looking for the scissors she'd misplaced for the millionth time or click-clicking her biro as she read through her papers in the lounge, no temptation to slip into the kitchen and make myself a coffee or a sandwich.

So I sat upstairs in my bedroom, sweltering in the heatwave that showed no sign of abating, forcing myself to memorize long quotes from *Macbeth* and page after page of irregular French verbs. Repeating them out loud over and over again with my eyes tightly shut, I learned the exact wording of Boyle's law and Charles's law, Ohm's law and Archimedes' principle. Working my way through box after box of tissues and gulping down the antihistamines Dr Lyle had given me, I memorized the day, month and year of the Reichstag fire, the invasion of the Ruhr, the Kellogg–Briand pact, the Munich putsch and the march on Rome. While the swallows darted around their nests in the eaves outside my window, I learned lists of statistics on Brazilian coffee production and annual rates of rain forest depletion until I could repeat them without even glancing at my notes.

It was only six weeks – six short weeks – since Mum and I had killed Paul Hannigan, and already I was back to thinking almost exclusively about my exams. It was only occasionally now that my mind strayed from my textbooks and I found myself thinking about the body rotting beneath the rose bushes.

I suppose I'd slowly come round to Mum's way of thinking in spite of all my doubts, in spite of having seen too many movies where something always happens to trip the guilty up. I suppose I'd finally come to accept that she'd been right all along: *we'd got away with it.*

If the police hadn't come to the house by now, then surely they were never going to. After all, they must have found Paul Hannigan's car – it couldn't have just sat in the Farmer's Harvest's car park week after week without being noticed. And Paul Hannigan must have been reported missing to the police after nearly two months. Somebody must have become concerned about his disappearance in that time. Hadn't someone been trying to contact him that very first morning? They must have alerted the police by now . . .

The only possible conclusion I could come to was that Mum had got it right – the police hadn't made any link between the disappearance of Paul Hannigan and us, and in all probability they never *were* going to make any link between the disappearance of Paul Hannigan and us.

Besides, even if the police did come to the house now, they wouldn't find anything. The kitchen had been scrubbed and disinfected so many times they wouldn't find the tiniest speck of Paul Hannigan's blood, not the faintest shadow of a fingerprint; the eight bin bags had gone from the spare room and the place Mum had hidden them was so perfect, so ingenious, that the police would never discover them.

We'd been lucky. We'd been very lucky. We'd killed a man. We'd hacked and beaten him to death on the tiled floor of our kitchen. *And we'd got away with it.*

35

It was Saturday the twenty-seventh of May. I got up at seven as my revision timetable dictated, put on my dressing gown and slipped out of my room, intending to make a quick coffee before starting work. I paused at Mum's bedroom door and listened. I could hear her heavy regular breathing and smiled. I knew how precious every second's sleep was to her.

I was coming downstairs trying not to make any noise and had just, with great difficulty, avoided stepping on the treacherous fourth step, when I saw it.

A white rectangle lay on the mat by the front door.

I knew at once it was something to be afraid of. The postman never came that early. *It had been hand-delivered.*

I picked it up and saw the ugly grease smear (*butter?*) where a thick thumb had pressed the flap down.

I turned it over. The face was blank. I hurriedly tore it open.

Inside was a small scrap of lined paper ripped out of a secretary's notepad. Halfway down the page was a message printed in block capitals with a dying biro. It read simply:

> I KNOW WHAT YOU DID.
> I KNOW YOU KILLED HIM.
> I WANT £20,000 OR I GO TO THE POLICE.
> DON'T LEAVE THE HOUSE.
> I WILL CALL TODAY.

I ran straight back upstairs and woke Mum.

Less than five minutes later Mum was sitting at the kitchen table in yesterday's work blouse, a pair of jeans and the brown boots she wore for walks in the country-side. She gnawed at her bottom lip and stared fixedly at the cheap, translucent piece of paper. The bags under her eyes were starkly etched on her face that morning, like the outward manifestations of a sick soul. She was brooding, sullen, exuding a bruised bitterness, her hair a frazzle of knots. She hadn't brushed her teeth and I could smell last night's wine on her breath. She didn't take her eyes off the letter for a second, not even as she reached for her coffee mug, brought it to her lips and sipped from the sticky rim.

I was still in my pyjamas and dressing gown, too numbed by the shock of the letter to go up and get dressed. I'd long feared that our fragile peace would come to a sudden end one day, but I'd always imagined the authoritative knock at the front door (polite but not going to be denied entry), the uniformed officers with their radios crackling, 'smiles' that were merely the faintest twitches of thin, unfriendly lips. I'd never imagined for one minute that it would end like this – a blackmailer's grubby note stuffed through our letter-box.

While Mum read the letter over and over again, I racked my brains trying to figure out who the blackmailer could be.

I remembered the farmer who'd driven past that morning when we were digging the grave in the oval rose bed and the body of Paul Hannigan was lying face-down in the grass beside us. Mum had always said he couldn't have seen what we were doing at that distance – but what if she'd been wrong? What if the farmer had seen *exactly* what we were doing that morning and now, after six weeks of weighing up his options, had decided to try to make some money out of it?

Four-wheel-drive Man was another distinct possibility. He'd looked every bit the soap-opera villain with that bald head and sinister goatee, and we'd definitely aroused his suspicions that night in the car park. Maybe he'd smelled a money-making opportunity and followed our taxi all the way back to Honeysuckle Cottage. If he'd discovered that the car we'd left in the car park belonged to Paul Hannigan and that Paul Hannigan was now missing, maybe he'd been able to piece together everything that had happened?

Or was it someone closer to home? Had I somehow given the game away to Roger the morning after the killing, in spite of my best efforts to behave normally? Had he seen the bloodstain on the back door? He was extraordinarily sharp, and I knew he was short of money; that was why he was giving me home tuition after all. But the cheap paper, the grubby thumb print, the letter shoved through the letterbox in the early hours? None of it seemed to bear any relation to the fastidious academic I knew. Then again, if there really was no such thing as 'character' (and Roger had been very excited by that idea), it could just as easily have been him as anyone else.

'Who do you think it is, Mum?'

'I don't know, Shelley,' she said distractedly, still not taking her eyes off the blackmailer's note. 'I don't know.'

'Do you think it could be Roger?'

'No!' she snorted with a dismissive shake of her head. 'It's not Roger. It's definitely not Roger. We're dealing with a criminal here, a habitual criminal.'

'What about Four-wheel-drive Man then? You thought he looked like a criminal – we both did.'

Mum considered this suggestion more seriously. 'I suppose so,' she said without conviction, 'but I still can't see how he could have found out. Only you and I know what happened here that night.'

Her attention was drawn back to the letter as if it possessed a magnetism she was powerless to resist.

'Anyway,' she said almost as an afterthought, 'we'll know soon enough.'

I must have looked blank, because she went on, 'The

letter says *I will call today*. Whoever it is, they're coming here – to the house – today.'

I imagined Four-wheel-drive Man swaggering arro-
gantly around the kitchen in his black leather car coat,
lounging in one of the kitchen chairs, chewing gum and
grinning at us menacingly, marking each and every
demand he made with a boorish slave-drum beat of his
fist on the table. I shivered with revulsion as if I'd turned
over a brick in the garden and disturbed a squirming
knot of earwigs.

'What are we going to do?'

Mum folded her arms tightly across her chest as if
she was suddenly cold.

'There's not much we *can* do, Shelley. If the blackmailer goes to the police, they'll have to investigate the
allegations. They'll come here looking for a body,
they'll have search warrants, sniffer dogs. I think it'll
all be over for us then . . .'

I could see the dogs digging frantically at the loose
soil of the rose bed, uncovering a thumb as white as a
new bulb.

Mum turned her attention back to the note and
suddenly screwed it up in a spasm of anger. 'I can't
understand it! How could anyone have found out?
We've been so careful! What's given us away? And why
now – after nearly *two months* have gone by?'

She grimaced as she drained the dregs of her coffee
and ran her hand agitatedly through her ragged hair.

'Do you want a refill?'

She nodded and held out her cup. As I filled it, I saw how violently it trembled in her hand.

'Is it really all over then?' I asked in dazed disbelief.

Mum flattened the note with the palm of her hand on the kitchen table and considered it yet again. 'I think we're trapped, Shelley.'

Trapped. I was struck that she'd used that word. We were still mice after all, mice caught in the spring of the metal trap, our little matchstick necks cleanly snapped in two.

'Isn't there *anything* we can do?'

She covered her face with her hands and dragged them down until they were pressed together at the point of her chin as if in prayer. 'Not that I can see, Shelley. Not that I can see. We've got very few options open to us.'

I thought about all we'd been through to avoid detection – burying Paul Hannigan's body in the oval rose bed, driving to town in the burglar's battered turquoise car, the terrifying run-in we'd had with Four-wheel-drive Man, Mum's late-night journey into the national park to dump the bin bags in the abandoned mine shaft. Had all that been for nothing? Were we going to be defeated now, not by brilliant detective work, but by some loathsome money-grubbing *blackmailer*?

'What options do we have?' I asked, the pitch of my voice rising sharply.

Mum turned her elegant, exhausted face towards

me. She was so tired that she was hardly able to keep her eyes open when shafts of sunlight managed to break through the morning clouds and fill the kitchen with bright spring sunshine.

'We can go to the police and confess everything before the blackmailer gets here,' she said. 'Whatever else, it'll be better that the police hear it from us first. A confession – even at this late stage – could still help us in court when it comes to sentencing.'

I saw the ghostly white tent erected over the oval rose bed, the scrum of journalists on the gravel, the back seat of the police car, its black upholstery hot to the touch. And what would come after that? Hours of questioning at the police station, the humiliation of mug shots, fingerprinting. Then, after months of miserable waiting, the trial. Standing in the dock on trembling legs while the prosecuting barrister unleashed the unanswerable question: 'If you really thought you'd done nothing wrong, Miss Rivers, if you really thought you'd been acting in self-defence at all times, why did you bury Mr Hannigan's corpse in the garden of Honeysuckle Cottage?'

If prison had been a real possibility the night we'd killed Paul Hannigan, it was surely inevitable now. Medieval horror in the twenty-first century. My brilliant career diverted into a siding to rot neglected for God knows how many years. Forced to share my most intimate space with girls more savage, more vicious than Teresa Watson and Emma Townley knew how to be. I knew I wouldn't be able to survive it. I wouldn't be able to bear the brutality, the philistinism, the filth. I knew I'd end up taking my own life . . .

'Isn't there anything else?' I asked, struggling for breath as if the noose were already tightening around my neck. 'Isn't there anything else we can do?'

Mum shrugged her shoulders helplessly. 'We can pay the twenty thousand pounds,' she said, but in a way that made it sound more like a question than a statement.

'But we don't have twenty thousand pounds,' I groaned. 'That's more than your salary for a whole year. It would take forever to find that amount of money.'

'I could get it, Shelley,' she said quietly.

'How?'

'I could borrow against the value of the house. I could take out a mortgage.'

The thought of Mum paying all that money to the blackmailer made me feel physically sick. She worked hard enough and went without enough as it was. The thought of her carrying the extra burden of the blackmailer on her back was just too horrible to countenance. And it was naive to think this would be the blackmailer's only demand for money. He'd keep coming back for more and more and more. We'd have to live the rest of our lives with this disgusting parasite feeding on us at will. It wouldn't be any kind of life at all. It would be the most miserable servitude imaginable. There'd never be any closure to the traumatic events of April the eleventh. It was a wound the blackmailer would pick open again every time it began to heal.

'It'll never stop, Mum,' I said. 'Once we give him money he'll just keep coming back for more.'

'I know, Shelley, I know.'

A stupid thought came into my mind and I gave it voice without thinking. 'What about Dad? Would Dad give us the money?'

Mum turned a face full of bitterness and hurt towards me.

'*I'd never ask him!*' she hissed. It was clear she would tolerate no further discussion.

I felt my skin prickle with anger. She was dismissing Dad with such cold finality that it was as if he were dead. But he wasn't dead to me. I struggled to swallow the words I wanted to shout at her. It was the wrong time, the wrong place, to have this argument.

There was a long silence between us. Mum eyed the blackmailer's note obsessively, as though still convinced the answer lay somewhere in those lines of biro block capitals.

'So is that it?' I said eventually, unable to believe that our road had run out so suddenly, so hopelessly.

Mum was silent. She chewed at her bottom lip and played with the note, folding it into a thin strip and snaking it between the fingers of her right hand. She studiously avoided my eyes.

I wanted to scream at her at the top of my voice. *Is that it? Is that the best that your razor-sharp intellect*

can come up with? Is that the best that the super-brain,
the woman-who-can-solve-any-problem can do?

I glared at her with contempt as she sagged listlessly
at the kitchen table, hardly able to keep her eyes open
because she'd barely slept, because she'd drunk too
much wine again the night before. If she hadn't been
so weak, if she hadn't started to fall apart after we'd
killed Paul Hannigan, she wouldn't have been such a
wreck that morning, she'd have been able to think of
a way out of the mess we were in! If she hadn't been so
weak, maybe Dad would still be here to protect us! If
she hadn't been so weak, maybe I wouldn't have been
such a mouse – maybe I would have been able to stand
up to the girls concerned and we'd never have found
ourselves in this situation!

The flood of anger I felt towards Mum also dragged
with it the sour realization that in spite of my sixteen
years, I still looked to her to act like a mother and
keep me safe; I still looked to her to perform a maternal miracle that would dispel this danger, that would
chase away the wolf circling our door. And I felt
betrayed when I realized that there was going to be
no maternal magic today, no miracle in the kitchen –
just the too-bright sunlight and the silence, occasionally broken by a flurry of soft, feathered bodies in the
eaves.

After a long, long time Mum spoke again. 'There is
another way, Shelley.'

'What?' I grunted sullenly, expecting no more than

some pathetic straw to clutch at. 'What, for God's sake? *What?*'

Mum let the blackmailer's note drop from her fingers onto the table and looked deep into my eyes, her face as ghastly as an alabaster death mask.

'We kill him, Shelley,' she said in barely more than a whisper. 'When he comes here today, we kill him.'

36

It's strange looking back on it now, but Mum's words didn't shock me. I wasn't appalled as I suppose I should have been. Just two months earlier, I would have been stuttering in disbelief – *Are you insane? Are you out of your mind?* – but now I simply considered the idea, coldly, dispassionately, *on its merits* . . .

And the first objection that sprang into my mind wasn't moral, it was practical. I remembered Four-wheel-drive Man, I remembered his heavy bulldog build, the shaven head, the dagger-shaped goatee, the mean, penetrating little eyes.

'How, Mum? How are we going to kill him? Four-wheel-drive Man's huge – he's built like a wrestler. What are we going to do to a man like that? The burglar was drunk, he hardly knew what he was doing. Four-wheel-drive Man will be a different proposition altogether.'

'We don't know that it *is* Four-wheel-drive Man, Shelley. You're jumping to conclusions again.'

'But what if it *is* him?' I persisted, refusing to be fobbed off. 'What if it *is* him? One hard punch in the face from a man like that could kill you. You won't be just covering the bruise with make-up and going off to work the next day, that's for sure. How are we going to kill a man like that, for God's sake?'

Mum said nothing. She just stared down at her large, awkward hands, which sat on the table like two sun-bleached crabs washed up by the tide. She seemed to be weighing something up in her mind; weighing, balancing, slowly coming to a conclusion that she reached only with the greatest reluctance.

'There is a way,' she said finally, looking up at me with a strange expression on her face, perplexed, a little shamefaced. 'I know how.'

'*How?*'

'Wait here.'

With a great effort she raised herself wearily from her chair and left the kitchen. I heard her boots clomping up the stairs, the groaning of the floorboards in her bedroom somewhere above my head, and then a prolonged silence.

Finding myself alone in the kitchen, I began to feel uncomfortably exposed and vulnerable. What if Four-wheel-drive Man came to the house now while I was downstairs all alone? What if his face suddenly appeared at the kitchen window? This last thought was so terrifying that I squeezed my eyes shut so that I couldn't see the kitchen window any more. There was only one thought running through my head while I waited impatiently for Mum's return: *HurryupMum hurryupMum – hurryupMum!*

The plaintive squeak of the fourth stair told me that she was on her way back down, and I opened my eyes.

I was surprised to see that she'd put her beige fleece on over her blouse, as it was clear it was going to be another scorching hot day. Both her hands were buried inside the large pouch-like pocket, which bulged strangely.

When Mum reached the table, she turned to face me and drew something slowly out of the fleece pocket. At that instant, a starburst of bright white sunlight flooded through the kitchen window behind her, momentarily blinding me, and it was only when I shifted position and put my hand up to shield my eyes that I saw what she was holding in her outstretched hand.

'You didn't get rid of the *gun*?' I gasped, astonished to see the loathsome object again. 'You didn't take it to the mine?'

Mum gave an almost imperceptible shake of her head. 'Why not?'

'I don't know,' she said shrugging her shoulders. 'I felt so insecure after the burglar broke in that, when the time came, I just couldn't part with it.'

After a long pause she went on. 'Maybe some part of me knew all along that we were going to need it . . .'

She placed it carefully on the kitchen table and sat down. I'd got to my feet, but my knees had turned to jelly and I sank back down into my chair.

The gun squatted on the table like some metallic

scorpion, its deadly sting secreted at the end of its blue-grey tail. I contemplated it with a mixture of revulsion and fascination. It looked so alien in the kitchen among the green glass pasta jars, the cookery books, the puppy calendar from Gran, the corkboard covered with photos of Mum and me and my Hello Kitty stickers – it was jarringly out of place, jarringly *male*.

'Is it loaded?'

'Yes. Six bullets.'

'Do you know how to use it?'

'It's not difficult, Shelley. You take the safety catch off and pull the trigger.'

I shook my head, numb, disbelieving, the physical reality of the gun starting to bring home the enormity of what we were considering.

'Why didn't you tell me you'd kept it?'

Mum shifted uncomfortably in her seat and looked away. 'I – I didn't want to unsettle you.'

'*Unsettle* me?'

It wasn't difficult to see through her delicate evasion: she hadn't told me the gun was in the house because she didn't trust me any more. Since the night I'd snatched the knife from the dining-room table and run out into the garden after Paul Hannigan, she no longer knew what I was capable of. She no longer knew what I might do if I was put under extreme stress again. Was she worried that I might shoot myself or that I might shoot her?

It piqued me, but not so much that I couldn't

appreciate the irony of the situation: while I'd felt that Mum had changed since the night we'd killed Paul Hannigan, that in some ways she'd become a stranger whose behaviour I could no longer predict, she'd been feeling exactly the same way about me.

'You should have told me,' I said. 'You shouldn't keep secrets from me. I'm not a child any more. And I'm not a *weirdo*, you know.'

Mum pulled a pained face and I could see that she regretted her dark suspicions. She placed her hand on top of mine and smiled apologetically. 'You're right, Shelley. I should have told you.'

I let her go on holding my hand, but steadfastly denied her a smile of forgiveness – until I remembered the secret I was keeping from her. Paul Hannigan's driver's licence, hidden upstairs in the bottom of my secrets box. My conscience pricked me hard, and guiltily I gave her the smile that she wanted. (*It's OK, everything's OK between us.*)

My attention returned to the gun, whose obscene black hole of a mouth was pointing directly at my heart.

'Are you *sure* you know how to use it?' I pressed her.

'Yes, I'm sure.'

I imagined Four-wheel-drive Man again, but this time he wasn't ordering us around. This time he was kneeling in a corner of the kitchen, blubbering and snivelling, begging for mercy as I aimed the gun at his head. What would happen if I pulled the trigger? Would it be like the movies? Would a blob of strawberry jam suddenly appear in the middle of his forehead? Would his eyes slowly empty as his soul fled? Would he crumple to the floor in a lifeless heap?

When he comes here today, we kill him . . .

Were we really thinking of putting ourselves through all that searing trauma again (*the blood, the body, the fear*)? Were we really thinking of committing murder? Because there was no doubt that that's what it would be. Last time, with Paul Hannigan, we'd been fighting for our lives, we'd been acting in self-defence – but this time it would be calculated, cold-blooded murder.

When he comes here today, we kill him . . .

But why did it have to be *we*? Why wasn't Mum taking this responsibility on herself like she did when she disinterred Paul Hannigan's body or took the bin bags to the national park? Why wasn't she telling me to go upstairs and hide in my room until it was all over? I shouldn't have to be there. I shouldn't have to see it. Hadn't I seen enough? Shouldn't she be protecting me?

But the longer she sat there lost in thought, saying nothing, the clearer it became that she wasn't going to say anything of the sort. She wasn't going to sacrifice herself for me. Whatever we were about to go through, she seemed to have made up her mind that we would go through it together.

'Are you really serious about this, Mum?' I croaked, my throat suddenly dry.

Mum didn't look at me. She reached out a hand towards the gun and cautiously – as if frightened it might suddenly bite her – turned the barrel with the tip of her index finger as she considered my question. When she stopped and looked up at me again, the gun was pointing down the hallway towards the front door. The direction in which the blackmailer would come.

'If he goes to the police, it's all over for us,' she said flatly.

We lapsed into an uneasy, agitated silence. This had all come at the wrong time! I'd been planning to spend the whole day revising global warming, my French vocabulary, the Treaty of Versailles. I couldn't suddenly switch now to the contemplation of this real-life problem. I didn't have the mental energy to scale such an enormous peak, not today, not now, it was just too much. I wanted to return to the manageable, finite problems that my exams posed.

'But kill him? Really *kill him*, Mum?'

'It's zugzwang,' she said with a bitter smile.

'What's zug—?' I couldn't even remember the rest of the word.

'Zugzwang. It's an expression from chess. When it's your turn to move but there's no move you can make that won't be disadvantageous to you.'

I thought about it. She was absolutely right. Whatever we decided – to give ourselves up, hand over the money or kill the blackmailer – we were going to suffer. All of our options were equally hellish. But we had to do something. It was our move.

'We're in so deep now, Shelley,' Mum said, 'we've come

so far down this path that we might as well keep going. Giving ourselves up would be every bit as awful as –' she clearly didn't want to say murder – 'carrying on.'

We're in so deep now. Her words reminded me of something else. One of the quotes from *Macbeth* I'd learned just a few days before. I tried to remember how it had gone:

> I am in blood
> Stepped in so far, that, should I wade no more,
> Returning were as tedious as go o'er.

Recalling where the quote came in the play discomfited me even more than the words themselves. Just before Macbeth orders the murder of Macduff's wife and child. Just before he commits his worst atrocity.

'You'd better go up and get dressed,' Mum said, gently cupping my elbow. 'He could be here any minute.'

'OK.' I sighed. 'But when I come down we've got to talk this all through properly. We can't just rush into something like this on the spur of the moment – we've got to think about it more, we've got to talk more. Maybe it isn't zugzwang. Maybe there's something else we can do that we just haven't thought of yet.'

I'd pushed back my chair and was beginning to stand up when I heard a noise outside.

I froze. Mum started to ask me what was wrong, but I thrust my hand abruptly into her face to silence her. She understood and turned her head to listen, the tendons in her neck standing out thin and taut like piano wire. *He can't come now*, I thought, *he can't possibly come now! We're not ready for him! I'm not dressed! We haven't decided what we're going to do! Please, God, let me have imagined it!*

But the snapping and crackling of gravel, the squealing of unhealthy brakes, the spitting and panting of exhausted metal wasn't in my imagination – a car was coming up the drive towards the house.

Mum heard it too and her eyes widened with fear, the unhealthy yellow sclera disfigured by a red graffiti of broken veins.

'It's him!' she whispered, and her whisper was as loud as a scream. 'He's here already!'

37

'What are we going to *do*, Mum?' I cried, but she was already on her feet, snatching up the gun and hurriedly secreting it in the fleece's front pouch.

She turned on me fiercely, bringing her face close to mine and clutched my wrist hard in her right hand. 'Leave everything to me, Shelley! Don't *do* anything, don't *say* anything! Let me do all the talking!'

The arrival of the blackmailer had transformed her. She was suddenly wired, suffused with a hard, determined energy. Every vestige of her jaded torpor was thrown off in an instant. She swept her hair impatiently out of her eyes and strode into the lounge. Slavishly I staggered to my feet and followed her.

The dining room and lounge were much darker than the kitchen, deprived as they were of sun until the afternoon. The fireplace, the piano, the armchairs and sofa, appeared dark, solid, funereal, and it took a few moments for my eyes to grow accustomed to the gloom. Mum, who was standing directly in front of the window, was just a silhouette. I felt the sudden need to be physically close to her as this unknown danger neared the house, and I walked towards her on legs as faltering and uncertain as a toddler's.

The crunching of gravel, the dry whining of the brakes grew louder and louder until a car suddenly lunged into sight across the lounge window.

I stopped dead in my tracks, unable at first to comprehend what I was seeing, unable to believe the evidence of my own eyes – almost, *almost* convinced by the physical impossibility of this apparition that I wasn't really awake at all, but wrestling in the coils of another monstrous nightmare.

The battered turquoise car, the car we'd got rid of weeks before in the car park of the Farmer's Harvest – *Paul Hannigan's car* – was coming slowly to a halt behind our Ford Escort.

The floor seemed to tilt suddenly beneath my feet and I had to put out a foot so as not to fall, like a gymnast who's mistimed her landing. It didn't make any sense! It wasn't possible! We'd got rid of the car! Paul Hannigan was *dead*! How on earth had the car found its way back here to Honeysuckle Cottage? How on earth had it found its way back *to us*?

So it was true, after all. The dead don't stay dead. Paul Hannigan had come back to take revenge on us for what we did to him.

Mum turned away from the window, her face grim, terrible, as white as bone. She started towards the front door, but I blocked her way and seized her hands.

'What is it, Mum? What's going on?'

She didn't answer me. A car door clunked shut outside.

'I don't understand,' I moaned. 'We got rid of his car! *We got rid of his car!* What's it doing back here?'

I could hear heavy footsteps making their way slowly across the gravel, coming closer to the front door.

'Leave everything to me, Shelley.'

She freed herself from my grip and tried to go into the hall, but I held on to her, seizing hold of her fleece, gripping the belt of her jeans.

'Don't open the door, Mum!' I pleaded. 'Don't let him in here!'

Mum pulled my hands roughly off her. 'Don't be *stupid*, Shelley!' she shouted. 'Don't get hysterical! We have to let him in! This has to be brought to an end one way or another!'

There was a resounding thump at the front door that shook the entire frame and set the chains rattling.

I followed Mum down the hall and leaned against the balustrade for support. I watched her undo each of the locks and chains and slip the bolts – one at the bottom, one at the top – and as she yanked the front door open, I fully expected to be confronted by the vengeful, bloody ghost of Paul Hannigan.

38

But it was no ghost.

A small, comical-looking man of about fifty, with an enormously distended pot belly, stood on the doorstep. He'd tried to cover his baldness by combing the long strands of hair that grew above his right ear over the top of his crown and flattening them into place with some kind of grease. The podgy swag of his double chin hung down almost as far as his sternum. A pair of large-framed plastic glasses perched on a small snub nose, a roll-up fag dangled from a flabby bottom lip. He wore a grease-spotted yellow T-shirt stretched almost to breaking point, baggy grey tracksuit bottoms and a pair of decrepit trainers.

But what caught my attention even more than his huge stomach was the man's arms. They were short, truncated, almost like a dwarf's, yet powerfully muscled, the bloated, marble-veined biceps covered in the faded hieroglyphs of ancient tattoos. On one hairy wrist there was a chunky identity bracelet and one of those copper bands that are supposed to cure arthritis.

On the other, a gold Rolex flashed in curious contrast to his otherwise shabby appearance.

He stood there jangling his car keys and the loose change in his pocket, waiting to be invited in. I don't know who Mum had been expecting, but she seemed as taken aback as I was. We both stood gawping at the fat man, speechless.

He peeled the saliva-sodden cigarette from his bottom lip and flicked it away across the gravel.

'I think you know what I'm here for,' he said, with a belligerent thrust of his lower jaw.

But I didn't. It was only slowly that my brain connected this caricature to the battered turquoise car, only slowly that I came to the only conclusion possible: that, in spite of all my hysterical expectations, *this* was the blackmailer.

'You'd better come in,' Mum said and opened the door wider for him to enter.

The fat man stepped into the hallway and for a moment all three of us stood there squashed close together, awkward and embarrassed, like strangers in a lift. The only sound was the fat man's strained breathing, the only movement the rise and fall of his enormous yellow gut.

Mum hesitated, seemingly unsure what to do next. Her hand hovered at the mouth of the fleece pocket. Was she going to shoot him right then and there in the hallway? Was she going to press the gun against that swollen belly and pull the trigger before he could take another step into the house? But her hand dropped back to her side and she turned and walked slowly down the hallway and into the kitchen.

The fat man followed her and, reluctantly, I followed him. Although I lagged several paces behind, I couldn't help noticing that he limped, his body keeling sideways every time he shifted his weight onto his left foot. One of his trainers made a squelchy fart sound at every step, like the comic honk of a clown's car.

When we were all in the kitchen, Mum turned to face the blackmailer.

'So I suppose you're responsible for *this*?' she said, holding up the note like a schoolmistress reproving a delinquent pupil.

'I am indeed!' he said jovially. Moving towards the chair Mum had just been sitting in, he asked, 'Do you mind?'

'Yes, I bloody well do mind!' she snapped fiercely, but he ignored her and eased himself into the chair.

When he was settled, he looked around with a self-satisfied smile, pushing his glasses back up his nose with an obscene jab of his pink index finger.

He had the perennially youthful face of many obese people, as if those full cheeks and dimpled chins are immune to the usual ravages of time. Sitting there at the kitchen table in a chair that his great bulk reduced to kindergarten proportions, he resembled a monstrously overgrown schoolboy, a bald, criminal Billy Bunter, who could no longer fit comfortably behind his desk. His face, with its pouty feminine lips and turned-up nose, could almost have been the face of a victim, of a mouse, if those soft features hadn't been contradicted by the short tattooed arms. They told a different story, of hours spent bench-pressing in the gym to turn them into lethal weapons, brutal pistons that broke jaws and snapped noses. He folded them now across the yellow egg of his paunch and calmly looked Mum up and down.

'So what's it to be then, luv?' he said. 'Are you gonna pay the twenty grand or do I go to the cops?'

'I'll pay the money,' Mum said, without hesitation.

'Good,' he beamed. 'Very sensible. Now, how long will it take you to get it?'

'I don't know,' she said, gnawing again at her bottom lip. 'I'll have to apply for a mortgage, but it shouldn't take long, no longer than two or three weeks.'

'I can wait a few weeks,' he said magnanimously. 'And how much can you give me today? Right now?'

'I've got about fifteen hundred pounds in the bank,' she replied, after a moment's thought.

'Can you get that for me today?'

'Yes, I can. If we go to my bank in town I can take it out of the ATM—' She inhaled sharply. 'No, I've just remembered – there's a daily limit on both my accounts. I can only take out three hundred from each.'

'That'll do for a start, that'll do for a start.' He slapped his thighs and beamed warmly at me as if all was right with the world and there was nothing for anyone to feel the slightest bit down about. 'What are we waiting for then?'

I was amazed at his light-hearted breeziness. It was as if he was completely unaware that he was committing any crime at all. He seemed totally untroubled by any guilt or bad conscience, as if he was merely collecting a debt that Mum owed him, recovering money that was rightfully his.

Mum took a few agitated paces around the kitchen and then came back to the table, her hands gripping the back of the empty chair like the claws of a bird alighting on a branch (*but what kind of bird – a songbird trapped in the hunter's net or a bird of prey with a victim in her sights?*).

'I'm not going to hand it over just like that!' she burst out.

'I don't see that you've got much choice, luv,' the blackmailer replied. The baby face darkened and the stunted arms unfolded themselves and dropped menacingly onto the kitchen table. 'I know you killed him. I know you killed Paul Hannigan.'

The name meant nothing to Mum. But it meant everything to me. To hear it spoken out loud like that made me flinch as if struck, and even though I was standing at the other end of the kitchen, as far away from them as possible, I shrank even deeper into my corner.

'Before I give you any money,' Mum persevered bravely, 'there are things I need to know.'

The fat man made a series of disgusting grunting noises from deep in the back of his throat, raking phlegm up into his mouth. He whipped out a handkerchief with surprising dexterity, spat a green wad into the dishevelled nest, then fumbled it away into his pocket. He impatiently poked his glasses back into place, and eyed Mum quizzically.

'Like what?' he said. 'What things? You ain't in a position to make demands.'

'I need to know how you found out.'

He gave a deep, treacly chuckle. 'That's easy enough,' he said. 'I know what happened, luv, because I was with Paul Hannigan the night he came out here to rob you. I was with him! I was *here*!'

39

Although Mum did her best to disguise it, I saw the shock register on her face, a crease like a crack in a wall breaking across her forehead, a sudden slackening around her jaw. We'd always assumed the burglar had been alone. It had never entered our heads that he'd had an accomplice. But that was exactly what the grotesque clown in our kitchen was saying.

'I want to know everything,' Mum said, recovering remarkably. 'I want you to tell me everything that happened that night.'

'You want to know everything,' the fat man repeated.

'Yes.'

'And why's that, then?'

'So that I can move on, so that I can put it all behind me. I have to know everything that you can tell me about that night.'

'Everything, eh? No details spared?'

'Everything.'

'And then we'll go and get the money?'

'And then we'll go and get the money.'

'OK,' he said, but for the first time a suspicious look clouded his features. He glanced at Mum and then at me as if he felt he might be walking into some sort of trap. What he saw must have reassured him, because the look disappeared as quickly as it had come. After all, what possible threat could there be from this neurotic, mousy woman and her neurotic, mousy daughter? He wiped his hands on his thighs and raked a little more phlegm up from his throat, which he was content to swallow this time.

'All right. Let's see – I bumped into Paul Hannigan in the pub that night. It was a Monday. Monday, April tenth. I didn't know him that well – I'd bought some knock-off from him and he'd come back to my flat a few times, but I wouldn't say we was close. More acquaintances, like. He'd only been down this neck of the woods a few months. He'd been in prison up north, and he said he'd moved down here hoping his luck would change.'

His luck changed all right, I thought to myself. But it had changed for the worse. It had changed for *the worst*.

'After closing time, he came back to my flat and we carried on drinking. We really gave it one that night. We got through the best part of a bottle of whisky and a bottle of vodka and God knows how much we'd had in the pub beforehand. Anyways, he kept going on about how desperate he was for money. He said he had an idea for a job, but he needed a car, and because he knew

I had a car he kept on nagging me to come in on it with him.

'His idea was to rob a secluded house in the country. He said that houses out in the country were easier to rob than houses in town – they had old windows that were easy to force, they often didn't have alarms, and there were no nosy neighbours nearby to call the police. Like I say, I didn't know him that well, and to tell you the truth I wasn't over-fond of him. There was something about him that weren't quite right. He had a bit of a screw loose somewhere, he talked a load of old rubbish most of the time. He was a real loose cannon, you know, always flashing this big hunting knife he carried around with him everywhere. He tried to tell me he'd been inside for murder, that he'd cut someone up who'd double-crossed him, but I knew from other people that he'd only been inside for drug dealing.

'Anyways, he kept on nagging and nagging me to come in on this job with him. He kept on about the antiques that people kept in these country houses, and that if we got lucky we could find something worth a fortune and we wouldn't have to worry about money for a good long time after that. Anyways, I was so drunk I ended up saying I'd go with him. We agreed that if any-one in the house woke up he was just to tie them up, there wasn't to be no violence. I found some old rope in the cupboard under the sink and we had a snack before we set off because we was both starving by that time.'

A snack. Paul Hannigan's last supper. I remembered

the loud, sour belch. *Sorry, ladies . . . I shouldn't have had them eggs. Them eggs was off.*

'Paul wanted to drive. He said he knew where to go. I didn't mind 'cause, to tell you the truth, I think I was in a much worse state than he was. I'd drunk so much I could hardly see straight, let alone drive in the dark.

'I couldn't keep my eyes open. I kept dropping off to sleep in the car. We seemed to be driving for ages, going round and round all these twisty country lanes . . . and then Paul spotted this place.

'We parked out the back there.' He gestured vaguely with his thumb in the direction of the lane, where I'd first seen the car from my bedroom window. 'It was late, round about three-thirty. The plan was that I'd stay in the car and keep lookout while Paul did the actual robbing. I was to honk the horn three times if anyone showed up. Paul got out the car and I saw him slip through the hedge back there and into your garden.'

He knew the date, he knew the time, he knew where the car had been parked. He wasn't lying. He really had been there that night.

'I waited in the car for ages but I was so drunk I couldn't stay awake. I was woken up by the sound of some girl screaming and Paul shouting – it sounded close, like they was outside in the garden. I got out the car to see what the hell was going on and went through the hedge the way I'd seen Paul go. I could see right into the kitchen – I only stood there for a few seconds but that was long enough for me. I saw Paul chasing her over there –' he nodded his head in my direction – 'round and round this table.' He prodded the table three times with his stubby index finger as if to prove the veracity of what he was saying.

(*Stabbing and slashing at the burglar's back. 'We're playing musical chairs now! We're playing musical chairs now!' The flailing knife snagging his neck and loosing a geyser of bright arterial blood.*)

'She was screaming her head off and I could see she was covered in blood,' the fat man went on. 'I figured she'd disturbed Paul while he was robbing the house and he'd gone psycho and started cutting her up with his hunting knife. I thought the kid's parents would come running downstairs to help her any second and Paul'd kill them too. I remember thinking to myself: *He's got the bloodlust on him. He's gonna kill everyone in that house. He's gonna cut them all up. There's gonna be a right royal massacre.*'

The fat man raked up a little more phlegm with a few short, violent pig grunts and slid his glasses back up to the bridge of his nose.

'Well, basically, I panicked. I mean, a bit of robbing's one thing, but I didn't want to get caught up in no murder. I decided to get out of there sharpish-like.

'But when I got back to the car I remembered that Paul had taken my car keys with him. I've never learned how to hotwire a car; nicking cars ain't my thing. But the screams coming from the house were bloody shocking, so I just legged it back the way we'd come. It was as black as a witch's hat out here that night, I can tell you, and I got myself well and truly lost in all them lanes, but I just kept going. All I knew was I had to get as far away from this house as I could.

'Anyways, I found my way out onto the main road finally and ended up walking all the way back to town. It must've taken me close on three hours. As soon as I got in I called the mobile number I had for Paul. It rang and rang but there weren't no answer.'

(*Soft, muffled, a series of musical notes like a bird or maybe even an insect. It stopped and then a few seconds later it started again.*)

'I was expecting Paul to turn up at my flat at any minute all covered in blood, saying he'd done something terrible, and asking me to hide him or help him to get out of the country. But he didn't show up. I called his mobile again, but now it was switched off. I left loads of messages, but he didn't call me back. I kept the local radio on all day expecting to hear that there'd been a bloodbath in a house out in the country, but there was nothing about no killings. All I could think was that they just hadn't found the bodies yet. As it got later, I started to think he must have done a runner in my car. Too scared to come back here in case the police were waiting for him. I figured he was probably miles away by now, lying low up north.'

It was a strange sensation to hear my own murder being described; it made my arms come up in goose bumps. And I couldn't help thinking that it could so easily have turned out that way. If we'd said the wrong thing while Paul Hannigan was holding us at knife point or if we'd tried to make a run for it, everything the fat man thought had happened so easily could have – and on the Tuesday morning Roger would have found Mum and me butchered like cattle on a slaughterhouse kill floor.

'I was a bloody fool to get involved with a kid like Paul Hannigan. I knew he weren't right in the head. Now I was worried sick that if the police caught him I'd get dragged into it and end up facing murder charges. As well as all that, my car had all my work tools in it – I'm a plumber, see – so I couldn't work neither till I got it back. And I couldn't exactly call the police and report it stolen, could I?'

He laughed and looked up at Mum as if expecting her to laugh along with him, but she remained stony-faced.

'Anyways, the next day there was still nothing on the radio about no murders and there was nothing the next day neither. I figured that if Paul had killed someone out here, the police would've found out about it by now. Why weren't it all over the papers and the TV?

'And that's when I started to think that maybe I'd got the wrong end of the stick and there hadn't *been* no killing. I called Paul's mobile again and again but it was always switched off. I didn't know what to do, so I decided it was best to do nothing – just sit tight and wait and see what happened.

'And then on the Friday morning I got a call from the police. My first thought was, they've caught Paul and he's gone and grassed me up. Now I'm gonna get done as an accomplice to murder. But it was nothing like that. They said they'd got a complaint from the Farmer's Harvest restaurant about a car that had been left in their car park. They said they'd run the number plate through their computer and it had me down as the owner and would I move it sharpish-like. And that was that! Nothing about Paul. Nothing about no murders.

'When I got down to my car I found it unlocked with the keys still in the ignition. Everything had gone from inside it! Everything except for the bag of dope Paul had with him that night. My work tools and my anorak had gone, my road atlas, Paul's trench coat that had been on the back seat –'

I saw Mum tense. Her left foot, which had been unconsciously tapping to a manic rhythm while she listened to the blackmailer's tale, had suddenly stopped moving. I knew what she was thinking, because I was thinking exactly the same thing: *Did he know about the gun?* But it was clear from the way he blithely carried on talking that he didn't.

'– everything had gone! I couldn't figure it out. Why would Paul leave my car there? Why would he leave it unlocked and with the keys still in the ignition? He'd left a hundred quid's worth of dope in the glove box! He'd taken my work tools, even though they weren't

worth nothing to him! Why hadn't he called to tell me
what had happened? What was he playing at?

'I asked around, but no one had seen him or heard
from him. It was as if he'd just disappeared into thin
air. The whole thing was doing my head in, I tell you.
So the next day, the Saturday, I drove back out here –
to *Honeysuckle Cottage*.' He said the twee name with
infinite contempt. 'Thought I'd take a look around.
I reckoned that was the only way I was gonna get to the
bottom of all this.

'I parked up round the side there, close under the
trees so's I couldn't be seen. I hadn't been there five
minutes when I saw the two of you come out of the
house. I recognized the girl from that night, and I could
see she was as right as rain. I watched you get in your
car and drive away – I was worried for a second that
you were gonna turn up where I was and see me, but as
luck would have it you went the other way. I followed
you all the way into town and when you stopped at
the supermarket I parked up behind you and went in
too – discreet like – I didn't want you to catch on.
I watched you do your shop, trying to overhear what
you were talking about, trying to see if I could pick up
a clue to what happened out here.'

The thought of this sinister clown following us
through the labyrinth of country lanes, shadowing us
up and down the bright aisles as we filled our trolley,
watching us select our most intimate personal items –
soaps and shampoos, Tampax and toilet rolls – filled me

with revulsion. I remembered the dream I'd had the night after we'd killed Paul Hannigan: the car parked in the narrow lane that began to follow the van taking us to prison, the shadowy figure behind the wheel. *Who's that?* Mum had asked me in the dream. *It's the watcher*, I'd replied. Was it possible I'd known all along that Paul Hannigan hadn't been alone, but at a level so deep in my subconscious it could only reveal itself in a dream?

'Like I say,' he went on, 'I couldn't work it out. I'd seen your girl covered in blood, I was sure Paul had been doing her in. Now here she was, out shopping, all hunky-dory. And Paul had disappeared off the face of the earth. No one had seen him, no one had heard from him. None of it made any sense. And when I tried his mobile, the line was just . . . dead.'

(*The strange grimace on Mum's face as she'd beaten the mobile into a masticated pulp.*)

'And that's when I started to think that maybe you two had done something to him.'

40

The morning clouds had dispersed completely now, and the kitchen was filled with bright golden sunlight. It reflected off the fat man's glasses so that when he turned towards the window his eyes disappeared behind two white rectangles of glare.

The ebullient spring sunshine was completely out of tune with the tense scene unfolding in the kitchen. I couldn't help thinking that if this were a novel or a movie, the blackmailer would have arrived in the middle of a ferocious thunderstorm, a day of growling thunder and lurid yellow forks of lightning, torrential rain lashing the gravel drive. But this wasn't any fiction, this was real life. There he sat in our sun-filled kitchen, slowly unpicking the stitches of the shroud that hid Paul Hannigan's decomposing corpse, while the day outside called for picnics and barbecues and ice-creams at the seaside.

He looked directly at Mum now, his hands holding his belly like a bright yellow beachball he'd just caught and was preparing to toss back to her. 'Yeah,' he said, 'that's when I started to think that you two might have done something to Paul.

'I tried to think back to that night and what I'd seen in those few seconds when I'd been standing in the garden looking into the kitchen. I could remember it pretty clearly, considering how drunk I'd been: the kitchen lit up like a TV set and Paul chasing the girl round and round the table. I went over it and over it in my mind. I *had* to be missing something, because Paul hadn't killed no one. It was driving me crazy – and then at last I cracked it!

'I'd been concentrating on Paul all the time, see, I'd been looking at what *he'd* been doing. But when I focused on the girl instead – well, the whole picture changed like magic. Paul weren't chasing *her* around the table any more – *she* was chasing *Paul*! And if she was chasing Paul,' he added, smiling, 'then maybe the blood she was covered in weren't hers.'

Mum's right hand slipped subtly into the fleece's pouch pocket. I knew she had her hand on the gun. Was she taking the safety catch off? Was she getting ready to shoot him?

The blackmailer hadn't noticed her surreptitious movement. He continued with his story, apparently suspecting nothing.

'If something had happened to Paul in this house, I was sure there'd be some sort of clue left behind. So I decided to come back to have a poke around and see what I could find.'

I saw Mum draw herself up to her full height and straighten her back. She knew there'd been no clues for him to find in the house; she'd taken care of that herself, she'd dotted every *i*, she'd crossed every *t*. But I had a horrible presentiment of what the black-mailer was going to say next, and I felt my knees start to tremble in my pyjamas.

'I'd seen you go shopping in town that Saturday morning, so I drove down here the very next Satur-day, betting that this was a regular weekly outing. Sure enough, at about ten I saw your car go past with the two of you in it chattering away like a couple of canaries. So I drove on up to the house and let myself in.'

'How did you get in?' Mum asked, horrified.

'Paul may have talked a load of rubbish most of the time, but he weren't wrong about the windows on these old properties – easy to force as anything. I see you've had new locks fitted to them now. Very sensible.

'Anyways, I searched the place from top to bottom and I couldn't find nothing. The whole place was as clean as a whistle and I'd almost given up, to tell you the truth, when I found *this*.'

He leaned forwards and reached into his back pocket, his face turning an unhealthy claret with the effort, his breathing coming in phlegmy rasps. Finally he tossed a pink plastic card onto the kitchen table. Mum picked it up, not understanding, having to squint closely at the childish signature with its silly arabesque and the postage-stamp-sized photo before – with an involun-tary grimace – she understood what it was.

She was unable to resist throwing a hostile, accusatory glance at me.

'It's Paul Hannigan's driver's licence,' the fat man said. 'I found it upstairs, hidden away in a little box in your girl's dressing table. I knew that if this was here... then Paul Hannigan had never got out of this house alive.'

Mum watched him struggle to put the driver's licence back in his pocket. She seemed somehow reduced, deflated. She collapsed in the chair opposite him as if she feared she'd fall down if she didn't move quickly.

She'd been defeated by the blackmailer, by the obese bullfrog grinning at her across the table. And she'd been defeated, ironically, by the person she'd been trying so hard to protect: *me*. I'd given the enemy the key that had enabled him to get inside our fortress, to get behind her carefully prepared defences and force our surrender. She couldn't hide her bitter disappointment, her sense of betrayal.

'It weren't difficult to work out what must have happened,' the fat man said, smiling smugly at his own cleverness. 'You disturbed Paul while he was robbing the house, and there'd been a fight. Somehow your girl here managed to get his knife off of him and in the struggle he'd ended up dead. You thought you could cover the whole thing up. You thought you could outsmart everyone and just carry on with your nice little lives as if nothing had happened. But you hadn't counted on me cropping up, had you?'

He put his muscled dwarf arms behind his head and leaned back in his chair.

'I'd bet money he's buried out there in the garden somewhere. Am I right or am I right?' He chuckled his phlegmy treacly laugh again. 'Yeah, I thought so.' He grinned, Mum's sullen silence all the confirmation he needed.

He stared steadily at Mum, obviously savouring every second of her misery. Her hand had long since dropped out of the fleece pocket and was hanging limply by her side.

'There you go,' he said cheerily, 'now you know *everything*. So are you gonna pay the twenty grand, or do I have to write a little note to the boys in blue?'

'How many other people have you told about this?' Mum's voice was hoarse and frail.

'None,' he answered flatly.

'How can I be sure about that?' she persisted. 'How do I know you haven't blabbed about this in every pub in town? How do I know you're not just the first of God knows how many blackmailers who are going to come crawling out of the woodwork?'

'You'll just have to take my word for it.' He shrugged, but after a moment's thought he seemed to accept that this wouldn't count for much in the circumstances, and he tried to give her a little bit more.

'Listen, luv,' he said. 'I've done three long stretches inside, and every time it was because someone grassed me up. I don't tell no one *nothing* no more. I've learned the hard way to keep my mouth shut.'

'Why did you wait so long before coming here?' Mum asked. 'You found the driver's licence –' she calculated quickly – 'on the twenty-second of April: that's over a month ago.'

He winked at me conspiratorially like a mischievous uncle. 'She don't miss a trick, your mum, does she?' He turned back to her and his smile faded. 'I was in hospital. I've got a dodgy ticker. I was in hospital almost a month. They only let me out the day before yesterday. Now, I think that's enough questions. When are we gonna go and get this six hundred quid?'

Mum ignored him. 'What about Paul Hannigan's relatives? What about his friends? Won't they be looking for him?'

'He didn't have no family,' he said with growing impatience. 'He was an orphan, so he told me. Said he'd grown up in care.'

'What about his friends?'

'He'd only been living down here a few months. He only knew a handful of people. He weren't the sort that made friends easy. I probably knew him better than anyone. No one's gonna miss Paul Hannigan, luv, believe me. And no one else is gonna figure out what happened neither. I'm the only one who knows. I'm the only one you've got to worry about.'

The fat man didn't realize it, but everything he said was making the killing option more and more attractive.

If he was telling the truth, then he was the last remaining loose end. Him and him alone. But now we were being given a second chance to tidy that loose end away.

'How do I know you're not going to keep coming back for more money?' Mum said.

If there'd ever been any real doubt that the black-mailer would be back for more money again and again, his reaction to Mum's question dispelled it for good. He jumped angrily to his feet, sending his chair scraping back across the tiles with such a lacerating screech that my hands automatically flew up to my ears.

'That's enough questions!' he yelled. The jolly, avuncular persona he'd assumed vanished, and now there was only an ugly pouting mask, a monstrous, bloated baby face that was going to scream the whole world down because it wasn't getting its own way. His truncated, muscle-swollen arms flew out from his sides, ready to punish, ready to hurt. 'I've answered enough of your questions! You ain't in a position to ask no questions! You ain't in a position to make demands!'

There was a tense, awkward silence. I felt my heart racing wildly. Mum had shied away from him as if fearing a blow. The fat man stood glowering at her, his lips twisted into a pantomime scowl, his arms twitching with malignant energy. Some thin strands of hair had escaped the grip of his hair grease, and now waved like antennae above his bald scalp.

'We go and get the six hundred now! No more questions! No more time-wasting!'

'There's no need to get aggressive,' Mum said, putting up her hands in a submissive gesture. 'I always said I was going to pay. We'll go and get the money right now.'

She stood up and looked around distractedly, muttering, 'Handbag. Where's my handbag?' She found it beneath one of the stools by the breakfast bench, picked it up and slipped it over her shoulder. 'Now I just need my car keys,' she said, patting her pockets and scanning the kitchen again, but at the same time not really looking, her mind detached, elsewhere. She was trying to make up her mind, I was sure of it. Trying to decide what to do: to pay the blackmailer or to kill him? To live with this gross leech sucking on her flesh for years to come, or, like a desperate gambler, risk everything on one more throw of the dice and take out the gun and shoot him dead.

'Don't worry about your car keys,' the fat man said. 'We'll go in my car. It's better that way.' He looked scornfully at Mum and for a moment I saw her through his eyes: a scatty, spoiled, middle-class housewife, a stupid plump hen for his vulpine teeth to devour at leisure, a meal ticket for the rest of his life.

'Are you sure you've got everything you need?' he growled at her. 'I don't want to get all the way there and then find you ain't got the right cards with you or you've forgotten your pin number or something.'

'No, I've got everything I need.'

'Come on, then, let's go.'

He walked out of the kitchen, his anger forgotten, back to his jolly avuncular self, a hand in his pocket merrily jangling his car keys and change. 'We won't be long.' He winked at me as he passed, like an old and much-loved family friend.

Mum still hesitated, a dazed expression on her face. She was trying to make up her mind, trying to decide what to do. Her hand went to the mouth of the fleece pocket but darted away again when the fat man barked at her: 'Come on! What are you waiting for?'

Mum walked past me, her eyes on the floor, and followed him into the hallway. I wasn't sure what she was going to do, but if she hadn't shot him by now, surely she wasn't going to – it had to be better to kill him inside the house than outside. There was no risk of being seen inside; the gunshots were less likely to be heard by someone passing. All I could think was that she'd decided to pay him the money after all.

I followed Mum up the hall, so close that I was almost tripping on her heels. The blackmailer had already opened the front door and stepped out into an idyllic May morning. He was walking across the gravel towards his car, and he was whistling, he was actually *whistling*, as if he didn't have a care in the world! He opened the passenger door, then looked round for Mum. When he saw her hovering in the hall-way, he called out angrily again, 'Come on, for Christ's sake! Hurry up!' He held the car door open, waiting impatiently.

Mum turned to me and seized my shoulders fiercely. She brought her cheek close to mine and under the cover of a goodbye kiss whispered urgently into my ear: 'What should I do, Shelley? What should I do?'

I stared straight at the blackmailer over her shoulder, at the bullfrog neck, the inflated dwarf arms, the obscene gut, the hand idly scratching at his groin, and with my face pressed close to hers, pretending to return her pretend kiss, I replied without hesitation.

'*Kill him, Mum.*'

41

Mum pulled sharply away from me and walked determinedly out of the house and across the drive towards the blackmailer, deftly switching her handbag from her right shoulder to her left as she went. When she was about two metres away from him she stopped and plunged her hand deep into her fleece pocket.

The fat man had started to move towards the front of the car on his way to the driver's side, but he stopped when he saw Mum pointing the gun at his head, clutching it tightly in both hands, her left eye closed, taking careful aim.

His hands shot up in surrender and he pressed himself against the car's front wing, arching his torso backwards over the bonnet, pathetically trying to increase the distance between his face and the gun as if those few extra inches could mitigate the bullet's brutal impact. He cringed, unable even to look in the direction of the gun, squinting desperately away to his left and right as if convinced that the slightest eye contact with Mum would induce her to pull the trigger.

'All right, luv,' he said, over and over again, 'all

right, luv, everything's all right now, luv, everything's all right now, it's all right, luv, it's all right, everything's all right.'

I hovered at the door, willing Mum to shoot. She shook her hair from her face and took a few shuffling steps closer.

The fat man tried to say something, but he could only talk in terrified tongues and his babbling sputtered out in confused silence. A dark stain spread over his crotch and down the thick trunk of his right thigh.

I held my breath, still waiting for the gunshot. *It must come now, any second now, any second now!* But Mum still didn't pull the trigger. From where I was standing I could see the gun in her outstretched arms start to sway from side to side, a dead bough in the breeze, but I only realized what was happening when I saw the expression on the blackmailer's face change. His eyes still darted anxiously all around him, but not because he couldn't bear to look in the direction of the gun any more – he was getting ready to make a run for it.

That's when I knew Mum had lost her nerve. She wasn't able to pull the trigger.

I ran out into the drive screaming: '*Do it, Mum! Do it! Do it now! Do it!*'

I was right beside her, screaming into her face, my hand tugging at the back of her fleece. The sudden, deafening whipcrack of the gun made me scream and jump high in the air. The recoil drove Mum backwards three huge strides and spun her around almost one hundred and eighty degrees, so that she ended up pointing the gun at the lounge window.

I stared at the blackmailer, looking for the blob of strawberry jam in the middle of his forehead, the slow emptying of his eyes as his soul fled, waiting to see him crumple to the ground in a lifeless heap. To my amazement, he seemed entirely unchanged. He still stood by the car, arching backwards as far as he could across the bonnet, his arms still raised, the fat pink hands waggling at his shoulders like starfish.

He realized what had happened – that Mum had missed him – much faster than we did, and with astonishing speed for a man of his size he pushed himself off the car and sprinted down the drive.

Mum was still recovering from the vicious recoil, dazedly trying to steady the leaden weight of the gun and aim.

'Shoot him, Mum! Shoot him! *He's getting away!*'

I knew that if he got out of the drive and onto the public road, we wouldn't be able to chase after him; the risk of being seen was just too great. If he made it to the road, if he escaped the tree-screened privacy of Honeysuckle Cottage, he'd be safe, and all we'd have to look forward to would be his terrible revenge, a revenge I was sure wouldn't be long in coming.

Mum pointed the gun at his receding figure and there was another ear-splitting explosion. A white wound appeared high up in the trunk of one of the ash trees at the top of the drive, and I knew she'd missed again.

The blackmailer had disappeared from sight around the corner of the drive where it straightened leading down to the road. I could just see glimpses of his yellow T-shirt flashing through the foliage. Mum and I set off after him.

It was impossible to run in my slippers in the thick gravel and I had to kick them off as I went. The sharp little stones stabbed into the soles of my feet, but I swallowed the pain – *we had to stop him getting to the road!* Mum was lagging behind me, bent double with a stitch after just a few paces, holding her side, hardly looking where she was going. I screamed at her to hurry up, that he was going to get away, and wincing with pain she forced herself to run faster and managed to catch me up.

As we entered the straight leg of the drive, we saw that the fat man's pace had slowed dramatically, his sprint declined to no more than a limping jog. And he was still twenty metres from the gate and the safety of the road.

Mum and I gained on him quickly. He looked back when he heard us coming up behind him, his face a shocking black-red like blood in a test tube. He tried to shout something at us, his lips curled up into a snarl, but he was so short of breath he couldn't form the words and all I heard was something like '*Ha! – Fa! – Pa!*' His face was drenched with sweat and he had to keep his finger pressed permanently to the bridge of his nose now or his glasses would have fallen off. He turned his attention back to the gate, the finishing line he was desperately trying to reach, but he was hardly moving forwards any more, he was virtually jogging on the spot, and I knew now that Mum and I would catch him before he could get to the road.

As we closed in on him, I became aware that I was giggling as I ran, giggling in excited anticipation of the moment when we'd overtake the fat man and Mum would shoot him. In those last few seconds before we caught up with him, running barefoot in the drive, my dressing gown flapping open around me, I felt something I'd never felt in my life before. It was a totally new emotion, a liberating, exulting sweetness that flooded through my veins like a drug. It was as if everything artificial in my life suddenly fell away and I was fleetingly in touch with a primitive truth, a reality older than life itself. And I felt like a giant, I felt like a *god*!

And then we were so close I could have reached out and grabbed hold of the fat man's filthy T-shirt. Mum, still clutching at her side as she ran, held the gun out until it was just a few inches away from the folds of fat on the back of his neck and squeezed the trigger.

The gunshot was so loud that I felt it rather than heard it, a reverberating thunder deep in my chest, and the fat man crashed face-down into the gravel like a felled oak.

42

Mum tried to click the safety catch back into position, but her hands were shaking too much. It seemed an age before she finally managed it and put the gun carefully back into her fleece pocket.

I was exhausted from the chase, my lungs burning and my breath coming in rapid gasps. Sitting down on one of the large whitewashed boulders at the edge of the drive, I put my head in my hands and concentrated on reining in my galloping breathing. The birds, scared away by the gunshots, slowly reassembled in the tree-tops, chattering and burbling as if excitedly discussing this latest twist in the drama they were enjoying from on high. I stared at my feet. They were black with dirt, and covered in hundreds of tiny indentations and cuts.

I was the first to break the silence.

'Do you think anyone heard the shots, Mum? They were so *loud*!'

Mum just made some noncommittal noise. She was circling the enormous mound of the blackmailer's corpse, which lay in the middle of the drive like a beached whale. He must have been dead before he hit the ground, because he hadn't even put those iron arms out to break his fall, and they'd ended up pinned fast beneath the copious folds of his belly.

Mum knelt down and put two fingers to his neck.

'There's no pulse,' she said, quietly, as though not wanting to wake him. 'He's stone dead.'

I didn't budge. I knew we'd have to move the corpse quickly, as it could be seen from the road, but I had to rest for just a little bit longer. I needed to get my breath back, I needed time to try to absorb what had just happened. I wasn't sure I could hold back the melt-down if I didn't. I wasn't sure I'd be able to go through with the next stage – the disposal of the body, the disposal of the car.

'That's funny,' I heard Mum say.

'What is?' I said, looking up.

'Come here. Help me turn him over.'

Reluctantly, I stood up and went over to her. She leaned over the corpse and seized its right shoulder, I grabbed the grey tracksuit bottoms at the hip and we pulled. There was a moment when we had to strain hard, but once we'd got it to a certain point the fat man's body rolled over easily and flopped onto its back. I wiped my hands furiously on my dressing gown, con-vinced I'd touched something wet.

The fat man's glasses had gone skittering across the gravel with the impact of the fall, and without them his face looked different, strangely naked, almost feature-less. His eyes were closed, and in death his face had lost all the snarling anger it'd had when he'd shouted at us over his shoulder. It was tranquil now, almost serene. The face of a favourite uncle, always ready with a funny story or risqué joke, passed out on the sofa after an enormous Sunday lunch. The stunted, over-muscled arms lay at his sides and I thought of all those wasted hours in the gym, straining to build up arms that could punch their way through doors only to find that at the moment of crisis they'd been useless, raised meekly in the air in surrender.

I felt nothing, absolutely nothing, looking at the blackmailer's corpse. No guilt. No pity. No regret. He was not a human being to be mourned, he was just a problem to be solved. We'd have to find a way to get rid of that huge corpse and the car – unbelievably, we'd have to get rid of the battered turquoise car for a *second time*.

'There's no blood,' Mum muttered, more to herself than to me.

'Huh? What do you mean there's no blood? There must be blood.'

'Look for yourself. There's no blood. *There's no bullet wound.*'

She was right. His head, which should have been blown apart by the exiting bullet, was completely intact. The great yellow hump of his T-shirt was spotted with greasy food stains and peppered with dirt from the gravel, but there wasn't a single drop of blood on it. Apart from a small graze on his chin and a little gash on his forehead where he'd crashed to the ground, there was no sign of a wound anywhere.

I went to say something, but Mum had already wandered off down the drive.

'You're right,' I called after her, completely astonished, not understanding. 'There's nothing at all!'

'And look at this!' Mum was standing by the right-hand gatepost, pointing at something near the top. The straight line of the post's edge was broken, as if a bite had been taken out of the wood.

'I must have missed him,' she said incredulously. 'Somehow I must have missed him. From two inches away!'

She began to walk back, stooping to pick up the blackmailer's glasses, which appeared completely undamaged.

'What killed him, then?' I asked when she was standing beside me again.

'What killed him?' Mum laughed a dry, humourless laugh. '*We* killed him, Shelley. We scared him to death. It looks like he's had a massive heart attack, but it's just the same as if my bullet *had* hit him – it's still murder in the eyes of the law.'

We scared him to death. We scared that enormous brute with those vicious little arms to death. The thought filled me with a curious satisfaction and pride which I would have liked to savour, but the thought of all the hideous work which lay ahead loomed in my mind and overshadowed everything else.

'We'd better move him,' I said. 'If someone drives past . . . '

'Yes, we'd better.'

I went round to his feet and bent down to pick up one of his legs, but Mum gently touched my back to tell me to stop.

'He's too heavy to drag, Shelley. Let's bring the car down and take him back up to the house that way.'

It was no easy task to get the fat man's body into the back of our car. He must have weighed nigh on sixteen stone, and although we could just about manage to lift him between the two of us, the problem was to man-oeuvre him onto the back seat before he got so heavy we had to put him down again. After several failed attempts, we decided that the only way we could man-age it was by Mum actually sitting on the back seat with the fat man's head in her lap and then dragging him back in on top of her while I held on to his legs, looking away, trying not to breathe in the ammonia stink of urine from his tracksuit bottoms. When half his torso was inside the car, Mum extricated herself from beneath his inert gelatinous mass, wriggling frantically like an insect trapped in jam, and let herself out of the other door. With me pushing from one side and Mum pulling from the other, we eventually got the body into position on the back seat.

Mum was very worried about injuring his head or legs when we closed the back doors, and she spent a long time trying to get his legs in a position where the sharp edge of the door wouldn't strike them. Eventually I had to lean over from the passenger seat and hold them until she managed to slam the door shut.

It was only a short distance back up to the house in the car, but we both automatically put our seat belts on. The irony almost made me laugh out loud – the two of us buckled up for a fifteen-second journey like the conscientious citizens we were, while the body of the man we'd just murdered lolled precariously across the back seat.

Mum parked the Escort exactly where it had been before, right in front of the blackmailer's car.

She turned off the engine and in the ensuing silence I asked, 'What are we going to do with him, Mum?'

She seemed miles away, lost in thought, and I mistook her silence to mean she didn't know.

'I've got an idea!' I said, turning to her excitedly. 'What about the mines? We could put him in his car, then push the car into the mine shaft that you used before. A car would be able to fit into the shaft, wouldn't it?'

'I've got a better idea,' Mum said flatly, turning to look at me now. 'But we've got to act *fast*.' She glanced at her watch and gnawed at her bottom lip. 'If we take too long it might not work.'

She leaned over and looked me intently in the eyes, her hand on my knee. 'I want you to do everything exactly as I say, Shelley. Do you understand? *Exactly as*

I say.' Paul Hannigan's driver's licence was still fresh in her mind and I nodded emphatically, determined to show her that she could trust me one hundred per cent from now on.

'Good. Now help me to move him,' she said, and started to get out of the car.

'Move him *where?*' I groaned, suddenly overcome with horror at the thought of digging another grave in our garden.

'There's no time to explain now, Shelley! *Just do what I tell you!*' she snapped.

Mum dragged the fat man's corpse out of the car, heaving backwards with her arms locked beneath his armpits until his buttocks were on the very edge of the back seat and I was able to take hold of his legs.

We carried him towards the house, stopping every few metres or so to rest. When we were roughly halfway between his car and the front door, Mum cried out to me to put him down and we lowered him gently onto the gravel. I noticed that his Rolex now had a large semi-circular crack in its lower half, which reminded me of the smiley faces I used to draw on my exercise books at junior school.

'We have to turn him over,' she said, and we turned him so he was lying face-down, his head pointing towards the house. Mum knelt down and vigorously brushed away the small leaves and smudges of dirt that the back of his yellow T-shirt had picked up from the gravel. When she was satisfied she stood up, and taking the gun out of her fleece pocket, handed it to me.

'Take this upstairs to my room and hide it under my pillow. Then get dressed and come back out here as quickly as you can. Go on!'

I did what she said at the double. I had no idea what she was doing; all I understood was that we were involved in some sort of race against the clock. When I came back downstairs, Mum was kneeling by the fat man's corpse, fishing through his back pocket. I saw her take out Paul Hannigan's driver's licence and I shrank back into the hallway, not wanting to provoke an outburst by appearing just at that moment. I waited until she'd slipped it into her jeans' back pocket before I stepped outside.

When she saw I was back, she said, 'Your slippers, you lost your slippers somewhere in the drive. Quickly go and find them, then put them upstairs in your bedroom where you usually keep them.'

I ran off into the drive, my feet actually stinging more now in shoes and socks than when I'd been walking around barefoot. I found one slipper straight away but the other one was nowhere to be seen. It was several minutes before I finally found it suspended in one of the rhododendron bushes.

When I got back to the house Mum was carefully placing the blackmailer's glasses on the ground a few feet in front of the body. When she was happy with the way they looked (lenses on the gravel, one arm closed, the other arm open), she left them and went over to the turquoise car. She closed the passenger door that the fat man had been holding open for her, then went to the other side and opened the driver's door. She walked right around the car, eyeing it critically, then made her way to the island in the centre of the driveway, glancing back over her shoulder as she went as if she didn't trust the car to stay as she'd left it when her back was turned.

Mum picked up her handbag from the shrubbery where she'd dropped it when she set off after the black-mailer. She didn't slip it onto her shoulder, but held it in her hand, and the long leather strap hung down and curled itself into the shape of a noose.

She looked back towards the car, but now she seemed to be looking *beyond* it into the farmer's field, in the direction of her first shot. Then she turned and squinted across at the trees, where her second shot had gone. I followed her gaze and found myself looking at the ash with the white tear high up in its trunk. Mum stood there frozen in contemplation, the only movement her long white fingers kneading the soft leather of her hand-bag, then set off resolutely down the driveway.

I waited until she'd disappeared from sight before discreetly following her, knowing full well that she didn't want me near her right now, and that any questions were likely to provoke a furious rebuke.

At the point where the drive dog-legged, I concealed myself behind a bush and spied on her through the foliage. She was down by the gatepost. She seemed to be clawing at it with her fingers, rubbing at it furiously with her sleeve. Then she dropped into a crouch and began moving slowly across the gravel on her hands and knees like an animal. What on earth was she doing? *Had she gone mad?*

When she finally stood up, clapping her hands and cuffing at her knees, I slipped back to the house and waited for her by the front door.

She reappeared a little while later and, after pausing for a moment as though running through a checklist in her mind, began walking towards me at a funereal pace, her eyes fixed on the ground in front of her. She stepped over the fat man's corpse with fastidious care – as if avoiding a dirty puddle – then stopped suddenly and picked something up. I took a pace closer and just managed to catch a glimpse before she dropped it into her handbag: it was the fat man's half-smoked roll-up that he'd flicked away before coming into the house. Mum snapped her handbag shut and stood up with a loud cracking of her knees.

She stood there intently surveying the scene like a film director who wants to be absolutely sure that every detail of the set is perfect, every prop is in the right place, before crying *action!* I surveyed the scene too – the loathsome car with its driver's door wide open, the blackmailer's corpse humped face-down in the drive, the glasses lying on the gravel with one arm erect like a cocked ear – but I understood none of it.

'I've got my slippers,' I said as I came up behind her.

My voice made her jump and she turned round abruptly, unsmiling.

'Good. Now put them upstairs like I told you.'

'OK. Then what? What's next?'

'Next?' She put her hands on her hips and looked at me strangely. 'Next, we call for help.'

43

I followed her into the house, completely confused now.

'*Call for help?* I don't understand. What's going on? What are you doing?'

Mum explained in a rapid machine-gun burst of words as she strode down the hall into the kitchen.

'I'm going to call the emergency services and say that we were sitting in our lounge when a strange car pulled up in our drive and a man got out, clutching his chest, and collapsed. I'll say that he's unconscious and he doesn't seem to be breathing and we don't know what to do and can they send an ambulance straight away!'

She glanced at me over her shoulder but it was all too quick for me to take in.

'He died of a *heart attack*, Shelley. There are no marks on him, there's nothing to make them suspect that we had anything to do with his death. They'll just assume he started to have a heart attack at the wheel of his car and made for the first house he saw to try and get help, but died before he could make it to the front door.'

She studied the face of her wristwatch, her lips moving with her thoughts, then snatched up the phone.

'But I've got to call them right away. It's ten o'clock already – he's been dead for half an hour.'

I stood there speechless as Mum's plan slowly sank in. Like all the best ideas, it seemed obvious once you heard it – but I was sure it would never have occurred to me. It was incredibly bold. And it would take nerves of steel to pull it off. The ambulance would get rid of the fat man's corpse for us. The police would get rid of the fat man's car for us. The authorities themselves would get rid of all the most incriminating evidence of our crime for us. We wouldn't have to do anything. We would be above suspicion – the good Samaritans who vainly tried to help a stranger.

Mum wedged the receiver between her cheek and shoulder.

'Take those slippers upstairs now and put them away like I told you,' she said as she dialled the number with a trembling index finger.

The ambulance arrived surprisingly quickly, given how remote Honeysuckle Cottage was. It came bumping up the drive at a quarter past ten, its siren wailing and blue lights flashing, full of earnest, boy-scout eagerness to do good. I was dreading meeting the ministering angels who were racing to save the life we'd just taken (*would they be able to see what had really happened when they looked into my eyes?*), but at the same time I was bored by the thought of the melodramatic rigmarole they were about to go through to try to save the fat man's life. All the king's horses and all the king's men weren't going to be able to put this Humpty together again.

Two paramedics – one in her wrinkled fifties with dyed blonde hair and frameless glasses, the other much younger, chipmunk-cheeked with a masculine crew cut – got out to attend to the fat man. They didn't run, but sauntered over calmly; smiling, experienced professionals who knew how important it was to keep everyone calm, how important it was not to rush. Meanwhile, the driver, a tall gangly youth with horrendous acne, started to unload equipment from the back of the ambulance: an oxygen cylinder and plastic tube with some sort of bag attached to it, a black box like a guitar amplifier that I could see from his limping gait was heavier than it looked.

Mum fussed around the two paramedics, playing the shocked householder who'd had her quiet Saturday morning shattered by the unexpected arrival of this human tragedy on her doorstep. She answered their questions with a well-feigned anxiety to help. *When did he collapse? Ten – no, about fifteen minutes ago. Have you given any CPR? I'm sorry, I don't know how, I'm sorry . . . Have you moved him? No, I haven't, I wouldn't dare . . .* No one would have thought that she was telling black lie after black lie.

The paramedics effortlessly turned the fat man onto

his back in one perfectly synchronized manoeuvre. 'No pulse, no breathing,' Dyed Blonde declared matter-of-factly, as if she were making no more than an idle observation about the weather.

I didn't want to stay to see the whole farce acted out, but I didn't think I should just disappear either – I didn't want to do anything that might arouse suspicion. So I went back inside the house but stayed in the hallway by the door, where I could still see and be seen. I was playing the role of the sensitive sixteen-year-old who couldn't bear to watch something so raw, something so real as the life-and-death struggle that was taking place in our drive. In reality, I just wanted them to go, I just wanted them to take the corpse and go away. Once they'd gone, it would all be over. The long nightmare would be over at last. The incredible piece of good luck we'd had with the fat man dying of a heart attack, and Mum's quick thinking, had suddenly, unexpectedly, brought us out of the complex labyrinth we'd been lost in, and I just wanted to be left alone with Mum to enjoy our miraculous escape.

I slouched against the wall, glancing from time to time at my watch, scratching nervously at the wallpaper with my thumbnail. What was taking them so long? Couldn't they see that he was dead, dead, *dead*? I glanced outside to see Chipmunk Cheeks cutting the fat man's yellow T-shirt right up the middle with a big pair of scissors, exposing the tangle of grey and black hairs, the tumid white hummock of his belly, the fat breasts with their enormous pink nipples.

When I looked outside again a few minutes later, Dyed Blonde was connecting curly cables to the black box on which – when Mum wasn't blocking my view – I could see a green light flashing.

Mum turned to look at me and, still in the role of the appalled householder, made a face that said, *Isn't this terrible, Shelley? The poor, poor man!* Then she turned back to the paramedics, a hand anxiously worrying at her mouth.

Dyed Blonde was now holding two black pads like flat irons above her head, while Chipmunk Cheeks methodically removed the fat man's Rolex, identity bracelet and copper arthritis band. The moment the green light changed to orange she plunged the pads down hard on his chest. The fat man's arms and legs convulsed violently for several seconds, as though he was having an epileptic seizure. Dyed Blonde rocked back on her haunches and got ready to do it again.

The shuddering and jerking of the corpse's limbs was sickening to watch, but at the same time it made me want to burst out laughing. I turned away, covering my smirk with my hand, and went into the kitchen, where no one would be able to see me. I just stood there, waiting for the fit of giggles to pass, wishing away the time, staring at the various objects on the breakfast bench without actually seeing any of them.

Alone in the kitchen, I started to worry about the discrepancy between the time the fat man had really died and the time we'd told the paramedics. All in all

I reckoned there was a difference of about three-quarters of an hour. Had the paramedics noticed anything odd about the body already? Had they been able to tell the moment they arrived that the fat man had been dead for longer than we were telling them? When did rigor mortis start to set in? With Paul Hannigan it had been within the first two hours – could it be earlier? Was that the telltale clue that had already caught us out in our lies? Were they already exchanging knowing glances, planning to pass on their suspicions to the police as soon as they could? Was the gangly youth running his hand over the blackmailer's car at that very moment and noting that the engine was cold when it should still have been warm if we were telling the truth?

Although I usually feared the worst in every situation, even I couldn't manage to build this up into a very real anxiety. I couldn't convince myself that the paramedics would notice anything suspicious about the corpse. The fat man was the victim of a massive heart attack; he was stone dead when they arrived. Surely they wouldn't bother to look into things much further than that? And I simply couldn't believe that a mere forty-five minutes would give rise to any significant forensic changes. We were safe, I was sure of it, we were safe . . .

When I went back outside, the paramedics were assembling a stretcher. The acne-pocked youth went over to Mum.

'Would you like to come with us to the hospital, or are you going to follow in your own car?'

Mum was completely wrong-footed by the question. The last thing she wanted was to have to keep this act up at the hospital, possibly for hours.

'But I don't know him,' she said pleasantly. 'As I explained to your colleagues, he just pulled up here in his car and collapsed.'

The young man seemed equally taken aback by Mum's answer. He was momentarily lost for words, as if no one had ever refused to come with them to the hospital before. 'OK,' he said finally, twisting at the fat teardrop of his ear lobe and trying to smile to cover his incomprehension.

Mum clearly felt the need to explain more, as if she were being accused of hard-heartedness. 'I've never seen him before in my life,' she said. 'He's a total stranger.'

The youth kept nodding as Mum spoke, but still looked unconvinced and slightly appalled.

The two paramedics had carried the fat man into the ambulance and were working on him indefatigably in its submarine-like confines. Dyed Blonde had put an oxygen mask over his mouth and was feeling his neck with two fingers of her right hand, while Chipmunk-Cheeks was tying a tourniquet around his arm and preparing to attach a drip.

The gangly youth walked back to the ambulance and closed one of the rear doors. He was starting to close the other one when Dyed Blonde suddenly cried out as if in pain. The youth froze with a grimace as if he thought he'd caught her finger in the door and peered anxiously inside. Then I saw his whole body stiffen.

I tried to see what was going on, but his white back blocked my view. I'd begun edging closer to the house when Dyed Blonde screamed again – all professional calm shattered now, consumed with excitement, uncontrollable, frantic excitement – 'There's a pulse! There's a pulse! I've got a pulse!'

Mum and I stood side by side and watched the ambulance accelerate down the drive, its deafening siren painting giant blue spirals in the air around it. We were still standing there long after it had disappeared from sight, both of us speechless and immobile.

When Mum finally stirred and turned to go indoors, she noticed the blackmailer's glasses still lying on the gravel where she'd placed them. The paramedics either hadn't seen them, or had forgotten them in all the excitement. She knelt down and picked them up and contemplated them. A symbol of her carefully laid plan that had gone so disastrously wrong.

A black look shook her features, and for a moment I thought she was going to hurl the glasses against the wall, but the rage passed, and instead she carefully folded the raised arm as gently as if it had been an injured bird's broken wing.

44

Mum and I sat in the lounge dazed, stupefied, as if we'd just been caught in a bomb blast and couldn't speak or hear each other for the ringing in our perforated eardrums.

We sat slumped on the sofa unable to process what had just happened (*There's a pulse! There's a pulse! I've got a pulse!*), unable to believe that the paramedics had managed to resuscitate the fat man after all that time. We'd been so close, *so close* to a happy ending, so close to a brilliant resolution that would have solved everything, so neatly, so perfectly – only to have it snatched away from us at the very last moment.

I sat paralysed, dumb, staring at the richly patterned rug under the piano, shaking my head in disbelief. We think we control the course our life takes, we think we're the captain of the vessel with our hand on the wheel, but in fact it's luck (or fate or destiny or God or whatever we choose to call it) that's really in control. We might as well take our hands off the wheel and go to the back of the boat and sleep, because it's this *other force* that really decides whether we make it to the shore or we sink without trace. We *think* we have all the control, but in reality we have none.

How could they have resuscitated the blackmailer after so much time had gone by? It was impossible, it was against all logic, it was against all common sense. But this other force had decreed that it should happen and so it had happened and that was all there was to it.

Mum was inconsolable. She'd been so worried about keeping the gap between the real time of 'death' and the arrival of the paramedics as short as possible that she hadn't stopped to think she might be giving them enough time to save the fat man's life.

She frantically flicked through the few medical books we had in the house – a medical dictionary, a reference work for personal injury lawyers, a criminal law book entitled *Forensic Evidence* – and at last found a relevant passage. It said that resuscitation after periods as long as an hour *was* possible, but would almost certainly leave the victim with severe brain damage, a vegetable incapable of thought or speech. Mum rallied a little after reading this, but she soon lapsed back into self-recrimination and black depression.

Unable to bear the torture any longer, she rang the local hospital to see if they could give her any news. She adopted the role of the anxious householder once more and went through her story all over again. *We were in our house this morning when a strange car pulled up in our drive and a man got out clutching his chest . . .* She was transferred from department to department and patiently went through her story word for word three more times. No, she didn't know the patient's name. No, she didn't know what ward he was in. No, she wasn't a relative. After almost a quarter of an hour of being transferred and left on hold, she was finally informed that they'd had no admissions that morning that fitted the description she'd given.

Mum was so tense when she finally put the phone down that she couldn't cope with ringing any of the other local hospitals he might have been taken to.

It wasn't until late that afternoon that we were finally put out of our misery.

The police car whose arrival I'd long imagined, signalling our imminent arrest and the end of our attempt to escape the consequences of killing Paul Hannigan, finally pulled into our drive just before six o'clock.

Unlike my premonitions, however, the police car's blue light wasn't flashing and the knock at the door when it came was timid, almost apologetic. Nor were we confronted by the black-uniformed goons with crackling radios that I'd always imagined. Instead, when Mum opened the door, there was a young officer in a white short-sleeved shirt, dangling his peaked cap in his hands because it was too hot to wear. He looked like a Renaissance cherub, with blue eyes and rosy cheeks and curly blond hair that lapped his collar and was surely longer than police regulations allowed. My first thought when I saw him was: *He can't be here to arrest us. They wouldn't have sent an angel with such terrible news . . .*

'Mrs Rivers?' he asked gravely.

Mum nodded, too nervous to trust herself to speak, and showed him into the lounge. The atmosphere around us was heavy, dense, like wading through water. We all sat down and the policeman took out a little notebook from his breast pocket and a miniature, lizard-green pencil. He flicked through the pages, looking for one in particular. (*Did it have that formula written on it that they had to read out every time they made an arrest? Did he have to read it because he could never remember how it went – 'Anything you do say may be used in evidence . . .'?*)

We waited in silence and I had the strange sensation of time slowing, slowing right down, almost coming to a complete standstill. I saw everything around me as if in slow motion: the young policeman turning a page of his notebook, the tip of his tongue protruding from the corner of his mouth with concentration; Mum sitting on the very edge of her chair, frown lines like claw marks across her forehead, her hands pressed to her face like the figure on the bridge in Munch's *Scream*.

In the next few seconds the young policeman would deliver judgement on us. The fat man was alive, he'd told the police everything and we were under arrest; the fat man was dead and we were safe . . .

And at that moment I felt a strange calm come over me, the calm that comes with resignation in the face of the final crisis. It was as if I'd been through so much that I was drained of emotion, and in its place resignation fell like a blanket of snow, numbing me, protecting me from the pain that was about to come. I wondered whether people who were about to be executed felt this same calm, this same sweet resignation, whether it descended to protect them in their final moments of agony, as the noose was tied around their necks, as their hands were tied behind the stake, allowing them to die at peace . . .

The policeman found the right page at last and looked sharply across at Mum.

'I'm afraid it's my duty to inform you,' he said, 'that the man who was taken ill here today – Mr,' he glanced down at his notes, 'Mr Martin Craddock – died before they could get him to the hospital.'

'Oh, how awful,' Mum said, with the perfect timing, the perfect intonation of a gifted actress – genuinely sad but with the tiniest dash of stiff-upper-lip stoicism. 'That's too bad. That really is *too bad.*'

I felt a rush of joy and relief that I had to struggle to control. I wanted to leap into the air and dance around the room, I wanted to fling my arms around the policeman's neck and cover his cherubic face in kisses.

He was dead! The fat man was dead!

The policeman pulled a pained expression that was meant to express his sympathy at Mr Craddock's sudden death that morning, but didn't quite succeed. I saw him sneak a look at his watch. He wanted to keep this short; he wanted to be somewhere else.

He went over Mum's version of events again but seemingly more out of politeness to her than because it was of any real interest to the police. He nodded and uh-huhhed in agreement, but didn't write anything in his notebook and had already put the miniature pencil carefully back in his pocket. He looked around the lounge as if he was hoping a little dog would suddenly come bounding in and give him an excuse to change the subject.

When Mum had finished, there was a long, awkward silence. The policeman, who was clearly anxious to go, struggled to find something appropriate to say.

'He'd a long history of heart trouble, I understand. He'd only just come out of hospital.'

'Is that so?' Mum said. 'How very sad.'

After another uncomfortable pause he tried some homespun philosophy. 'Oh well, that's life for you. Every minute someone's born, every minute someone dies. That's the way of the world, isn't it?'

There was a cringingly embarrassing moment while his words hovered in the air, which Mum sensibly brought to an end before either of us could burst out laughing. She jumped to her feet and said, 'Yes, well, you must be a very busy man. We do appreciate you taking the time to come out here and let us know how it all ended. It's very kind of you.'

I stood up as well, and, seeing me, the policeman

sprang out of his chair with rather more eagerness than was fitting. The three of us stood there uncertainly, each of us hiding our relief that the interview was over.

'Oh, before I forget.' Mum took the fat man's glasses from the top of the piano. 'The ambulance people left these behind.'

The policeman held up the large frames, and seemed to be about to make a joke about them when he remembered the circumstances in which they'd been lost. They just fitted into his breast pocket.

We walked the policeman to the door and out onto the drive.

'Is that his car?' he asked, pointing with his cap.

'Y-yes,' Mum said, unable to conceal the nervous catch in her voice.

He went around to the driver's side of the battered, turquoise car and leaned inside. He stayed there for several minutes. I threw Mum a questioning glance, and she just shrugged her shoulders back at me, but I could see the frown lines had returned to her forehead.

The policeman finally closed the driver's door, then walked right around the car and stood with one hand on his hip, the other scratching his temple.

'That's strange,' he said, with a perplexed smile.

'What is, Officer?' Mum's whole demeanour was suddenly less convincing than before. Her expression was strained, fragile.

'Well, it's parked so *neatly*.' At last he'd found something to interest him in this tedious little errand he'd been sent to run. 'I mean, he was having a heart attack, but he managed to park his car perfectly behind yours. And not only that, he's put it in neutral, he's put the handbrake on, he's turned the engine off and he's pocketed the keys – all while he must have been in excruciating pain. It's amazing!'

He beamed at Mum, but she seemed unsure how to respond; she was having great difficulty meeting his clear blue gaze.

'Force of habit, I suppose,' she said drily.

'It must have been,' he laughed, hooking a thumb into a trouser pocket, 'it must have been. But it's incredible, isn't it?'

'Yes,' Mum was reluctantly forced to agree. 'It's hard to believe.'

The policeman stared at the car with amused bewilderment for a few moments more, then with a final shake of the head that said he'd never cease to be amazed by the things he saw in his line of work, he turned away and walked back to his patrol car.

'We'll get someone out to you tonight to tow it away,' he called over his shoulder. 'I'm sure you don't want that blocking your drive for weeks on end!'

And with that he started his engine and, with a casual mock salute, drove away.

45

The next day, Sunday, Mum and I slept in. We broke our routine and treated ourselves to a huge cooked breakfast – eggs, bacon, mushrooms and fried tomatoes – and ate it sitting at the kitchen table, flicking through the numerous supplements in the Sunday paper.

Mum looked ten years younger, the exhaustion, the dreadful strain of the previous morning, had vanished from her face.

'Did you sleep well?' I ventured.

She smiled broadly. 'Very well, thanks, Shelley, very well indeed. Like a baby.'

I smiled too. Mum was sleeping again. That was a good sign.

That day had a special, magical quality to it, like Christmas Day. After everything that had happened the day before, after everything we'd been through since the early hours of April the eleventh, the nauseating roller-coaster ride that our lives had become, the relief that it was all finally over was exquisite.

I was in a state of bliss. I felt like the survivor of a shipwreck who, after drifting for weeks in an open lifeboat, lashed by storms, capsized again and again by waves the size of houses, is rescued against all the odds and suddenly finds herself sitting before a blazing fire, wrapped in blankets, sipping a hot drink. I relished every small, mundane detail of the world around me as if I were witnessing a miracle: the way the mushroom cloud of milk slowly spread its looping tentacles into the darkest depths of my coffee, the motes of dust gyrating like miniature solar systems in the sunlight slanting through the kitchen window, the minuscule purple veins on Mum's lowered eyelids as she read the paper, the distant church bells that merged into one faint, crystalline note and seemed to speak of an idyllic, chocolate-box past. I relished all of it, I loved everything that there was for being.

We didn't get dressed until eleven, and even then we just sat back down at the kitchen table and carried on reading the paper and made yet another pot of coffee.

We didn't talk very much about the events of the previous day, but every now and then a thought would float into our heads and one of us would speak.

'Do you think the blackmailer was telling the truth?' I asked. 'You know, when he said he hadn't told anyone else that we'd killed Paul Hannigan?'

Mum considered. 'Yes, I think he was. He told us the truth about his heart condition, after all.'

'And about Paul Hannigan not having any close family who'll come looking for him?'

'That's harder to say. That's just what Hannigan told

him. All I can say is that my gut feeling is it's over now. I really believe it's over now.'

A little later Mum exclaimed, 'Imagine if I'd hit him, Shelley! We'd have had his body to get rid of, *and* that blasted car. *Imagine!*'

I shook my head, appalled at the thought of how close we'd come to having to enter that chamber of horrors all over again. What on earth would we have done with the fat man's body? Buried it in the garden? Dug a grave in the vegetable patch? And what would we have done with the car? Abandoned it somewhere else with all the risks that entailed, or would it have been possible to sink it in one of the mine shafts in the national park as I'd suggested? It didn't bear thinking about . . .

'Thank God you're so cack-handed,' I joked, but Mum didn't laugh as I'd expected.

'It's like a *miracle*,' she said. 'I mean, how could I have missed from that close? The gun was virtually touching the back of his neck. It's not possible, Shelley. It's just not possible.'

Later still, thinking about the conversation we'd had the day before (*Zugzwang. It's an expression from chess.*), I said, 'It's all been a bit like a game of chess, hasn't it?'

'I suppose so, in a way. We certainly had to think hard about every move we made.'

I thought about all the decisions Mum had made since she'd brought the chopping board crashing down on Paul Hannigan's skull: to bury him in the garden instead of calling the police, to keep on with our routine as if nothing had happened, to dump the bin bags in the abandoned mines where they were never going to be found, to keep the gun, to stage the fat man's death for the paramedics the moment she realized he'd died of a heart attack. So many difficult decisions, so many right moves.

'You played a brilliant game of chess, Mum.'

'We both did, Shelley. We both did.'

When my back was starting to ache from sitting in the wooden chair for so long and I was tired of reading about new fashion trends and new diets and new movies and new starlets, I said, 'I don't feel guilty about what we've done, Mum. I'm glad they're both dead. I don't feel guilty about any of it – not even about yesterday. He got what he deserved. Good riddance to bad rubbish, I say. Everything we've done, *everything* – it's all been in self-defence. Even yesterday.'

After lunch we drove into the countryside and went for a long walk through the water meadows by the river. It was another glorious day, and the colours of the landscape seemed incredibly vibrant. The yellow of the rape flowers was so bright I could hardly bear to look at it; it was like staring into the broiling heart of the sun. The sky was a deep cerulean blue, the distant hills an exquisite lavender, the young trees along the riverbank a lime green verging on yellow, the tall tussocky grass a rich emerald and the wild flowers that grew among it the purest zinc white.

'It's like being in a Van Gogh painting,' Mum said. 'It's as if the colours haven't been mixed on the palette at all, they've just come straight out of the tube.'

When we reached a secluded part of the river where the stinging nettles had been left to grow out of control, Mum made sure there were no walkers or fishermen around, then took the gun from her handbag and quickly tossed it into the river. It disappeared with a pleasing *plosh*.

'What about water always giving up its secrets?'

'Let it. They'll never be able to trace the gun back to us. I just didn't want it in the house any more.'

'Are you sure we won't need it?'

Mum put her arm around me. 'Yes, Shelley, I'm sure. After everything we've been through, I'm not going to be frightened of anything ever again.'

In the shade of a weeping willow, in a little dip in the bone-dry earth, we burned Paul Hannigan's driver's licence. Mum held a lighter to it and slowly it turned black and the corners began to curl back on themselves in the heat. It produced a foul-smelling black smoke, which I thought was only fitting for the cremation of Paul Hannigan's toxic soul. I felt immense relief as I watched his face melt and blister into unrecognizability.

The fat man's revelation about the licence hadn't triggered the horrible row with Mum I'd thought was inevitable – not even the day before, when we'd spent so many miserable hours indoors anxiously waiting for our fate to be decided. And now that the card was smouldering in the little dry hollow between us, I knew we were never going to have that argument. Mum was never going to question me about it, she was never going to reproach me, she was never going to bring the subject up again. I knew that she'd forgiven me.

Mum looked at me and smiled sweetly. 'No more secrets?'

'No more secrets,' I agreed without hesitation.

When the flame had gone out and the heat had cooled, I poked the twisted black insect that was all that remained of Paul Hannigan's driver's licence, and it crumbled away to ashes.

Later that afternoon we both felt like sitting outside in the garden. Although my scars were healing well, I still had to be careful, and we looked around for a suitable swathe of shade to sit in.

'What about there?' Mum said pointing to the far end of the garden.

I blanched. She was pointing to the oval rose bed and the frothy exuberance of pink roses that gushed from it like an enormous floral fountain.

She saw my expression and realized her mistake. 'Maybe it's better over there by the—'

But I interrupted her. 'No, by the rose bed's fine.'

So we took our plastic garden chairs and sat in the cool shade of the roses just a few metres away from Paul Hannigan's shallow grave. I mastered my revulsion, controlled it, philosophized it away. Whether I was near

Paul Hannigan's corpse or not, he was always going to be with me. In fact, I'd come to believe that he was a part of me now in just the same way that the tribesmen I'd seen on TV believed the wild pig or the monkey they killed became a part of them. There was no escaping him, there was no running away from him. Paul Hannigan was with me forever now. For better or worse.

The surreal scene even gave me an idea for a picture I thought I'd like to paint one day: two genteel Victorian ladies taking tea on the lawn, while in the flower bed behind them could just be made out a greening corpse in its grave clothes. I'd call it *In the Midst of Life We Are in Death*, from the line in the Christian burial service. Its message would be that no matter where we are or what we're doing, death and horror are always near us. The challenge is to get on with our lives and be happy even though we can always see them out of the corner of our eye, blurred, but still recognizable in the background.

We dozed and chatted lazily, and when the whole of the front garden was painted in violet-blue shadow I lightly touched Mum's shoulder.

'Mm?' She smiled drowsily without opening her eyes.

'I want to go back to school, Mum,' I said.

She opened her eyes now, and there was surprise and anxiety in them; the jagged furrow had returned to her brow. 'But there's only a few weeks to go to your exams, Shelley. All of your year is on study leave right now, isn't it?'

'Yes, it is,' I said, 'but there are some revision classes I'd quite like to go to. Mrs Harris has all the details, and I'd like to see some of the teachers again before the exams – especially Miss Briggs.'

Mum hadn't expressed her real concern, and her brow remained furrowed. 'What about those girls – Teresa Watson and the other two? What if they're there?'

'I don't think they will be, Mum, I doubt revision classes would be of much interest to them, but if I do see them . . .'

I remembered how I'd taken the knife from the dining-room table and plunged it into Paul Hannigan's back; I remembered how I'd chased the fat man down the drive with bloodlust in my heart. If Teresa Watson touched me, I'd have her up against the wall with my hand crushing her windpipe before she knew what was happening to her. When she looked into my eyes, when she saw what I was capable of, she'd run a mile. I'd killed two men; I wasn't going to be frightened of any schoolgirl.

'Don't worry. They won't do anything to me. I'm not frightened of them any more. If anything, *they* should be frightened of *me*.'

I knew those words had come out of my mouth, but their sentiment was so unfamiliar to my ears it was almost as if someone else had said them. It wasn't a mouse speaking any more; there'd be no more scurrying along the skirting board looking for a safe place to hide, no more keeping very still and hoping not to be seen. I felt stronger, more confident, more *capable* than I'd ever felt before. Life was brutal. Life was savage. Life was a war. I understood that now. I accepted that now. And I said: *Bring it on*. I wasn't going to be anyone's victim. Ever again.

'And there's something else, Mum. I want to call Dad.'

Her arm flinched as if she'd been stung; her jaw clenched.

'Well, that's your decision,' she said, her voice dry and tremulous. 'I'm not going to stop you.'

No, she was not going to stop me, and neither was Zoe. If Zoe answered the phone I wouldn't be deterred ('Tell him it's his *daughter*.'). He wasn't going to reject me that easily. Not without an explanation. Not without being held to account. *Not without hearing what I had to say*.

Mum stroked my hair back over my ear and left her hand nestling at my neck.

'Those scars are healing beautifully,' she said.

'I know, I know. A few more months and you'll hardly be able to notice them.'

She gently caressed my cheek and smiled. 'As good as new.'

'No,' I purred. '*Even better*.'